BETTER THAN BEFORE

BLAIR BRYAN

The best way to buy my books is direct at tealbutterflypress.com There you can save 20-25% and find autographed paperbacks. They are available at most booksellers too.

I write under two pen names, Ninya for Non-Fiction and Blair Bryan for Contemporary Fiction.

Non-Fiction

Scotland with a Stranger: A Memoir

Treehouses with a Teenager: A Memoir

First You Then Him

Fiction By Blair Bryan

Back to Before

Better than Before

The Sweetest Day

The Funologist

When Wren Came Out

AnaStasia Lived Two Lives

Steamy Sexy Series Velvet Guild

Velvet Guild Collection 1

Velvet Guild Collection 2

Velvet Guild Collection 3

Velvet Guild Collection 4

Velvet Guild Collection 5

ONE

S now-capped mountains started to spring up in the distance amid fields of thick waving yellow grasses as Holly coasted down hills and chugged up valleys. The morning sun played peek-a-boo with the clouds and dappled the fields where cows and horses grazed in lazy clusters. Holly had glanced at the GPS frequently during the drive, watching the hours burn down into mere minutes. It had been two long days and nights in the van, only stopping at a Motel 6 when her eyes were so weary, she couldn't keep them open any longer and the road started to shift and blur. It was the final leg of their journey, and now that they were only a few miles away, she paid more attention to her surroundings, drinking them in as she drove.

Murph stood at attention on her lap, scraping one paw against the glass and whining, eager to get out and run. Holly rolled down the window a crack, and he pressed his nose into the opening at the top, feasting on the smorgasbord of scents of the West.

"We're almost there, buddy," Holly murmured as she stroked his thick curly fur. "I should have taken you in for a groom before we left." His brown eyes were practically covered by fur, and the thick knotted coat made him look twice as large as he was.

"I didn't expect the mountains to look like bacon," Dillon piped up from the back seat where he had been sleeping for the last several hours. He sat up and pressed his nose against the glass just like Murph. Holly glanced over at a range of them that lined the road they were on and had to agree. The yellow gravel trails running up the red clay mountains *did* look like marbled bacon.

"You know what, buddy? They kind of do," Holly agreed, laughing. "Or are you trying to tell me you're hungry?"

"That too." He smiled and stretched his hands above his head.

"We're meeting the realtor to get the keys, and then we can celebrate with some pancakes."

Holly focused intently on the GPS. According to the screen, they were only a mile away from their final destination. The first bit of anxiety and doubt bloomed in her belly and set off a flood of what if's swirling in her mind.

What if they don't like it here?

What if uprooting them was a mistake?

What if Chance relapses?

Her worries popped up like dandelions in the lawn, annoying and relentless, and she chopped them off at the root, one by one.

You don't have the time or the energy for this pity party. Suck it up, buttercup.

"Take the next right. Your destination is on your left." The female robotic voice cut in, distracting Holly from her worries.

She turned off onto the last turn and eased the minivan up the long gravel driveway that curved between banks of pine trees. At the end of the driveway, a gray, fully tricked-out pickup sat parked in front of a log cabin. Holly pulled into the makeshift parking spot beside it and shifted the van into park.

Forcing a smile on her face and pushing down her anxiety, she turned back to face the boys in the back seat. "Okay, guys, we're here."

"That was the longest drive ever!" Dillon exclaimed and yanked open the door, eagerly putting his feet on solid ground with Murph jumping down behind him.

Inside, Holly's stomach churned. She was not someone who did things on a whim. She thoroughly researched every move she made carefully—from which brand of dishwasher was the quietest to finding the highest-rated school for the boys. This move felt a little out of control and reckless, and for a second, she was terrified. Frozen in her seat, she let the chill pass through her, and then she plastered another smile on her face and stepped out of the van and onto the red Montana soil. Chance finally woke, stretched with an open-mouthed yawn, and then followed her. Standing again at his full height, Holly wrapped her arm around him and pulled his shoulders toward hers for a side hug.

"Dang! Did you grow two inches on the way down here?" It always took her breath away that she saw her boys every single day, but at certain moments, when the light hit them just right, a significant change was suddenly blatantly obvious. Most days, transformations went unnoticed, but then Father Time would smack her upside the head and whisper, "You're running out of time. He's turning into a man right in front of you."

Holly smiled and waved a little greeting at the woman standing next to the pickup truck as they walked closer.

"You must be Holly," a thick woman stated, dressed simply in what could only be considered semi-formal western wear complete with polished cowboy boots, denim skirt, and bolo tie. She smiled and held up a basket with a purple bow on it. Ever the optimist and desperate for clues from the universe to prove she'd made the right choice, Holly took the bow in her favorite color as a sign. The older woman's face was sun-bleached beautiful in its unassuming, plain way. She wasn't the kind of woman who spent a single second twisting self-consciously in front of a hallway mirror. She projected confidence and strength, and her solid handshake reinforced the entire package. It didn't hurt that she looked like she was strong enough to bench press both the kids.

"I am," Holly confirmed, offering her a hand.

"I'm Jill. Welcome to your new home!" She held up the keys between her thumb and forefinger and jingled them together, then handed the basket to Holly. Tucked inside were thick packets of beef jerky and candy, paper towels and cleaning supplies, and a bottle of local wine. Practical and useful, the kind of gift Holly appreciated most.

"This is so kind of you! Thank you very much."

"The Celtic sea salt caramels are to die for." She patted her thick denim-covered haunches. "I must confess, I have an addiction, but the first step is admitting you have a problem, am I right?" she asked with an oblivious smile and a carefree wink. Holly glanced over at Chance and saw his shoulders stiffen.

Addiction. The word stopped her cold, and her smile faded slightly, casting a darkened pall as the sun hid behind a cloud. She used to joke about it, too, but now the word held so much power. She could barely bring herself to say it anymore. Brushing the feeling away, Holly turned the corners of her mouth up into an obligatory smile as Jill dropped the keys in her outstretched palm. "These are my sons, Chance and Dillon."

"It's nice to meet you. Are you going to be helping your mom out around the acreage?" Jill asked.

Around the acreage. It was the first time Holly had heard those words uttered out loud, and it was terrifying to think she was personally responsible for everything she could see. Every one of the twenty-two acres was hers to maintain.

As a coping mechanism, her worried brain called up an old movie reference from *The Lion King*. "As far as the eye can see, Simba." Acres of land stretched and unfurled for several miles. Outbuildings, a barn, and her home, plus two additional cabins on the property, were now entirely her responsibility. When Holly first moved to her home in New Hope, she thought the townhouse would be a lot for her to handle, but this was a whole new level.

What was I thinking?

She was relieved to hear Chance answer, "Yes. We're the grunt labor."

"Well, I won't keep you," Jill said. "I bet you're exhausted. I know you're at the end of a long journey, so I'll let you get right to it. Is it okay if I check up on you in a few days?"

The gesture took Holly by surprise. Their real estate transaction was complete, and Jill had fully earned her three percent commission. Holly was so dumbfounded the woman would willingly choose to spend more of her own time on them that she accidentally uttered, "Really?"

"It's just the way we do things around here," Jill answered without skipping a beat. "We like to take care of each other."

"Well, I have to admit it is going to take some getting used to, but I think that sounds really kind and I would appreciate it." Holly mused that at least one other person in the world would know where they were and had verbally committed to checking up on them. That small act of kindness put Holly's jumpy heart a little more at ease.

Jill turned and hoisted herself up into the pickup truck with the grab bar. It was so high from the ground it looked more like a tank, then disappeared in a cloud of dust as the truck rambled down the long gravel drive.

"Well, what do you think, guys? Should we go inside?"

"Yes!" Dillon exclaimed and ran up the wooden stairs of the front porch. The main house was a classic A-frame log cabin, with timbers that were notched together like the Lincoln logs Holly spent hours building with her father when she was a kid. The front porch wrapped around the entire small house, doubling its square footage and taking advantage of the sweeping panoramic views of the prairie grasses and mountains far in the distance. She envisioned rocking chairs and a little table and enjoying her morning coffee outside. Murph would love hanging out there, basking in the sun or tucked under the table by her feet.

"Wow!" Dillon exclaimed once they were inside. "This is a real log cabin. I've never been in one of those before." His mouth gaped open wide as he stared up at the cathedral ceiling revealing a spacious loft tucked in the second story. Thick branches spiraled up a huge tree trunk, creating the stairway up to the second level. "This is so cool!" Dillon shouted as he raced up the stairs, and Holly fed off his excitement and followed him up the staircase.

If only I could bottle that energy.

"So, I was thinking we could put the TV here. You guys can play games and hang out with friends in this space, and then I'll get a bunk bed for your bedroom."

Dillon's excitement faded and his forehead tensed.

"What is it, buddy?" Holly asked.

"Do you think people will like me at my new school?"

"Doubtful." Chance's deepening voice carried from the kitchen below.

"Be nice to your brother," Holly reprimanded and waved Dillon close with her fingers. "Come here." She felt his arms wrap around her middle and bent to kiss the top of his head.

"It *is* scary to start all over again, isn't it?"

His dark blond head nodded up and down.

"You know how to be a good friend, right? All you have to do is talk to people. See if you have common hobbies. Take an interest in them and ask questions to see if you match up on anything. I bet if you ask, there might be one or two boys in your class who like to play video games and fart." Holly threw the joke in to break through the tension, and it worked. Dillon rewarded her with a mischievous giggle, pulling back in time to shove his hand down his shirt and proudly produce a significant armpit fart.

"See? If nothing else, you can teach them your armpit technique." She ruffled his thick hair with her hand, and it stood on end. "You're gonna find your people, honey. I promise. Who wouldn't want to be friends with Dillon Simon?" She smiled and then redirected, hoping his excitement would return. "Let's go check out your bedroom."

There were two decent-sized bedrooms on the main floor, an adorable birch kitchen, and a single bathroom. Large windows were cut into the logs, letting enough light in to make it cozy. Thick, knotty beams made up the ceiling and were stained a rich caramel color. Not a single wall was a flat surface.

How am I going to hang pictures in here? Holly wondered as they descended from the loft.

"I call top bunk!" Chance announced when they entered their bedroom.

"Oh, man!" Dillon lamented, his age always making him slower on the draw.

"Don't worry about it. To make it fair, we'll rotate top bunk every month."

The concession made Dillon smile knowing he would have a chance at the top bunk, and Holly was surprised that for once Chance didn't even argue about it. The boys walked into the kitchen and opened up the cabinets one at a time. After looking inside seeing they were empty, they shut them and turned the water on.

"Let's get Murph's water and food station set up. Dillon, can you go out and get his dishes?"

"Sure, Mom." He returned with the dishes a few minutes later and filled the water bowl before setting it on the floor for Murph, who lapped it up eagerly.

The boys ran outside to the back deck, and she followed them, lingering at the rail. It overlooked another incredible million-dollar mountain view. Billowing white clouds danced across a perfect blue sky. Holly couldn't believe her luck; it was like a little piece of paradise had been gifted to her. The price she had paid made it all worth it. She closed her eyes and breathed in the pristine air.

Two apple trees studded with baby apples the size of the tip of her thumb and a small overgrown vegetable garden were cut into the backyard.

"Looks like you boys are going to have to learn to garden. We get to grow some of our own food! I've always wanted to try that," Holly enthused. "We're going to get a glimpse into what it was like living in the 1800s!" She lapsed into her comfort zone—teacher mode. "It was called homesteading. You either grew your food or you went hungry. It won't be that dire of a situation for us, but it will be fun to learn how to be more self-sustainable, don't you think?"

The boys were silent. It was a lot of new information to absorb and a massive change from their lives in New Hope. The weight of it seemed to finally settle on their shoulders, so Holly quickly shifted the subject. "Isn't it beautiful here? Listen to that!"

The boys strained to hear what she was talking about. Puzzled looks washed over their faces and crinkled their foreheads in confusion.

"I can't hear anything," Chance answered.

"Me neither," Dillon chimed in.

"Exactly! It's so beautifully quiet here, isn't it? The serene calm is going to be amazing. We will finally be able to catch our breath." Chance shot her a look. Quietude definitely wasn't as big of a priority for her sons as it was for her. Holly glanced down at her watch. "The movers will be here in two hours, so why don't we drive into town, have some lunch, and grab some groceries. Then we can come back and start unpacking."

She and the boys jumped back into the van, and Holly set the GPS to drive into Garden Brook. The town was small and quaint, and in the center of it was a square surrounded by tiny mom and pop shops—a handcrafted chocolate candy company, a soup and sandwich bar, and an insurance agent. There wasn't a single chain store in the mix. Trailing petunias in full showy displays of fuchsia and yellows cascaded down baskets on every lamp post. Small groups of people congregated, chatting on the sidewalks, and waved as Holly drove by. At the main traffic light, cars stopped in all directions to allow a mule deer and its fawn to cross the street.

"We are *definitely* not in Indiana anymore," Holly said out loud as she watched the skittish deer dart past and escort her baby to safety, feeling a kind of kinship with the animal.

"That's obvious," Chance deadpanned. "Is this place for

real? It feels like we're living inside one of those sappy Hallmark movies you make us watch at Christmastime."

"I've never seen so many smiling people in one place," Dillon observed.

"Yeah," Chance agreed. "It's kind of creepy."

"Well, I guess that's something else we're gonna have to get used to. It's not the worst thing in the world, is it?" She pulled in front of the general store and parked the car.

"Mom, what's a general store?" Dillon asked.

"Well, it's the kind of store that has a little of everything. It has food, probably camping and hiking supplies this close to a National Park. Maybe some Yellowstone souvenirs. Remember when we read *Little House on the Prairie* and Pa would ride to town to trade his goods at the general store? It's kind of like that."

"Great, so we're going *back in time*," Chance groaned, the teenage snark reflecting the annoyance he clearly felt.

"No, not back in time, smarty pants." Holly explained, "But things will definitely be slower here. It will be an adjustment, but it will be awesome."

"You keep saying it's going to be awesome here." Chance leaned forward. "Are you trying to convince us or yourself?"

Holly pinched her lips together; he had a point.

"It's just that I think we could all use a little break from the craziness. I know I could." Chance's brown eyes met hers then shame darkened them as he broke her gaze and glanced away. "It will be good for *all* of us," Holly corrected and tried to reassure him.

"What's there to do here," Chance asked, "besides watching paint dry?"

"There's *so much* to do here!" Holly gushed desperately wanting her boys to find solace *and* fun in their new home. "After we get settled and the movers are finished, we will plan a day trip into Yellowstone, then you'll see what makes this place so special. But for now, let's go grab some groceries and get some supplies before the movers arrive."

The bell attached to the door jingled as Holly walked into the store. Immediately distracted by the colorful rainbow of rock candy and pastel taffies wrapped in wax paper, Dillon stopped the first few feet inside the store. Rough-hewn wood floors that were scuffed and worn from a century of punishment creaked under Holly's feet. Wooden barrels filled with t-shirts and knickknacks lined the ends of the aisles that were packed with food items arranged in neat rows and minor camping and hiking supplies. A sign advertised park-approved firewood was available outside and permits at the register. Next to the wall of candy was a long vinyl bar with seats that swiveled in circles and an old-fashioned soda machine. Seated on a stool tucked in the corner was an old man nursing a cup of coffee and the last dregs of a sundae in the bottom of a fancy sundae glass. The stretched-out spoon lollygagged to the side then clanged against the glass when he scraped the edges in search of the very last melted drop of ice cream.

"Look!" She got Dillon's attention. "I think this is an old-fashioned soda fountain like they had in the 50s! The kind where you could go get an egg cream with two straws for your date."

"What's egg cream?" Dillon asked.

"It's like custard. Tastes like eggy ice cream."

"That sounds disgusting." His gaze lingered on the candy counter. "Can we get some taffy, Mom?"

"I don't see why not." Holly wanted to indulge the kids a bit. She pulled the shopping basket from the pile near the door and began to fill it with the essentials. Cereal, milk, pasta, and sauce. A bag of apples and three pears. A brick of cheese and a bottle of rosé.

The rosé made her heart pang for Stacey.

"Come here, darlin'." A white-haired old lady wearing an apron and a bun smiled and beckoned her closer. "Pardon my intrusion, but you look a little teary-eyed. Is everything okay?"

Holly laughed at herself. "Just a little homesick for my best friend."

"You must be new in town." A network of lines and wrinkles formed around her bright eyes that rippled and tugged when she smiled to reveal white teeth inlaid with silver and gold fillings.

"We are. I'm Holly and these are my boys, Chance and Dillon. We relocated from Indiana."

"Goodness! That's a long way away. I've never been to Indiana. I'm Ruth, by the way." She turned and pulled out three sticks of rock candy in bright pink, blue, and purple and held them out. "This is to make your first day in Montana a little sweeter."

"You don't have to do that. I can pay for them," Holly offered and quickly opened her wallet to search for cash.

"Nonsense," the older woman said abruptly.

"That is so nice of you. Thank you so much." The phone vibrated in her purse. "Sorry, I have to take this. I think it's my movers."

Holly turned to take the call. "This is Holly Simon."

"Ms. Simon, this is Pat from Four Brothers Moving Company."

"Awesome! When can I expect you?"

"I'm sorry to tell you that the truck broke down and the earliest we can deliver is tomorrow by noon."

"Tomorrow?" Holly repeated, her voice cracking under

the weight of the delay. "But all our furniture is… our beds… What are we going to sleep on?" Pure exhaustion from the drive made it difficult to get a full sentence out.

"I'm so sorry to inconvenience you like this, but we are stuck until the axel can get fixed, and the earliest the repair shop can get the parts is tomorrow morning."

"Okay. Thank you for the call." Holly accepted the news with a heavy sigh, pinching the bridge of her nose and closing her eyes to get her bearings. The idea of sleeping on the hard wooden floors of the house with the paper-thin blankets still in the van from the ride down made her cringe.

I should have been better prepared.

"Well, *now* I can see things are definitely not okay."

Holly jumped. "Oh, it's just my mover, they broke down and our truck full of furniture is stuck on the side of the road."

"Oh no!" Ruth commiserated.

"What?" Dillon said, instantly teary and worried. "Did they lose all my stuff?"

"It's just a delay, buddy," Holly said, ruffling his hair. "They are coming tomorrow."

"What are you going to sleep on in the meantime?" Ruth asked.

"The floor, I guess," Holly answered. "It's just one night."

"Absolutely not, I won't hear of it!" Ruth declared. "I'll have my son, Deacon, run some sleeping bags by tonight. And don't even try to talk me out of it. I've been told I'm a stubborn woman." She laughed out loud at her own joke. "Right, Al?" she asked the man at the counter.

"They don't make 'em any stubborner," he agreed with a smile and a twinkle in his impossibly blue eyes.

"Wow. Again, so kind of you, Ruth. I feel like I'm already starting this friendship in the hole."

She smiled. "Don't worry, sweetheart. Come winter time, I'll find plenty of ways for you to pay me back." Her words were punctuated with a wink.

Holly wrote down her address and handed it to Ruth, who pulled her into a squishy, comforting hug that thankfully dropped her rising blood pressure into the normal digits again.

———

A few hours later, after dinner, Holly was kneeling on the bathroom floor, in her yoga pants that never saw the inside of a yoga studio, wearing thick yellow gloves next to a bucket of hot soapy water. She wrung out the sponge and wiped down the floor, blowing a stray curl out of her eyes. It was physical work that was making her sweat.

Through the open window, she heard the sound of spitting gravel and stood to see a cloud of dust swirling up the driveway as Murph started to howl. She dropped the sponge back into the bucket and swiped her forehead with her forearm. Acknowledging in the reflection of the dusty mirror, she was grubby and frazzled, not exactly ready to make a first impression on anyone. But her desire to sleep on something softer than the hardwood floor won out, and she pulled off the vinyl gloves with a snap and laid them next to the dirty sink.

"Mom? Mom," Dillon called from the kitchen. "There's someone at the door."

"At least we'll always know when someone is coming or going, thanks to our fluffy guard dog," Holly remarked as she headed toward the door.

She wiped her hands on her pants and opened the screen door. On the porch stood a mountain of a man. Strawberry blond hair tinged with white peeked out from under a well-worn cowboy hat. His cheeks were ruddy and dotted with patches of freckles and stubble that told the story of a man who spent most of his life outdoors. With strong shoulders and thick legs, he was in good shape, but not the artificial cross-fit type that had been the norm in Indiana. This was a guy who was born and raised on meat and potatoes. She could tell he probably wasn't rocking a six-pack under his flannel shirt and jeans, but every inch of him was solid and he oozed capability and strength.

"Yes?" Holly asked, tipping her chin up to make eye contact with his toffee-colored eyes.

"Mama sent me. I'm Deak." The word Mama made Holly's heart twinge. She had never heard a grown man use it in reference to his mother, and the man standing in front of her was as grown as they come.

He thrust out an enormous hand, his thick forearm covered in fine golden hairs. Her hand disappeared into his firmer one.

"I'm Holly."

"Well, Holly, I've got some sleeping bags for you." His words were drawn out and deliberate, slow like honey.

"Oh! Yes! Thank you so much!" Holly smiled, still standing in the doorway holding the screen door open awkwardly. "Your mom is a life saver."

"She is," he admitted with a grin. "But it's amazing how she's always able to wiggle out of the actual work her good deeds create. I think half the reason she named me Deacon in the first place is because the name means servant." He laughed a loud booming laugh that echoed into the empty house and instantly reminded her of Ruth.

"Can I help you unload?" Holly offered.

"No, ma'am. If that ever got back to Mama, I'd never hear the end of it." Walking back to his pickup, he gathered all the bags in one hand and a pile of pillows in the other then walked them back to the porch. Dillon appeared next to her, nudging under her arm for protection.

"Whoa!" he said with wide eyes, taking in the pure size and weight of Deacon.

"Dude, that's rude," Holly reprimanded then turned to Deacon while hiking a thumb toward Dillon. "Sorry. Apparently, being exhausted also makes this one forget his manners."

"No worries, ma'am. I've been getting that kind of reaction from people since I was twelve."

"Ma'am?" Holly asked, amused. "You don't have to call me that."

His eyes twinkled, and his full lips twisted up in a smirk. "Yes, ma'am, I do."

"Let me guess, Ruth?"

"You're catching on fast. She rules the roost here in Garden Brook and we let her." He smiled and then added, "If you'll hold open the door for me, I'll bring 'em in."

Holly held the door open, feeling a tingle when he brushed across her as he navigated the sleeping bags and his huge frame through the small door. Murph wandered over, tail wagging feverishly, and then splayed on his back to offer his belly to the big man who bent down to rub his undercarriage.

"You're a good boy, aren't ya?" Deacon asked as Murph became putty in his hands.

"Hey, traitor," Holly chastised the dog. "Somehow, I don't think you're going to make much of a guard dog here in the Wild West."

"My dogs would eat this one for breakfast," Deak said with a smile. "Although when it comes to swallowing, that hair might give them a run for their money."

"His coat is not practical in the country, but we couldn't leave him behind. He's part of the family."

"I hear you. Dogs are better than people any day. All they know is love." He stood up to his full height Holly guessed was close to 6'5". "I've got to be going."

"Thank you and please thank Ruth for me."

"Of course." He ambled away in his worn work boots, and Holly marveled again at his sheer size and the length of his limbs. Then she turned back to the task at hand, getting sleeping bags set up for the night for her and the kids.

TWO

The real heart-hammering, on high alert-style panic didn't set in until later that night when the boys were asleep. Holly sat on the floor and leaned against the wall in the kitchen with a pad in hand. Line by line, she neatly wrote a to-do list, downloading all the scattered details from her brain that popped up like squirrels in her mind making it impossible to settle down and sleep. It was a conscious act that gave her the illusion of control and arranged the panic into bite-sized tasks that could be accomplished and ticked off a list.

#1 Get the boys enrolled in school
#2 Clean and photograph the cabins
#3 List on Airbnb

Holly pulled up her online banking accounts and noted the balance was dwindling. Moving across the country came with more expenses than she planned on. Tipping the movers, buying curtains, hook-up fees for cable and the internet. Sneaky little costs she had overlooked, but that would be reflected in her available balance over the next week. She needed to begin generating some kind of income as soon as possible, especially since it was high season. Tourists flocked to Yellowstone throughout the summer, and she needed to capitalize on tourism over the next several months to be able to survive the first long winter that was only a whisper away.

The terror unfurled in her belly, opening up like a flower blooming in the sun. An all-consuming fear being so far away from everyone she knew. She picked up the phone and dialed Stacey.

"Hey, woman! You made it! I was hoping you'd reach out. I've been waiting by the phone for your call." Hearing her best friend's voice and suddenly feeling so far away, Holly burst into tears. "Oh no! Take a breath, start at the beginning, and tell me what's going on."

"There's nothing here. The kids have no beds. We're sleeping on the floor. My mover broke down. What if this is a sign? What if this is proof we aren't meant to be here and I made a mistake?"

"Whoa," Stacey chastised. "In through the nose, out through the mouth." Holly followed her directions, inhaling and exhaling deeply. "Now you need to listen to me. What you are doing right now is a huge undertaking. Anyone in their right mind would be terrified. I am so proud of you for taking a leap of faith. Starting over is hard. Instead of thinking about the whole huge, overwhelming task, just focus on one thing. What is the most important thing right now?"

"The boys. Getting them settled."

"Exactly. And how will you do that?"

Holly sniffled and ripped off a paper towel then swiped at her nose with it, unable to answer.

"So, I know a few things about teenagers," Stacey began.

"Food. That's a big one, especially for the boys. Did you find a grocery store?"

"Yes. We have some essentials. I'm planning to stock up later tomorrow."

"Well, there you go! Food… check. Way to go, Mama!"

Holly chuckled at the compliment.

"When are the movers arriving with the furniture?"

"They should be here tomorrow morning," Holly said. "I told the boys it's an adventure, that it's like camping."

"Nice job, spin doctor," Stacey praised. "That's half the battle. This *is* an adventure. And once all of the furniture shows up and you start developing a routine there, you're going to be so glad you did this," she continued warmly. "See how far you've come? New Hope Holly would have never had the balls to do this. *Montana* Holly? That girl is unstoppable!" Holly chuckled and wiped the tears from the corners of her eyes. "Look at where you are right now! You live in one of the most beautiful places in the entire country. You're getting a do-over with your boys. You saved yourself and them from Mick. This is just a tiny bump on your road to complete and utter happiness!"

"It's just that the learning curve is so steep. I don't know why I thought I could handle the upkeep of an acreage."

"You *can* and you *will*," Stacy said resolutely. "I promise you are going to figure this out, and once you've climbed up this mountain and you are standing on top of it like the badass I know you are, you'll be so proud and will have created an entirely new life. One that fits you. One that protects your boundaries and your heart. And someday, your sons will look back at this pivotal moment of their lives and finally understand and be so proud of the courage it took for their mother to start over."

"I know you're right. I just wish I could fast forward a

little. I'm currently stuck in the terrifying part where I question every single decision I've made."

"That's the thing, sweetie; you don't get a fast forward. Anything worth doing, any mountain worth climbing changes you. It's not the end result that's the most important. It is the person you are forced to grow into along the way." She paused and her voice softened. "You're one of the strongest people I know. You're scared. I get it. It's an absolutely normal and valid reaction in this type of situation. Honestly, I would be worried if you weren't terrified, but here's the thing. I know you, Holly Simon. I know how strong you are and what you've endured. The battle you fought this year prepared you for the next one. Growth is uncomfortable by design, but every day you are getting stronger and more solid, and I am so proud of the woman you are becoming."

"Thank you," Holly said weakly. "The me that decided to uproot the boys and start over has disappeared, and the me that overthinks and sits in fear is back in full force. I hate that I keep reverting back to the old me."

"Change isn't a linear thing, babe. It's starts and stops. Some days you are proud of the progress you've made, and others it's learning to give yourself a break and just getting through the day. Trust me, it's all part of the messy process. The best way to judge progress is to look at it from a distance. The girl I met at the grocery store who was buying four kinds of cereal to keep everyone happy and who bowed to Dr. Remington is not even remotely close to the woman who moved her sons across the country to give them a fresh start. You have to at least be able to acknowledge that."

"Mmmhmm." Holly nodded, reluctantly agreeing to Stacey's accurate assessment.

"What's one good thing that happened today?"

"The owner of the general store in town took pity on me and sent her son over with sleeping bags and pillows."

"See? That is proof that the universe wants you there. Don't doubt what you're doing for one more minute."

Holly sighed in relief and turned the conversation to something lighter. "I'm hoping to take the boys into the park in a couple of days. I want to make this fun for them."

"That's a great idea," Stacey enthused then added, "Give me your address. I want to send you a care package."

Holly brushed the rough paper towel against her cheeks. "How did I get so lucky to have a best friend like you?"

"You really *did* hit the jackpot with this one." Stacy laughed. "Don't worry, you'll get to pay me back when I plan my trip to Montana soon. I'll need adequate lodging."

"You have an open invitation to stay here any time you can get away. I miss you."

"Aww, girl, I miss you too."

"Thank you for talking me off the ledge. I feel a little bit better."

"Good. That's what I'm here for, honey. I'm always in your corner. I'm always here for you. So, you put that smile on your face and put those party pants on and help your boys fall in love with Montana. And when you fall apart, do it in a secret place where they can't see you. Where you can call and tell me all about it."

Holly laughed. "I hope you know that I'm seriously gonna be taking you up on that offer."

"I want you to. Remember, you can handle this. You are a strong and capable woman. Good things are coming your way, honey. Believe it."

Holly pressed end and settled back down into her sleeping bag, finally drifting off to sleep.

THREE

At the sight of the moving truck rambling down the dirt driveway, Holly let out a huge sigh of relief.

"They're here! They're here!" Dillon ran down the stairs from the loft and yanked his shoes on. "I have been waiting for this moment my entire life. I thought they'd *never* make it." Dillon exaggerated dramatically.

Chance's interest was also easily piqued at the prospect of freeing his precious Xbox from its cardboard container, and he quickly shoved his feet in his shoes. "Hope they unload our TV first."

Holly followed the boys out, and four exhausting hours later, there was an enormous pile of furniture still on the grass outside their cabin. Defeated, Holly sank into a leather sofa on the lawn she had drastically underestimated the size of. It was so overstuffed and wide the movers couldn't wedge it through the front door. Even after taking the door off the hinges, it still wouldn't clear and had been placed back on the grass while they unloaded the rest of the truck.

The overwhelm ballooned and tightened her chest as she surveyed the rest of her oversized possessions sitting on the grass around her. She didn't even notice a pickup truck rambling down the lane until it was coming to a stop in the driveway. Too tired to even move, she expected the truck to turn around and back out, obviously lost, but instead, it remained parked. Seconds later, Deacon's boots were on the ground.

"Are you sure you want to put your sofa there?" he drawled out as he walked closer. "It's not the most obvious choice, but I like it."

Holly was too tired to even laugh as she sat on the sofa with her feet resting on the ottoman. "You wouldn't happen to have a shrink ray gun in that truck of yours, would you? None of this will fit."

"I thought you might run into problems with that narrow doorway. Long day?"

"The longest," Holly muttered with a yawn, self-consciously covering the extra bit of pudge around her belly with her arm and not understanding why she felt the urge to do it in the first place.

"Mom!" Dillon shouted out the window. "We can't get our Xbox hooked up. MOM!"

The screen door slammed, and Chance stood outside on the front porch. "We need help, Mom. I can't figure it out either."

Holly yawned again, ignoring the request for a moment. Just the idea of spending twenty minutes juggling the cords and controllers to their appropriate positions seemed like too much work. "Just a second, guys." She sat up and rubbed her tired eyes with her dirty fingers.

"I'm sorry to pop in on ya, but Mama sent me because there's a pretty nasty storm coming this way," Deacon began. The news popped Holly up onto her feet, and she shielded her eyes from the sun, scanning the blue sky and white puffy clouds.

"I know it looks like nothing now, but in a couple of hours, it'll really turn into somethin'." He stood with his thumbs hooked into his belt loops, assessing the pile of furniture and what needed to be done before the first drop fell.

"Think you can help me get this into the barn?" he asked over her head to Chance who was still standing on the front porch. To Holly's surprise, Chance walked over to the sofa, picked it up, and hauled it with Deacon to the barn. She heard Chance laugh in the distance, a rare sound when he was tasked with any kind of manual labor. After a few long minutes, they returned.

Chance said, "Deak is going to help us get the Xbox hooked up after we get all this furniture moved."

Deak? Well, that was quick.

"Hey, Dorkus!" Chance shouted up to Dillon. "Get out here and help us move this stuff!" A few minutes later, the screen door slammed and Dillion appeared. Over the next twenty minutes, they worked quickly to move the furniture into the protected area of the barn as the sky began to fill with billowy white clouds that darkened into an angry black. When Holly was tired, she grew silent, observing from a distance. Holly listened to Deacon banter with them easy as pie. She watched in awe as the boys snapped to attention when he belted out orders, teasing them the entire way and finding ways to make mundane tasks seem fun. He had Dillon load their arms full of boxes and then asked Holly to time them to see who got to the barn the fastest.

He's like a Cowboy Mary Poppins.

"Okay now, boys, let's go take a look at that Xbox," he declared when the last chair was safely stowed away in the barn and the door was padlocked. He followed Holly up onto the porch, and she cursed the yoga pants she still had on from yesterday. Instantly aware he was likely seeing the flash of hot pink from a hole in the pants at the bottom of her tail-bone, she felt a flush of warmth in her cheeks as she tried to reach back to cover it, pretending she was rubbing a sore spot.

"Welcome to the insanity," Holly apologized as she opened the door wide and Deacon followed her in.

"Whoa! You weren't lying when you said it was stacked to the rafters," Deacon said, his mouth gaped open in awe. He pulled his cowboy hat off his head and rubbed his head with one of his meaty hands drinking in the mountain of moving boxes.

"I didn't realize how much we were downsizing. The wide-open spaces of Montana may have seduced me a bit," she admitted as she shot him a weary smile.

"She has a way of doing that," Deak answered, the *she* making Holly grin. Dillon appeared at his side, rocking from side to side, waiting impatiently to be acknowledged.

"It's not working," he whined.

"Looks like this one is mighty persistent." Deacon told him, "Take me to that TV and I'll see if I can help you out."

The heavy steps creaked under the weight of Deacon, and watching him navigate the spiral staircase up to the loft was like watching the giant climb up a beanpole and made Holly laugh.

"What's so funny?" Deacon asked.

"Nothing," Holly answered and turned toward the moun-tain of boxes blocking the kitchen sink. Mentally, she ran through the hastily scrawled contents she had written back in New Hope, which suddenly felt a million miles away.

First order of business—locate my Keurig.

She shuffled the boxes from side to side and then

exclaimed, "Ah-ha!" when she found it buried at the bottom. She ripped open the box with glee and felt her heart lift, setting the coffee maker in its perfect spot next to the window. In the loft, she was hyper-aware of Deacon's soft-spoken directions as Dillon's boyish laugh burbled up and echoed into the open space. Deak's louder one chorused with his and boomed into the area.

"Mom!" Dillon yelled over the railing. "What's the wi-fi password?"

"Mommasboy79," she called up to him and heard Deacon laugh at it and tease Chance.

Ten minutes later, she heard Deacon navigating his way back down the spiral staircase. Holly pinched her lips together to stop the smile from spreading across her face as she watched him step down delicately. Each tread required him to twist his massive form toward the final destination.

"They're all set," he said.

"Really? Thank you so much!" Holly continued to distract herself with putting dishes away, painfully aware of how close Deacon was now. He stood with his hat in his hands as his hair tufted and stood up. Her palm itched to smooth it down. "Once I get a little more settled, I think I owe you a home-cooked dinner," Holly heard herself say and wondered briefly if that was the only reason she made the offer. Something deep in her center stirred, and she immediately knew it wasn't.

"Oh no, ma'am. You don't owe me a thing." He palmed the hat in his hands, wringing it between them. It was faded and cracked by the sun. "If I didn't check in on you, Ruth would have my hide."

Holly smiled. "Okay then. Thank you."

Calm down. He's obviously not interested.

Murph whined and sat as close to Deacon as possible, and

he bent down to scratch him behind the ears. His thick fingers were tanned by the sun with a network of small scars mapping across the back of his hands. "You know what's comin,' don't cha, boy?"

"Sorry about that. He's a big baby. When a storm is coming, you can usually find him glued to the biggest human in the room."

She heard it first. Tings and dings on the tin roof like tiny pebbles dappling the metal lengths of the roofline. Holly looked out the window and took in the sky that had darkened to charcoal gray and the sheets of rain that pulsed out across the tall grasses.

"Looks like you were right about that rain," Holly said.

"It'll pass in a bit, but when she unleashes, it's quite a spectacle. Mind if I wait it out here?" He asked.

"Of course not. Wish I had something to offer you."

His eyes met hers and locked for a minute, making Holly's face flush with warmth. She cleared her throat, trying to gain control. Waving a hand in front of her face, she said, "It's so hot in here. Are you hot?"

"Soak it up. Our summers here go by fast. If you blink, you'll miss 'em."

"I was hoping to take the boys white water rafting sometime in the next week."

"That's a great idea. One of my best friends runs an outfitter. Hold on, I have his business card for occasions such as these." He pulled out his worn leather wallet and paged through it, finally pulling out a scuffed card and handing it to Holly. "Looks like I'm going to have to buy him a beer. We've had a running bet I'd never find a use for one of his business cards. Now look at what you've made me do."

"Me?" Holly teased him back. "I had nothing to do with this."

"His name is Cal. Tell him I sent you and he'll take care of you."

"I will," Holly said solemnly "and I won't even mention having seen this sad business card."

"You'd do that for me?" he asked with a lazy smile and a devilish glint that made his eyes hard to look away from.

"It's the least I can do." Holly slipped easily into playful banter that surprised herself.

He picked up a pen on the kitchen table and wrote out a series of digits. "I only live a few miles from here. I want you to have this just in case." He looked down shyly, and the gesture caught Holly by surprise when she noticed a warm pink tinged the tips of his ears. She picked the pen back up, warm where his thick fingers held it moments before, tore off the bottom of a scrap of brown kraft paper, and wrote her own number before handing it to him.

"Just in case," she said softly, then had to clear her throat. His warm hazel eyes bored into hers then darted away again as he stuffed the paper deep into his pocket.

The rain started to let up, and the pings and pops came more infrequently. "Hear that? It's almost over. You just survived your first Montana downpour."

"I feel like I earned a commemorative t-shirt or something."

He laughed and the deep creases just made his face even more ruggedly attractive. Auburn scruff coated his cheeks, and Holly squeezed her hands into fists to prevent them from leaving her sides and rubbing across their sand-papered surface.

"Do you know how to shoot a gun?"

"Um… no." Holly swallowed a lump in her throat. "Do you think I need to learn?"

"I think every woman needs to," Deak admitted. "The boys, too."

"We are *definitely* not in Indiana anymore," Holly said, sitting down on a box.

"Lock the doors," Deak said, and a cloud passed through his usually sunny disposition. "Every night. Do you understand me?" His voice was tighter, his expression clenched. "Just because we're in the middle of nowhere doesn't mean you're safe."

Holly's brow wrinkled in misunderstanding. "What do you mean?"

"Nothing," he muttered. "Just promise me you'll lock up."

"Yes," Holly said, stunned. "I will."

"Then you might be cowgirl material after all." He put his hat back on his head and excused himself. He walked onto the wet porch, and she heard his truck start up a few minutes later, still wondering what he meant.

FOUR

F our days later, on a sunny late June day, they were seated in a big green bus as it bounced down the long gravel roads that allowed traffic only one way further into the valley. It was a perfect blue-sky day. The vibrant blue contrasted with the red clay dirt that lined the finger creek beds that flowed into bigger streams the deeper they drove.

"Class 3 rapids," their guide Cal said, sitting in the seat in front of them. "It's a solid rush and as high as I am willing to take first-timers out on." He was in his forties and rough around the edges, and Holly could picture him sitting around a campfire with someone like Deak. When she mentioned his name, Cal just raised one eyebrow. It was his only tell.

"Are you sure we shouldn't start at a two or a one?" Holly asked, pulling uncomfortably at the neck of her t-shirt. Underneath, she was wearing her only existing swimming suit, a stretched-out black number that lost most of its elasticity around the same time her waist did.

"Come on, Mom!" Chance said, "You only live once."

"Lucky for me, both my boys are adrenaline junkies," Holly admitted.

"It's going to be awesome," Dillon agreed. He was glued to the window next to her, his eyes peeled for any sight of white rushing water.

Finally, the bus pulled up to the drop-off point, and they descended into the gravel parking lot and waited for instructions.

The boys bounced from side to side on the balls of their feet with pent-up energy. Dillon's fingers immediately went into his mouth, and he chomped on the fingernails. He was a worrier and adept at conjuring up death blow scenarios. She reached out to squeeze his shoulder, and he smiled up at her. She yanked at the straps on his life jacket, testing the fit, then tugged him toward her open arms for an impromptu hug.

Then she tried the same with Chance. "Mom! Seriously." His face reddened, and she followed his gaze to a girl enduring the same family bonding experience with her own family twenty feet away with their own guide.

Cal passed out three oars to them and motioned for both families to follow. Two bright yellow rafts sat on the shore at the edge of the water that seemed calm at first glance, but further away, Holly could hear the rush of the water.

"You guys ready for this?" Holly asked as Cal gathered them close for their rowing lesson.

"The oar should be held between the joint of the thumb and the face of the fingers. At no time should the palm fully make contact with the oar's handle. If you have big palm blisters, you are holding the oar too tightly. If you have blisters on the span of your thumb, you are holding the oar too tightly."

"38 Special Grip. Got it," Holly confirmed, and Cal cracked a smile to let her know he understood her joke that flew right over the boys' heads.

"Let's load up!" Cal encouraged and was the first one into

the water. He held the raft steady while Chance and Dillon stepped from the bank into the raft. Cal directed the boys to sit on opposite sides to evenly distribute the weight. "Tuck your toes under the side to anchor in." He instructed, and reached back to offer a hand to Holly, who took it and picked her way onto the boat, her rubber shoes squeaking in protest. There was already an inch of cold water in the bottom of the raft, and she curled her toes up to avoid it. He untied from the post and climbed in, crawling to his steering position at the back of the raft. Once seated, he picked up his longer oar and continued, "The water is going to be cold. Rafting in June is the best for rapids, but I'm not gonna lie, it's going to be a shock to your system. The water here doesn't really get warm until August, but by then, the rapids are calmer."

Holly reached a hand down to feel the water. Cal wasn't lying; it was ice cold.

"Alright, Simons, when I call out a side, you paddle like your life depends on it. Got it?"

"Got it!"

Satisfied with their response, he settled into his perch on the back of the raft pushing against the bank to navigate the boat into the river, but they were stuck on a rock. "Chance, can you get out and push us?"

"Sure." Chance jumped into the frigid water without hesitation, knees deep, and it sent him howling from the cold.

"Man up," Holly teased him, and he cracked a smile then jumped back into the boat and tucked his feet in as Cal directed them to paddle.

"Left, right, left, right." He used his oar as a rudder in the back, guiding them into the middle of the pristine water. Minnows danced away and then congregated back together into a mass underneath them. The sunlight pierced the crystal clear water, revealing moss, water polished pebbles, and snail shells. The air was calm and clear and the sun felt warm on her shoulders. Holly closed her eyes and soaked it in, a moment of tranquility floating, feeling free.

She heard them before she saw them. Popping open her eyes, she scanned further down the stream that was widening. Massive boulders penned in the sides of the banks, containing the water that rushed across their surface, swirling and crashing into the water rushing from the next boulder. The raw power of the water effectively transformed the river into a violent washing machine.

"Tuck in, paddles in the boat!" she heard Cal shout out behind her as they rocked into the first dip. His voice lost power as it fought the ferocity of the river.

Ever the thrill-seeker, Chance squeezed into the front of the boat as the first white wave crashed into him. Shrieking, he pulled back with a huge grin on his face. Holly dipped her head, but the water smashed onto her cheeks and chest anyway, the shock of the cold leaving her breathless. Her chest pounded. The raft dipped and dodged, hitting the rocks as Dillon and Chance shouted out into the void. Cal's paddle pushed the raft off from the rocks and then dipped down even lower as Holly's stomach lurched. The force of the water sent the back of the raft rocking up so high for a second Holly was sure they would capsize. A terrifying vision filled her mind of losing consciousness as her brain splattered across the boulder that was so close, she could reach out and touch it. At the last possible moment, the back of the raft bounced back down, restoring order as Cal pulled them out of it, the first set of rapids soaking and instantly freezing them all. It should have been annoying, but it was exhilarating. Holly felt her senses awaken in the moment, enjoying the play of emotions that danced across her boys' faces. Chance shook his hair in the cold spray and roared a battle cry into the choppy waters with a huge open smile, the biggest one she'd ever seen on his teenaged face.

This is why. Joy flushed up Holly's torso, warm and jubilant. There was no greater joy you can feel as a parent than being able to give your child a life-changing experience. She felt the power of it changing her, too, but she kept her eyes glued on her sons. Proud in this bright shining moment, providing the highlight experience of their year, her eyes recorded it as it unfolded in front of her. Time slowed down for a second as their utter enjoyment confirmed her decision to uproot them.

Cal guided them to a quieter place. "You can get out and swim alongside the boat if you want to, on this stretch." He barely got the words out of his mouth before Chance jumped into the water with a whoop. Dillon stayed on the raft, his feet tucked in as he watched his brother.

"Come on, dude! What are you waiting for?" Chance called out.

Dillon glanced back uneasily. "You're already wet, buddy. Don't you want to see what it's like swimming in a Montana River?"

"But what if the boat crushes me? Or a fish bites my toe, or I get a cramp and can't swim fast enough?"

"We have one rule at Garden Brook Outfitters, no man left behind," Cal answered. "First of all, you are wearing a life jacket. It's going to do most of the work for you. The current will carry you down this part of the river. You don't even have to swim at all; you can float just like the boat."

"See, honey?" Holly assured him. "Live a little. You miss out on everything cool by being afraid."

He mulled that over, and Holly could almost see the wheels turning in his anxious head. He stood up, looked back at her once more, and asked for confirmation, "You're sure nothing bad will happen?"

She crossed her heart with two fingers. "I promise. I'll count you in." He nodded and stood. "Three, Two, One!" On the last number, Dillon plugged his nose and jumped into the cold water then came up with a sputtering gasp.

"Look at you!" Holly enthused. "So brave."

Dillon smiled and swam toward his brother.

"Thanks for the pep talk," Holly said to Cal. "He's become a little reluctant and fearful lately. I hate to see him limit himself like that."

"They're good kids," Cal said. "I can see that."

"Thanks," Holly responded as she watched Dillon splash Chance. "So, how do you know Deacon?" Holly asked, trying to make small talk with the guide.

"Known the guy since sixth grade," Cal answered. "Ms. Ruth caught me swiping candies from the store, and instead of telling my parents, she let me work it off for the summer. Deacon hated my guts when I first started there, but I grew on him. He's a good one."

"I got the same impression." Holly wanted to ask more questions but was afraid that her interest would get back to Deacon. She learned enough about the power of gossip in small towns from New Hope.

"He's had a rough couple of years, but when the chips are down and you need someone in your corner, there is no man better to have there than Deacon Cartright."

Holly felt a flutter, the briefest brush of butterfly wings inside her belly.

Stop it. You're being ridiculous.

"He's got a bad habit of rescuing broken birds, killing himself to heal them," Cal offered.

"I'm not a broken bird," Holly blurted, offended.

"Sounds like I ruffled some feathers…" He then laughed at himself. "Oh man, bird… feathers… that was terrible. No offense. That came out wrong."

Holly laughed in spite of herself. It was hard not to like Cal. "No offense taken. I have a full plate of my own. Almost too full," she remarked as she watched the boys playfully splashing each other several feet away. "Ruth sent Deacon to help me out with a few things. I tried to tell her it wasn't necessary."

He snorted. "Yeah, I can guess exactly how that went down. When Ruth gets something in her head, that's the way it is. She's as inflexible as steel, but it always comes from a good place."

"Deacon definitely saved us that first night. Sleeping on the floor at my age would have put me down for a week."

"Is there a Mr. Simon?" Cal asked, and the hope flickered that maybe Cal was tasked to find out the dirt on her.

"Not anymore. I mean, there is, but he's eight states away, likely through half a bottle of vodka by now, and not in the picture."

"Bad divorce?"

"Wasn't the divorce, just the series of events immediately after." Holly looked down.

Stop talking. Everything you say will get back to Deacon. Don't become his next broken bird.

"I don't want to be rude," Holly stated, setting a boundary with the guide. "This is the best day my boys have had in a long time, and I want to focus on that instead of taking another ugly turn down memory lane."

"Of course," Cal said. "I'm sorry to pry. Deacon…" He stopped abruptly and then continued. "He's a big guy, but his heart is the biggest part of him. I guess I'm a little overprotective."

"There's no need. I promise you don't have to protect him from me. I've got more than enough going on in my own life. Speaking of that, I am going to be renting out my place on Airbnb and would love to add you to the listing. I know lots of people coming here are looking for an adventure in nature. You're so close to us, I would love to help send people your way."

"That's incredible. And I'll do the same. It's important to make hay while the sun shines. The tourist season up here is short. We have to stick together."

They floated closer to the next swell of rapids. "Boys! It's time to get back in the boat," Cal shouted, and Dillon, ever the rule follower, instantly began a breaststroke back to the raft. Chance lingered a minute longer, then followed. Cal reached down and yanked them up easily by their life jackets. "How was it?"

"Amazing!" Dillon answered, his teeth chattering and his lips taking on a blue twinge.

"The water is so clear," Chance said. "This is so awesome, Mom. Thanks for bringing us here."

Holly grinned.

"Maybe next summer you could be one of my guides," Cal offered, and Chance's eyes lit up at the idea. "Let's see how you do on the level three we've got coming up next."

With something to prove now, Chance tucked his feet into the space between the bottom and the side of the yellow rubber raft, and Dillon followed suit. No longer afraid of the water, the raft tipped and plunged down into the icy water, whose white foamy peaks slapped their faces. Hollering with delight, both boys followed Cal's directions perfectly, and when they finally came to rest at the pick-up point, both boys were equally disappointed the adventure was over. Chance jumped out of the boat as instructed by Cal and pulled them to shore, shaking the water out of his hair like a soaked dog.

Exhausted and exhilarated, Holly accepted Chance's outstretched hand to help her back onto dry land, then pulled her sunburned and chilled boys into a half hug on either side as they walked back to the bus.

"Wasn't that incredible?" she asked them.

"Maybe Montana won't be so bad," Chance admitted.

FIVE

S*nap!* A loud clapping sound later that evening startled Holly awake from the deep sleep brought on by all the physical exertion from the white-water rafting trip. Thinking it was nothing, she adjusted her sleep mask and rolled back over.

Four seconds later, another loud *Snap!* Her heart started racing as she froze in bed, her senses on high alert and her ears straining to decipher what the source of the noise was. Hearing it again, she yanked off the quilt and placed her feet on the cool wood floor. In the darkness, she tiptoed closer to the door and crossed the darkened room, her eyes scanning the night-drenched shapes of walls and furniture that still hadn't become familiar.

Snap! The sound got louder as she got closer to the kitchen, then she saw it. A fat gray mouse was stuck in the mouse trap she set out after finding droppings when she cleaned the kitchen cabinets. It flopped helplessly against the wall as the animal thrust his tiny body violently to free himself. The poor mouse squeaked in pain, and Holly's heart broke.

"Sorry, buddy." He snapped again at the trap in vain. Holly glanced at the clock. She knew the humane thing to do was to put this guy out of his misery, but the idea of killing him made her stomach queasy. She glanced at the clock on the wall and saw it read 10:17 pm. Not having another option, she picked up her phone and sent a text.

Holly: Sorry so late. There's a mouse in a trap that is still alive. Can you help a girl out?

The incoming text bubble immediately appeared, and she breathed a sigh of relief.

Deacon: On my way.

Ten minutes later, she heard gravel spitting from under his tires as he came up the lane. The door squeaked as she let him in and walked him over to the trap where the poor mouse was continuing to fight to free himself.

Deacon picked up the trap and disappeared for a few minutes, giving Holly the chance to look down at the faded gym shorts and tank top she was wearing. Noticing for the first time she wasn't wearing a bra—"Shit!"—she ran into her bedroom and slipped on a sports bra and then ran back to the kitchen before Deacon appeared in the doorway again.

"All set," he confirmed and walked to the sink, rolling the faded blue flannel shirt sleeves up to his biceps, exposing his thick muscled forearms, and began scrubbing his hands.

"Did you have to put him out of his misery?" she asked shyly.

"I don't think you want to know the answer to that."

"You're probably right."

"I'll bring over a flip trap that won't hurt them. It's basically a five-gallon bucket with a trap door. You smear a little peanut butter or a little cheese at the end, and they won't be able to help themselves. But instead of getting stuck in the trap, it will flip them into the bucket and hold them there."

"So, you can catch and release them?"

"Yeah, we'll go with that," Deacon said with a smile that teased the corners of his eyes.

"Can I get you a drink or some coffee for your trouble?"

He hesitated.

"If you don't already have…" Holly interjected.

"You know, I think that sounds pretty nice," he relented and brought his eyes to hers.

"Glass of wine okay?"

"I'm more of a beer guy, but what the heck?"

I'll have to remember to get some for next time. She felt a blush creep up her cheeks. *Next time? Girl! You're getting ahead of yourself.*

"Give me a second." She walked into her bedroom and punched in the number to unlock the closet, then pulled a bottle of chardonnay out of the small refrigerator. When she returned, Deacon's expression was puzzled but he said nothing. Holly poured two glasses and produced a sheath of peppered crackers, a block of white cheddar that she cut into fat slices, and two sprigs of crisp green grapes.

"Look at you, buttering me up with snacks." He smiled, sat down on a stool, and piled a cracker high with cheese, devouring it in one crunchy bite.

"Well, you *did* save me from becoming a murderer tonight." She picked up a slice of cheese with a flirty smile and popped it into her mouth. He leaned forward toward her on the countertop. The faded blue of his shirt only made his thick auburn hair more appealing. Her pulse quickened and she inhaled too quickly, forcing the chunk of cheese to get lodged in the back of her windpipe and sending her into an embarrassing choking fit. Deacon rushed around the countertop to help and smacked her on the center of her back. Completely mortified, her eyes bugged as she tried to cough, starting to panic.

This is how it ends. A piece of cheese is my downfall.

She clawed at her throat and struggled as Deacon delivered one more solid hit to the center of her back. Seeing it wasn't working, he wrapped his arms around her, and with one quick Heimlich thrust, it flew out and hit the refrigerator with a *thunk*.

"Are you alright?" He rubbed the middle of her back, and her flesh seared from his touch. She gasped for air, and it was filled with his cedar and sandalwood scent, unable to discern if it was him or the near-death experience that was making her lightheaded. Her face was beet red and she took two deep breaths before pulling away from his touch, afraid of what would happen if she stayed too close.

"I'm fine," she coughed out weakly and then gulped two long dregs from her wine glass.

Deacon watched the exchange, completely unaware of the effect his proximity was having on her. His forehead knitted with concern. Holly pulled out a stool and sat on it, mortified and desperate to change the topic.

"Well, the white-water rafting was a hit with the boys."

Deacon smiled his long lazy smile. "I'm so glad to hear that."

"Cal is great, and we are going to work together a little bit. I hope that's okay."

"Why wouldn't it be?"

"Um…" Holly swallowed awkwardly.

"You're a little skittish, did you know that?"

Holly blushed. "Unfortunately, it's something I'm working on, to be a little more assertive."

"You need to remove the word little from your vocabulary. It weakens everything you say."

His criticism stung, and she recoiled as though the words were physically wounding her.

"I'm sorry. I'm direct—too direct, one might say. In fact, *many* would say." He laughed at himself then took a sip from his glass and looked over at her with a smirk. "We seem to have a true goldilocks situation brewing here. I'm too direct and you're not direct at all. How about we meet in the middle?" He raised his glass in a toast.

"I'll drink to that." She raised her glass and delicately tapped it against his. She could feel the wine loosening her shoulders and then her tongue.

She tipped the bottle towards his glass to refill it. He quickly covered the top of his glass with his hand. "No more for me. You go ahead." She poured one more glass for herself and then the rest down the sink. When she turned around, she was met with another puzzled look from Deacon. Again, he didn't question her about it.

"What brought you to Montana?"

"I needed a do-over," she admitted and then sipped and studied his warm eyes, still trying to decide how much of her sad story she wanted to reveal to him. She looked down. "We had a rough year last year. Chance got into something that almost killed him." Her hand started to shake, her body betraying her fear and anxiety. Even though she tried to heal her mind, her body would never forget. The trauma was lodged deep in her tissues and bones, and knit into her soul.

She felt a warm, meaty hand engulf hers, and her eyes pulled up to meet his. The gesture was comforting and sweet and she began to melt.

Stop it. You're just another broken bird to him.

"He experimented with drugs. He ran away, and it was terrifying," she confided in a rush. Her eyes began to swim as tears welled at her lashes.

"Ah." He nodded. "So that's the reason for the bedroom liquor cabinet."

"Yeah. I need to provide a safe environment for him."

"Makes sense. What did your husband do?"

"You mean my *alcoholic ex*-husband?" she emphasized as she blurted, claiming her independence. "I found out he was lying to me, the whole time helping the kid engage in risky behavior. It was such a betrayal, and when I discovered it, I knew deep in my gut I had to start over. I knew there was no way Chance wouldn't backslide, or worse, go deeper if he was returned to the same environment that broke him."

Deacon nodded and sat in the pain with her quietly. It was a completely foreign concept to Holly. He didn't rush to fix anything or offer advice. He sat there quietly holding her hand, sheltering it in his own.

"So, I quit my job, sold my house, and left everything I had and everyone I knew so Chance could have a fresh start and a real shot at a new life."

"That's truly admirable. It takes guts to do that."

"You sound like my best friend."

"She sounds like good people."

"The best," Holly agreed. "I don't know why I'm telling you all of this."

"Your story is safe with me," he stated. The words anchored her deeper in his gaze until she felt like she was falling. "But definitely watch what you say around some of the old hens at the store," he warned. "Mama would never say anything, but some of her friends aren't so inclined."

She smiled and swallowed hard on the knot in her throat. "That's good advice."

"I'm assuming he's been through some sort of treatment center. Does he have a sponsor?"

"Not yet, that is one of my highest priorities now."

"I have someone you might want to introduce to him." He plucked a pen off the table and scrawled ten digits out quickly. "My buddy Kent struggled in our twenties, but he's been sober a long time now and runs the AA and NA meeting in Bozeman. He might take him on or know someone that would." He handed the paper to Holly. She was stunned.

"I want to say thank you, but it doesn't seem like enough." She paused and then decided to press her luck. "Cal said you were too generous, rescuing the wounded and trying to heal all the broken birds."

"Is that what you are, Holly Simon?" His voice lingered over the syllables of her name, drawing them out like taffy.

"Last year I might have said yes, but now I think I might be able to fix myself."

"You *are* able to fix yourself," he corrected.

"Yes. I *am* able." Holly's eyes locked onto his warm ones, the shift in her center making her deliciously dizzy.

"Good." He decided and knocked back his glass to finish it off before standing. "Thanks for the wine."

"I should be thanking you for dropping everything to rush over here."

"Not much around to drop anymore," he admitted, and Holly felt a thrill of happiness that he was sitting at home alone and not already entangled and off the market with a relationship. She walked him to the door.

"Can I invite you to dinner next week to thank you?"

"I'd love that," he answered and opened the door, his

boots heavy on the wooden deck, and then she heard him rambling down the lane.

She hugged her arms to her chest, awash with a giddy crush. She grinned and did a little dance as she put their glasses in the sink and then headed to bed.

You're smiling like an idiot. Her cheeks hurt from the permanent smile that was now plastered there after Deacon's revelation that there was no one waiting for him at home.

You got it bad.

SIX

After a short night, Holly woke up and stretched, forgetting for a second where she was in those few precious pre-dawn moments before the kids woke up. In the lingering pitch-black darkness, a coyote howled for its mate, a forlorn cry that pierced her heart and left her feeling isolated and alone. Hearing the howling, Murph stood on the bed and shook, his tags jingling, then he jumped down and pushed closer to her, nuzzling her ankles. Holly reached down to stroke his fluffy fur until they were both slightly more content. She padded barefoot to the kitchen in a trance to the coffee maker. Absentmindedly, she poured in water, plunked the coffee pod into the place, and waited for it to brew while recycling her conversation with Deacon the night before. Feeling the same tell-tale flush of warmth when his hand encased hers. Frustrated that the coffee still hadn't begun to brew, she looked at the settings again. The lights were dark and she laughed at herself.

"Gotta turn it on, dummy," she said out loud, then heard her therapist, Susan's voice in her head, and rephrased it as the stream of dark brown loveliness began to percolate into the waiting cup.

The Skype jingle rang, and Holly raced to her phone to answer it. The boys were still sleeping and likely wouldn't be making an appearance any time before noon since she declared the night before they were going to have to help her clean out cabin one on the property. Nothing like the threat of hard labor to keep the boys at bay.

"Hey, Stace!" Holly raised her mug in a mock salute. Seeing her friend's sleepy familiar face tugged at Holly's heartstrings. Stacey's hair mirrored her own, stuffed into a messy bun on top of her head, still in her pajamas. No matter where she landed in the world, she always had Stacey. Not even being a thousand miles apart could break that bond.

"Well, don't you sound better already!" Stacey gushed.

"I am," Holly admitted. "The white-water rafting trip won the boys over. I'm starting to think we are going to be okay here."

"You will be. Got a busy day ahead?"

Holly sipped at her coffee, feeling her senses come alive, and her mind started to spin. "Yes, I've got to get one of the cabins up on Airbnb as soon as possible. And last night we had a mouse in the house. You know, big Montana-style excitement." She laughed.

"I bet."

"It actually turned out to be slightly traumatic. It was still alive in the trap thrashing about, smacking the wall trying to escape."

"Oh my God, what did you do?"

"I had to call for reinforcements. I didn't have it in me to put it out of its misery."

"Reinforcements?" Stacey's tone was teasing with a smirk.

"Don't get too far ahead of yourself, but Ruth's son, Deacon, came over and helped me out."

"Who's Ruth?"

"She owns the general store, but she's the unofficial mayor of bean town around here."

Stacey leaned in closer to the camera. "Hmm…" she pondered. "I think there's more to this story than I'm being led to believe."

Holly shook her head and laughed at her friend.

"Are you blushing?" Stacey called her out on the carpet the way only best friends can. "Spill it."

"There's nothing to spill," Holly answered, hiding her smile with the cup as she took another sip.

"Don't be coy." Stacey snapped her fingers. "Come on! You know an old married woman like me has to get her cheap thrills from her single best friend."

"You're the worst," Holly said. "You're jumping the gun. There isn't anything but the glimmer of a possibility, and as far as I can tell, it's pretty one-sided."

"How could it be?" Stacey questioned. "You are a catch."

Holly rolled her eyes and looked down at her worn tank top and running shorts that were her pajamas. "Sure I am."

"It's true. You are the treasure. Don't forget that, Holly. You deserve a partner who works as hard as you do in relationships." She paused, knowing that it was always hard for Holly to stomach compliments. "So, tell me about him."

Holly exhaled and then leaned in with a huge grin, propping up her chin on her hand and strumming her fingers on the coffee mug to dispel some of the energy surging through her. "I don't know. It's been a while since I felt anything close to this."

"Ooh, girl!" Stacey said. "I like the sound of that!"

"It's probably nothing, but the man is *capable*. With

Mick, I felt like I was raising another kid. Deacon can handle himself and has a knack for showing up out of the blue right when I need him."

"You deserve a real man. Someone who shows up for you and the boys."

"Maybe." Holly looked away through the window at the hint of the impending sunrise. The navy sky was lightening with streaks of brighter light washing up from the horizon. Deacon's rugged face popped into her mind again, and she relived the warmth of his hand on hers as a horde of butterflies tickled her insides.

"Ooh! I have an idea. Sneak a pic and send it to me," Stacey urged.

"That would be weird, Stace," Holly admonished her. "We aren't there yet."

"Fine. I might need to come up there this fall and see him with my own eyes anyway."

"I would love that. Open invitation, any day, any time." Holly took a sip of her coffee, building up her confidence to ask the question that plagued her mind since the rafting trip.

"Do you think I'm a broken bird?" Holly blurted.

"Where is this coming from?"

"On the rafting trip, our guide was one of Deak's friends, and he told me Deak is attracted to broken birds."

"You're not a broken bird, you're a freaking eagle."

Holly chuckled.

"Seriously, woman, you are badass. Life threw some pretty horrific consequences at you, and you rose to the challenge. Broken birds lay in the grass and die. You fought through the pain to rise and soar."

Fresh tears welled up in Holly's eyes.

"I love you, Stace."

"Back at cha, sista."

———

Later that morning, the Skype jingle rang again. This time it was Mick. Holly exhaled a sigh and pressed the button to connect.

"Hey, Hols," Mick said flatly. He was haggard and tired. He palmed his face and let out a sigh himself.

"Is everything okay?" Holly couldn't stop herself from asking.

"Nah," Mick admitted as she heard the flick of a lighter before a hazy puff of smoke obscured her vision slightly. Mick scratched at his jaw line. "I need to talk to you about something."

Holly's radar instantly went up, and the first finger of fear tickled her belly. "Yeah?" she said to fill the awkward silence.

"It's going to be hard for me to pay the next few support payments."

"Jesus, Mick, it's court-ordered. I am not a bank. Figure it out."

"It's been hard to find work since the kids left." He took another long drag on his cigarette.

"You seem to be able to buy the cancer sticks. What's a pack of cigarettes cost now? Six bucks?"

"More like seven."

"As always, your priorities are perfectly aligned with your commitment to our sons." Holly spat her words laced with sarcasm she didn't even try to hide. "You staying away from the booze?"

He rolled his red-rimmed eyes. "Is that all I am to you now, a walking paycheck?"

"These are your *children*. I am not getting paid for services rendered. I am taking care of *our children* and that requires money. They need food and shelter and clothing for school that starts in a few months."

"I never get to see them. It's not fair that I'm supposed to send you all my money but never get to see what any of it buys."

"Seriously?" Holly fumed. "I don't know why I didn't see this coming. You've been a disappointment from the beginning. I know how you make your money, Mick. It's all under the table, shady shit outside of the system."

"I am a freelance *musician*."

"No. You are a *father*, and sometimes, it will require you to set your guitar down and step out into the real world to get a real job. I have let you slide for decades. It's time for you to step up now and be a man."

He looked away, lost in his own thoughts, backing down from the confrontation as he always did.

"Is that all you needed?"

"Yeah," he muttered and took another long drag.

Holly was shocked. "Didn't you want to talk to the boys?"

"Yeah… Sure, okay," Mick said offhandedly. Fresh anger welled up in Holly's belly from his blatant ambivalence.

"Dilly! Chance! Your dad is on Skype," Holly shouted upstairs. "After you talk to him, we have to get going. There is a lot to do." Suddenly, there was a lot more to consider. If she didn't have regular support payments coming in, life would become infinitely harder. The idea of it made Holly shudder. Jumping up and pulling her hair into a ponytail, she started the task of gathering cleaning supplies.

Tension gathered deep in Holly's gut. Her lips set in a hard line, she yanked open the cabinet drawers and stuffed toilet bowl cleaner, a brush, and anti-bacterial wipes into a caddy. She wanted to scream but was forced to tuck her rage deep inside her ribs where it grew and festered.

She remembered the Kids in the Middle Class she was forced to complete before her divorce was final.

"Don't speak ill of the other parent. It hurts the child when you express hatred toward them. The child will think you hate part of them. Do not dump your adult problems on your children. This is already a time of upheaval in their lives, and they are not built to handle adult issues."

In her heart, she knew the balding instructor who taught these principles was right, but it didn't make it any easier to carry the burden of a deadbeat father. What started out as pity turned into anger when she discovered Mick's betrayal last year. Now, the anger seethed into a trickle of rage. It spread inside her cell by cell, infecting her with negativity, consuming her from the inside out.

She shook her head to break the hold it was gaining on her emotions.

You cannot live in hate. It destroys everything.

From their bedroom, she heard Dillon's muffled laugh and it angered her even more.

Taking a deep breath, she exhaled the hot hatred. He was still the fun one. Even with all his shortcomings, Holly was afraid they loved him more. A small part of her yearned to tell them the truth, for them to know who and what their father truly was, but she pushed it away and gave herself a pep talk.

Nothing good can come from that conversation. This isn't helping. Stay busy. Get the cabin listed. This is the only thing you can control. You have to let go of what you cannot change. You can't control Mick's behavior or his shirking of real responsibilities. Focus on what you need to do to support your children on your own. Then, if he comes through, it's icing on the cake. Put yourself in a position of power where you don't need Mick for anything.

A few minutes later, when the boys appeared looking for cereal, she asked, "Did you have a good visit with your dad?"

"Yeah," Dillon said. "Dad is having a really hard time. He misses us so much." He burst into tears.

"Come here, sweetheart." Holly opened her arms, and Dillon rushed into them. She squeezed him closer to her while her anger roiled.

Grow up, Mick. Classic, making everything about you.

"I miss Dad."

"I know you do, but he can come visit us whenever he wants," Holly stated, hoping it would calm his fears. "When we left, I told him he was welcome to visit any time. He knows that."

"But he's a million miles away now," Dillon sobbed.

"Do you really see Dad driving sixteen hours to come see us?" Chance asked his brother while he poured cereal into a bowl and doused it with milk. Standing shirtless in the kitchen, wearing khaki shorts, he sat on a stool and shoveled spoonsful of cereal into his mouth. Holly was shocked at his uncanny ability to see through Mick's bullshit at sixteen.

"He might," Dillon offered and wiped his eyes with the back of his hand.

"Yeah, right," Chance muttered with his mouth full. "Dad does what's good for Dad." Holly was shocked at his stunning teenage clarity. Away from the influence of his father, she could see Chance maturing and discerning correctly that Mick was a selfish man. Relief flooded Holly, and the valve on the hatred released slightly.

"Let's focus on something else. If we get cabin one cleaned and photographed today, I'll take you guys to town for ice cream." She mentally calculated how much that was going to cost and cringed for a second before recovering.

"Yeah?" Dillon victory punched the air and tore away from her to gather up his shoes. Chance was quiet and disappeared into himself. She felt him harden and shut down. Ice cream wasn't going to have the same effect on him. She watched him read the cereal box as she ate her own bowl of cereal.

As they walked to the car, she slung one arm around Chance's shoulders to pull him in for a quick squeeze.

"You okay, buddy?" Holly asked.

"Yeah, Mom. I'm fine."

"Fine? That's what I was afraid of."

Chance sighed. "Quit worrying."

"Can't stop, won't stop," Holly answered, trying to inject her fears with humor.

"You have to find some other way to occupy your time."

"Speaking of occupying your time, Deacon knows a guy that runs a recovery program in Bozeman and gave me the address."

Chance stiffened and pulled away. "What? You told Deacon?"

"I'm sorry, honey, it just came out. He asked how we landed here, and I didn't want to lie."

Chance's jaw tightened. "It wasn't your story to tell."

"Honey, it affected me. It affected all of us. Hiding the facts isn't going to help the situation at all. I am proud of you and what you have overcome. Besides, we can trust Deacon."

"How do you know?"

"I just do."

"No offense, Mom, but your track record with men is pretty terrible."

Holly laughed and pushed his shoulder playfully, trying to

reconnect. "How'd you get so insightful at the tender age of sixteen?"

He puffed up with her praise. "Last year grew me up quick. I guess that is the one good thing that came from all of this."

"I guess," Holly agreed, but the truth wounded her heart. She had to acknowledge that he grew up faster than she wanted. Away from her influence, Chance forged relationships and learned healthy habits and beliefs that he adopted on his own. He came home with an interest in Buddhism, an influence from the center, but something he would have never been exposed to otherwise. He was creating a whole life for himself outside of her.

The last year robbed her of precious time with him, and the slighting stung. Chance had been fused to her entire being the moment of his conception, and even though it was natural for him to pull away, each tear toward his independence hurt. Detachment was a part of growing up. It was supposed to be normal and healthy, so why did it hurt so much?

SEVEN

Lost in her thoughts and motivated by her financial fears, Holly gave the boys boxes and a broom and told them to clear out the first cabin. It was a one-bedroom miniature version of her own with a charming little kitchen and matte black wood stove set in the corner of the open main living space. She scooped the ashes out of the ancient stove and reset the grate with logs and newspaper in the teepee formation that her dad taught her during the only camping trip he was able to take her on when she was eight.

Grief comes in waves. It had been over three decades since her dad left, and she still missed him. The primal wound left in her soul from his unexpected death was covered now by layers and layers of scar tissue, but pieces of him would surface and peek through, and it would only take a scent or a song to bring him flooding back in waves. The first several years, moments like that would bring her to her knees and leave her gasping for breath daily, her bottomless despair profound and overwhelming. But as the years passed, the anger from how he was taken so early faded into the background, and all that remained were the sweet memories.

The ice cream cones and the bowling alley lessons. The mornings she would wake up to a hastily jotted note with a Bit O' Honey candy bar weighing it down. It was an old-fashioned honey-flavored taffy with almond bits that was hard to find anywhere but Amazon anymore, but when she stumbled upon one in the wild, it would bring her to tears. His insistence that she learn how to change a tire and check her oil. It was like he somehow knew he'd be leaving early, so he tried to pack in as many life lessons as he could in their precious time together.

She was never as close to her mother, who always seemed to keep her at a distance. Always providing the basics—food, shelter, and clothing—while her dad was on the road. But she never figured out how to give Holly the one thing she needed most—love. When he'd return, Holly would rush to his side, unaware of the subtle bitter tang of competition that was taking shape as she vied for his attention, unknowingly pulling his focus from her mother to herself.

After he died, her mother's heart hardened even more. Holly made it through the rest of high school, then when her mother drove her to her college dorm, they both relaxed into an unspoken sense of relief that their obligation to each other was finally over. She had a fatal heart attack seven years ago, leaving Holly an orphan. It was barely a blip on Holly's radar that left her feeling guilty she didn't grieve her parents equally. The sting of the loss wasn't as all-consuming and gut-wrenching. She thought about her mother from time to time, but it was her father who had stamped his love on every chamber of her heart.

Holly scrubbed at the layer of greasy grime on the kitchen cabinets, consumed with fresh worries about her financial situation. The fear was like ingesting a tapeworm; it began to eat at the edges of her. She scrubbed harder, the stress giving her a burst of energy. She plunged her hands into the hot, soapy water and wrung out the cloth then scrubbed harder, breaking out in a sweat at her hairline. In cutoff jean shorts, she knelt down to get closer to the grime on the base cabinets, sitting back on her heels. Holly scrubbed and scrubbed the worries away, getting some level of satisfaction from the physical effort.

"You're going to take the finish off those cabinets if you aren't careful," a warm voice behind her said, making Holly jump as he laughed. It was a warm baritone sound that filled the room.

"You scared me." Holly wiped her forehead with the back of her hand and forced a smile on her face.

"Don't be afraid, timid little creature," he teased as he squatted down to her level, and she inhaled the scent of him, Irish Spring soap and maple. "I am here to save you."

She bristled at the word.

"I don't need you to save me. I can do that myself," she answered as she scrambled to her feet, the proximity making her heart hammer in her chest. "But if you're bringing sandwiches or coffee, I wouldn't turn that down." He opened his palms face up.

"I come empty-handed, with nothing to give you except my time."

"Well, beggars can't be choosers." Holly grinned at him. "Can you check the sink? I think there's a leak, Deak." She chuckled at the rhyme. "See, I'm a poet and you didn't even know it."

Her corny line made him grin. "Let me just grab my tools from my truck." He sauntered out to the truck, his long, muscled legs making short work of the journey. Holly watched him walk away. It had been a long time since she watched a man walk away and enjoyed it. He turned around and caught her eyes that lingered a little too long, and she quickly glanced away, but not before he noticed.

So busted.

He returned with a red toolbox and a smirk. "Did you see something you liked?"

Holly flushed red and looked down, pressing her lips together to stop the smile from spreading across her face.

He bent down and opened the cabinet to assess the damage. Bent down on one knee, one hand gripped the countertop while the other hand felt underneath for the leak. His forehead knotted in concentration.

"Ah! Gimme your hand." Before she could answer, he reached out and pulled her hand toward the sink, guiding her closer to him and pressing her hand deeper into the cabinet. Her chest quickened the closer she leaned. Then his eyes met hers. "There. Feel that?"

Holly blinked hard, trying to refocus on the leak instead of the callused hand wrapped around her own.

"Yeah." She nodded. "Can you fix it?"

"Honey, there ain't nothing inside a house I can't fix with these two hands."

I bet. Including me?

She was like a moth to a flame. He was magnetic and she was powerless to fight the pull.

"What are you guys doing?" Dillon asked innocently from the doorway, where he and Chance were observing the interaction with interest.

Holly jumped and pulled away, standing to lean against the countertop at a respectable distance, trying to look nonchalant. She tried to rest her chin on her hand but missed, and Chance laughed as she flushed warm again and tried to recover.

"Yes, *Mother*, what *are* you two doing in here?" he asked

with a smirk, studying her like she was an exhibit at the zoo. He'd never seen this side of his mom before, and he was amused. She reddened at his word choice. Chance only called her Mother ironically.

"Checking for leaks, my man, and we found one. Ready to begin your master fixer apprenticeship?" Deacon asked Dillon. "And what about you, Chance? Ready to learn some skills that will be valuable your entire life?" Deak was still on his knees, his enormous form like an overgrown mastiff.

"I guess so." Chance shrugged, bored to tears with the typical teenager response at the idea of learning a basic home repair skill.

"Now *that* is the kind of enthusiasm I can work with." Deacon laughed at his own joke. "Mind helping me make a run to the hardware store?"

"Can I come?" Dillon asked.

"Next time, buddy," Deak said. "I have something to talk to Chance about."

Chance's eyes darted to Holly's with a pinched look as he followed behind Deak to the pickup truck like he was headed to a firing squad.

Holly watched them leave from the window and then disappear in the dust down the gravel lane.

She heaved a sigh and turned back to Dillon. "Let's wipe down the rest of the kitchen, and then you can help me get lunch started before the boys come back."

"Dad says that's women's work."

"Did he now? Did you know that most famous chefs are men?"

"No," he admitted.

"It's true. Your dad's got it all wrong. There's no such thing as women's work. When you get married, you are part of a team. One of my jobs as your mother is to turn you into someone who is a capable partner for your future wife."

"Eww. Gross, Mom."

"Someday, it won't be so gross."

"I'm never getting married. I'm going to stay with you forever." He smiled up at her and wrapped his arms back around her. Holly closed her eyes and savored it because she knew it was a lie, but the sweetest lie he'd ever tell her. Someday, not far from now, he was going to stop giving her the hugs and his affections would find another girl to focus on. "He was holding your hand." Dillon's voice was muffled by the cotton of her t-shirt. "I've never seen you hold hands with anyone other than Dad."

"He was just showing me where the leak was, honey. That's all. I promise."

———

An hour later, the truck rambled back down the driveway, and an animated Chance held a brown paper bag of plumbing fittings. Holly observed them walking back to cabin one. Chance was laughing and they were rough housing each other. She grabbed a towel to dry her hands and walked out onto the porch.

"Lunch is ready!" she shouted over to them. At first, they didn't answer, but Dillon took over cupping his hands around his mouth and shouting even louder.

"Food! Come and get it!"

Immediately, Deak and Chance reversed direction and started walking to the main house.

"Your mama needs a cowbell out here like my mama used to have so we knew when it was chow time." Deacon's quick smile creased the fine lines by his eyes.

"Always add more cowbell," Holly joked and felt a giddy thrill when Deak's smile was directed at her.

"This guy never misses a meal." Deacon rubbed his belly affectionately and followed her into the house, stopping at the sink to roll up the sleeves of his shirt and begin washing his powerful hands. He grabbed the bottle of soap and tossed it over to Chance, whose hand lurched up just in time to catch it. "C'mon, you degenerates. Get over here and wash up for your mama."

Thick sandwiches bursting with turkey and cheddar cheese sat on a platter with fresh peaches and a bag of salty kettle chips. They sat down and filled their plates. Holly watched them together from her perch at the head of the table. It had been a long time since a man had sat at her table with her sons. Deak teased them both mercilessly. The boys lapped up the male attention bloated with testosterone and laced with insults. She could see them opening up, especially Chance. Whatever had transpired during the road trip to the hardware store had righted his hurt feelings.

Holly was quiet, watching their interactions and seeing how effortlessly Deak used humor to wrap them all around his enormous fingers. He had a way. When Deacon Cartright asked you to do something, you did it. Not because you were intimidated or afraid, but because you wanted to help him. You wanted to become valuable to him. You wanted to bask in the sunshine that radiated from his warm personality.

And when she realized this was happening, to all of them, not just her, it was terrifying. Because when you cared about people, when you let them in or even loved them, you got let down and hurt. She was used to getting hurt. She was used to being let down, but she would do anything to stop that from happening to her boys.

EIGHT

A few days later, Chance was running around the house looking for his shoes in a panic. "They're going to be here any minute."

"Who?"

"Deak and Kent."

Holly did her own little dance of panic, where she finger-combed her hair, pulled it back into a high ponytail, and quickly moistened her fingers to swipe them through the flyaways. Having skipped a shower, she squirted on a little perfume, then brushed on some mascara and two swipes of blush. Seconds later, there was a knock at the door.

"Come in." Holly crossed the room quickly and opened the door. "You must be Kent." She held out her hand.

"Yes, ma'am," he said, removing his hat and shaking her hand.

Chance jumped into his newly found shoes, yanking them up over his heels without untying them.

"It's a bit of a drive to Bozeman, and after the meeting, we usually head over to Bertie's Pie Shop. We'll be back by 10:30 if that is alright with you."

"Well," she considered. Having her son spend several hours with a complete stranger was unnerving. Hesitating, she glanced at Deacon who gave her the briefest nod. "I think that will work. This is important, but at least let me…" She paused and glanced around the room, searching for her purse. When she found it, she dug in and handed Chance a twenty. "He'll pay for the pie since you are so kind to drive him over."

"That's not necessary." Kent was dumbfounded by her gesture. He was solid with a soft belly slung low on his hips and a weather-worn face that matched the hat in his hands. Holly guessed he was nearly fifty and wondered how Chance was going to take to him. She knew that finding a sponsor Chance could really connect with was important to his sobriety. If it didn't work out with Kent, she didn't know what she'd do.

"It's my pleasure. I appreciate your offering to pick him up. The idea of him driving to Bozeman every week in the dark scares me."

"Looks like this deal works out better for both of us," Kent said with a wink. "Chance gets a sponsor and I get free pie."

"I feel like I should be asking you more questions, but if Deak vouches for you, then that's enough for me."

Deacon nodded. "You have nothing to worry about with this one. I've known him my entire life."

"Okay. Have fun!" She blurted awkwardly.

"Well, we've got to step to it to get there on time. You can't participate if you show up late. Ma'am," Kent acknowledged her, bowing his chin slightly, then put his hat back on and left with Chance. The screen door slammed closed behind them.

Deacon remained on the porch. "Have fun?" he teased.

Holly laughed and rolled her eyes at her own awkwardness. "Terrible, right? Kent will think I'm a total loon."

"Most likely." He smirked.

"Hey!" She shoved his shoulder playfully, appreciating the muscles in his shoulder her hand connected with. Dillon wandered out onto the porch and over to Holly for a hug.

"You smell weird," Dillon said, and Holly's face flushed pink. He sniffed the air, trying to place it while Holly shifted from one foot to the other uncomfortably. "Like flowers or something sweet. Are you wearing perfume? Why are your cheeks so pink?" Dillon was staring up at her face, confused, and Holly was so mortified she wished the floor would open up and swallow her whole. She glanced over at Deak, who was clearly enjoying her unease.

"Go get a snack," she offered as an easy distraction Dillon wouldn't be able to ignore. He walked to the kitchen cabinets and rifled through them, finally settling on a bag of Cheetos then leaving without another word.

"I better be going," Deacon said. He leaned in so close she could feel his warm breath on her neck, sending goosebumps down her arms, "And for the record, you don't smell weird at all."

NINE

After fielding an endless barrage of emails and phone calls, Holly was finally hosting her first guests. They were newlyweds who loved the proximity to the national park and had over fifty reassuring five-star reviews from other hosts. Staying an entire week, their fee was going to ease her first upcoming mortgage payment significantly, and with Mick's shady financial situation, she couldn't book her rentals fast enough. Holly was running through the cabin placing crisp white towels on the towel racks in the bathroom. To the table, she anchored a bucket of ice filled with cheap but chilled champagne and placed some chocolate-covered strawberries from the little chocolate shop on the square, and then added a heart made of red rose petals on the bed. She knew from all the research she did, it was the little touches that increased the chances of a guest leaving a five-star rating. Immaculate bathrooms, fresh towels, and comfortable bedding were important as well as quick resolutions of any issues during a guest's stay. Living on the property gave her an edge, and she wanted to use it to her advantage. Ratings and reviews were gold, and earning the elusive Superhost status was a goal of Holly's. It was going to take a long time to achieve it, but she had her sights on it anyway.

She locked the door behind her and waited for them to arrive. Cleaning out the second cabin and reading comments on Reddit boards, she learned about running a successful rental property. At dusk, the weary travelers knocked on her door weighed down with backpacks and exhausted smiles.

"Welcome to Montana, I'm Holly," she said with a bright smile as she handed over the keys to a blonde couple that looked like they had been handpicked from an outfitter catalog. "It can get cold here at night, so there are some extra blankets in the hall closet. There is also some wood on the back porch for a fire. Let me know if there is anything else I can do to make your stay with us more comfortable."

Quick smiles revealed toothpaste commercial perfect teeth. "We're Elsa and Franc," the model gorgeous woman said with an accent that Holly couldn't place but sounded Scandinavian. "Thank you. We've been hiking all day. We're very tired." Franc nodded in agreement.

How is that possible?

Elsa looked bright, shiny, and flawless after hiking through Yellowstone for an entire day. Her long glossy hair was pulled into a ponytail, and she was wearing a thermal shirt, skin-tight leggings that left little to the imagination, slouched wool socks, and hiking boots. An interested Chance appeared at Holly's side, unable to tear his wide eyes from Elsa.

"Do you need help with your bags?" he offered, and Holly had to press her hand to her mouth to hide her smile.

"You're very kind, but we are okay on our own."

"You are welcome to join us for breakfast," Holly offered.

"Yes!" Chance declared. "My mom makes the best pancakes."

Elsa smiled again, and it was like fireworks going off. If Chance was a cartoon, there would be a floating sea of love-struck hearts swirling above his smitten head.

"We have other plans for the sunrise, but appreciate the invite."

Chance was crestfallen.

"Okay then, we'll let you get settled. Enjoy your stay."

She watched them walk toward the cabin like Barbie and a blond Swedish Ken. "Pick your chin off the floor," she teased Chance.

"She's *beautiful*, Mom."

"And *married*, son," Holly replied. "And *too old* for *you*." Chance ducked his head sheepishly as a pink twinge dusted his cheeks. "I hope when an old man who smells like peas and vinegar shows up here, you scramble to offer him the same level of top-notch service you just offered our gorgeous Swedish guest."

"Mom." He sighed, embarrassed.

———

The week passed uneventfully and easily. Sometimes she forgot they were even there. Their rental car would be gone before she woke up in the mornings and would come rambling home at dusk. She purposely stayed away, giving the couple privacy, but close enough to respond quickly if they needed anything. They asked for nothing, and when they left, posted a five-star review.

Charming log cabin minutes from the North Entrance of Yellowstone National Park. Host was very responsive and accommodating. Easy check-in and check-out.

It was our honeymoon, and we arrived to chocolate-covered strawberries and champagne. Highly recommended for any romantic getaway. Will be back.

They included a photo of the heart Holly had made from rose petals. When Holly arrived to clean out the cabin, she found two unopened bottles of a fantastic Pinot Noir, an unopened tin of Macadamia Nuts, a dark chocolate bar, and almost an entire box of Starbucks coffee pods in the cabinets. Inside the refrigerator, she found gourmet relishes and condiments and an entire carton of free-range brown eggs.

The couple even included a thank you card with a $50 tip. The small gesture bit back the ever-present fear of being able to make ends meet.

See? The universe provides.

She hauled the gourmet windfall to her house and reset the cabin for the next night. Fresh white sheets snapped out and were folded and tucked under the bed. She cleaned every inch of the cabin and turned on an organic lavender warmer. Feeling calm, capable, and in control, she felt life was finally beginning to settle.

TEN

The second round of guests, Holly wasn't so lucky. It was a last-minute booking of four twenty-something girls. They were a gaggle of legs, elbows, freshly straightened hair, and cowboy boots. In town for a music festival, they even offered to pay Holly an extra hundred to provide drop-off and pick-up services. She gladly agreed, adding the total to her growing winter stash, grateful for every job that allowed her savings to grow. Each tick-up released a level of the pressure that was building the closer the days moved to winter.

On the surface, they seemed normal. All of their pre-booking communication was standard, not a red flag to be seen. Four sorority sisters who'd just finished their second year of college and wanted to cut loose. When she brought the blow-up mattresses over to make the tiny cabin more comfortable, they thanked her profusely. She walked them through the operation of the appliances and gave them her usual spiel about the danger of flushing feminine products down a septic system.

"Just toilet paper," she directed. "It's all it can take. Everything else should be thrown in the trash can."

Their heads nodded in unison, like dogs with a ball, but there was a vacant look in their eyes.

At seven p.m., she knocked at the door and waited. After another couple of hurried knocks, they finally stumbled out onto the porch where Holly immediately knew something was off. Their eyes were half-closed slits and they pitched side to side as they walked to the van.

"Are you guys alright?" Holly asked warily.

"Fine. We're fine," the leggy brunette named Kendall said, clearly the leader of the group. Along with a curvy blonde, she half-carried, half-dragged their other two friends to the van and set them inside the two bucket seats before crawling into the back.

"There's some water in a cooler back there," Holly offered as the two girls in the seats behind her dozed off, their eyes closed.

"Oh my God! Thank you!" Kendall said, sucking down the entire bottle in one long drink that made the bottle squeal in protest. When the bottle was empty, she crushed it on the floor of the van with her boot.

"Is this your first trip to Montana?" she asked them, trying to make small talk. Kendall either didn't hear her or ignored her, so Holly turned on the radio and started to sing along.

They were ten minutes from the festival when the puking began. The first girl directly behind Holly shot up like she had been electrified and began to dry heave. After three constricted thrusts, she projectile vomited so fiercely that Holly heard liquid hit the back of the headrest and felt droplets hit the back of her neck, making her cringe. The sour smell of stomach bile filled the van, and Holly rolled down the windows, gasping for fresh air. Holly's worried glance darted from the road to the girl behind her.

"Are you okay?"

"Hayley can't handle her liquor," Kendall answered, her tone bored and unconcerned as she continued to text and watch TikToks.

Then the girl seated in the other bucket seat roared to life, her thin limbs convulsing and flailing about the interior of the vehicle. Another wave of sour stench came and Holly gagged. What was it about the smell of vomit that made you puke? She pulled her t-shirt up higher over her mouth and nose and begged the pizza she'd eaten earlier to stay down.

The two vomiting girls flopped back into their chairs, pasty and pale. Their stomach contents were spewed all over the inside of Holly's van.

"We have to turn around," Holly said, making the decision on her own.

"But we're almost there. Can't you just drop us off?" the ring leader asked. She was an insensitive girl Holly was beginning to hate.

"Seriously?" Holly shrieked, twisting her head over her shoulder, alternating continuously to try to look Kendall in the eye and then back to the road as she drove. "Aren't you even a little bit concerned about your friends?" She was shocked a person could call themself a friend yet be so callous. "These two are in no condition to be in the middle of a crowd at the music festival. Someone could take advantage of them. It's not safe."

"No offense, but you don't know Hayley and Rachel. I've seen them rally before." She remained focused on her godforsaken phone that Holly wanted to rip out of her hand.

The girls vomited again as if to prove a point, and this time Holly had enough. She jerked the steering wheel to the side of the road and whipped the door open. Yanking the keys out of the ignition, she ran out into the fresh air gulping it in eagerly. Then she reached into the cooler between the front seats and grabbed more water bottles.

"I can't in good conscience drop you girls off at the festival. We're going back."

Kendall fumed and huffed her displeasure, then feverishly started texting again. Holly climbed back in the smelly van and stuck her head outside the window like Murph did on car rides, gulping in the fresh air to keep herself from getting sick.

Thirty minutes later, a grateful Holly pulled up into the driveway and opened the doors, thinking the two girls in the back would help get their friends settled. Instead, they stomped into their cabin, leaving their friends passed out in the bucket seats.

Holly dialed Deak's number and he answered on the first ring.

"I've got a couple of guests under the influence, passed out in my van, and I can't just leave them out here, can I?"

"What were they doing in your vehicle?"

"It's a long story." She sighed, standing in the dark next to the van. Even with all the doors open, the sour smell was awful.

"On my way," he said, and minutes later, she heard his truck barreling up the gravel driveway. She had guilted Kendall and the blonde into trying to help get Hayley and Rachel out of the van when she heard Deak's voice behind her.

"Holy Jesus, what is that smell?"

Holly frowned. "You don't want to know."

"What did they take?" he asked Kendall, whose eyes widened at the sight of him. Suddenly more interested in being of service now that he was around, she reached out and wrapped one manicured hand around his forearm and squeezed it. "Just some whiskey. They can't hold it like a real woman can."

She tipped her head down and batted her eyelashes at Deacon, who promptly pulled her fingers away from his forearm. Holly swore it sounded like Velcro being ripped apart, it was a deliberate act that nearly made Holly cheer. Then he asked, "Does that act really work for you?"

"You'd be surprised just how well," she cooed up at him with a wink. Walking one finger up his arm from his elbow to his bicep, her dark eyes ogled the pull of the fabric that strained to cover it. The blatant flirtatious act incensed Holly, who felt a wall of heat rise from her belly to her chest.

He ran back to his truck and reappeared with a battered leather bag. He produced a stethoscope from it and a small flashlight. Putting the ends in his ears, he listened to their chests and checked their pupils. "Vitals are good and pulse is normal. They are going to have a bad day tomorrow, but they just need to go to bed now." Taking off the stethoscope, he tucked it back in the bag and zipped it shut.

He lifted one of them effortlessly from her seat, walked her into the cabin, and placed her on the inflatable bed as Holly spread out sheets and pulled a bucket from the shed to place near the bed. Not taking no for an answer, Kendall pranced around Deacon, asking questions that he answered with single words, still trying to find her opening. She was like an annoying wasp, buzzing around his head as he ignored her.

After making sure both girls were safe inside the cabin, Holly closed the door and walked him to the truck. Still, she smelled vomit; it was a scent that suffocated her, making her crave a shower.

He leaned closer, his face wrinkled into a grimace.

Holly's nose scrunched up as she sniffed herself. "She got me." Holly smacked her lips together, her nose crinkled in disgust. "I swear I can taste it." He picked a loose chunk out of her hair and chucked it to the side.

"You saved the day again." She thanked him. "What else you got in that bag of tricks?" she teased, the jealousy of watching Kendall fall over herself for his attention lighting the fire of competition in her.

"Someday I'll show you," he answered. "Mama taught me to always be prepared. Parts of Montana are so rural, if a true life or death situation popped up, you wouldn't be able to get medical attention when you need it."

Holly sighed and pinched at her nose where a headache was beginning to form.

"You're white as a sheet." He took a step closer and assessed her, pressing the fingers of his hand to her cheek.

Holly rubbed her beleaguered face with her hands. "This is the punishment I get for taking a last-minute booking without checking references."

"Well, the good news is, no one is going to die here tonight."

"Fantastic," Holly deadpanned. "Because that is not exactly good for business." She was trying to be lighthearted when all she felt was sick to her stomach. "These girls are going to hate their choices in the morning."

"We all have days we regret."

"Oh really? What days does Deacon Cartright regret?' Holly teased, using the segue to try to pry open the door to his heart he kept locked and dead-bolted.

His face clouded, and her heart skipped a beat wondering if he was finally going to bend a little and let her in. The idea made her nearly giddy; she was anxious to even the playing field. To know something deep and dark about him would make her feel less exposed.

After a long pause, he said, "You wouldn't have time to hear them all." He gave a sad smile. "Get a shower and I'll come help you in the morning."

"Fine," she answered, "but someday you're going to have to open up and let me in."

"Maybe someday I will." And then he pulled away.

———

The next morning, her worst fears were confirmed. The girls didn't leave until 10:59, using every available minute of their rental. Wearing sunglasses and looking pale, without so much as a wave goodbye, they got into an Uber and disappeared without a trace.

"Holy shit," Deacon exclaimed, letting a hot breath blow past his teeth. Surveying the damage to the cabin, he was able to articulate what Holly wasn't. "I hope you kept their deposit."

"I did, but I don't think $200 is going to be enough."

"Whoa!" Even Chance was stunned at the condition of the rental.

"Whoa is right." She handed him a folded-up garbage bag and a set of rubber gloves. "Can you get started with the trash?" Chance put his headphones in and started to clear the stacked fortress of beer cans and empty take-out containers.

Deacon opened the windows to air out the lingering smell of smoke with a hint of vomit that was stagnant in the room from the night before. Holly checked the bathroom, and as she feared, the toilet was clogged.

"Even after I had that entire discussion with them about the septic." She pulled on rubber gloves and filled a bucket with hot soapy water, hit it with a healthy dose of Lysol, then for good measure, hit it again. The chemical rainforest scent was a huge welcome improvement already.

"How did they even…?" Deacon held up a door that was lying next to the cabinet it was supposed to be attached to.

"They were here less than twenty-four hours," Holly remarked. "The amount of damage, it must be some kind of world record."

Holly was furious at herself for accepting the booking.

Never again.

It took six hours of hard work, two trips to the hardware store, a pressure washer for the van, and an upholstery cleaner rental to right the damage the girls had done. She had to throw away the towels that were stained with mascara and greasy foundation.

Thank God for the magic eraser.

Her back ached from being on her hands and knees. Her arms were weary from all the scrubbing. It had been a long day and such a waste, but the lesson was learned.

ELEVEN

As a reward for Chance and Dillon's hard work, Holly got up with the sunrise the next morning and made an early run to the General Store for park passes. Ruth sent her home with all the picnic supplies she needed and was even able to sneak a caramel apple pie in the bottom of the bag while Holly picked through the produce. The sweet gesture was an appreciated unorthodox breakfast she downed with her coffee, fueling her after surviving the world's worst Airbnb guests. As she cut a second piece and gobbled it down, she didn't even feel guilty. Cinnamon and sugar dusted the flaky pie crust with thick chunks of gala apples topped with copious amounts of soft, gooey caramel.

Energized by the sugar and caffeine, Holly cut thick slices of crusty fresh bread and layered on turkey, ham, and Swiss cheese. She splurged on two cylinders of Pringles since, after working hard to clean out Kendall's pukefest, she thought the boys each deserved their favorite. Pizza for Dillon and Honey BBQ for Chance. She also made a pan of Rice Krispy treats with peanut butter, cut thick slices of them, and tucked the squares into the cooler. Bottled water and some Capri Suns were nestled into ice at the top for easy access while they were driving.

Holly drove the boys to Gardiner and the North Entrance to Yellowstone National Park. They waited in the beeline of cars to enter, creeping forward toward the massive hand-hewn stone entryway. It was a rock archway that perfectly framed the bright blue sky and puffy clouds that floated peacefully by and featured a snow-capped mountain range in the distance. Next in line, Holly leaned toward the steering wheel to read the inscription aloud. "For the benefit and the enjoyment of the people." Holly craned her neck as they drove through it. "Teddy Roosevelt commissioned this entrance. Isn't it beautiful?"

"It's just *rocks*, Mom." Dillon was not impressed, already jaded but at least awake next to his snoring brother.

"It's more than rocks, buddy," Holly explained. "These *rocks* have been around since the dinosaurs."

Suddenly, the rocks seemed slightly more important in Dillon's eyes, and he sat up and looked out the window. Dinosaurs had captured his imagination since he was five. Every rendition of *Jurassic Park* equaled a popcorn-fueled trip to the theater. He was obsessed.

"Look at that! *Snow* in the middle of summer! Can you believe it?" Holly exclaimed louder, making Chance stir and rub his sleepy eyes.

"Did you know there's a good chance this park is littered with dinosaur fossils?" Holly continued. "There's a museum in Bozeman I need to take you to someday soon. There have been some pretty amazing finds out here, buried under all this dirt and rock. Yellowstone is actually an active volcano."

"Yeah," Chance chimed in. "We're driving over a super volcano that is *long* overdue for an eruption. If it blows, we're all..." He dragged his finger across his throat in a dramatic gesture and pulled a croaking face that instantly made Dillon anxious.

"Is that true, Mom?" His glance darted between Holly and Chance, looking for confirmation.

"It's what killed the dinosaurs," Chance declared. "An eruption of that magnitude would cover the entire United States in ash and disrupt everything. No more cell phones, no more going outside. It would cover our house in three feet of volcanic ash and completely turn Murph into an ashy kickball."

Dillon's eyebrows raised dramatically and his thin lips pursed as Holly made eye contact with him in the rearview mirror, trying to diffuse the tension.

"A seismic event like that is *highly* unlikely. It's only happened three times in the last two million years."

"It's still possible, though." Chance liked to egg on his brother, and Dillon's eyes widened as he continued on dramatically. "Right under our feet, at this very moment, is an ocean of liquid magma five miles deep. Just biding its time, sitting and waiting for the perfect moment to erupt and blow us all sky high."

"Dude, stop. You're making your brother worry," Holly chastised him.

"Relax, Jack. I'm just messing with you. You seriously make it too easy." He yanked his brother's head toward his armpit and gave him a noogie.

"Your pits reek," Dillon plugged his nose as he fought off his older brother's attack, "and all that hair in them, yuck!" Dillon's words were muffled by Chance's red t-shirt as he wrestled to get away.

"That's what happens when you turn into a man!"

Holly ignored their antics and eased the van onto the

shoulder, parking the car near the long trail of others haphazardly parked along the road.

"C'mon," She urged them. "First stop, the Boiling River!" She grabbed the canvas bag with towels and began to pick her way down a crushed gravel path. "It's a hot spring you can actually wade in."

"Where is it?"

"It's a little bit of a hike to get there, but all the best places are off the beaten path." Holly was glad she was wearing her hiking boots. The path was flat and wide as they neared the river and they followed it down until they found huge log posts creating a bridge and saw sweatshirts and towels slung over them.

Finding a clear spot, she sat on the bank and began to take off her socks and shoes, taking the time to tuck the socks deep inside, as the boys flung theirs off like it was a race who could dip their toes into the cool water first. She gingerly picked her way across the stream bed across satiny river rocks that had been smoothed by water and made slippery with algae. She shouted out a couple quick warnings to the boys' backs. "Guys, don't get too far out! The current can become dangerous in the blink of an eye. And don't put your head under the water. You can get sick."

Chance piped up, "Yeah, we read about these brain-eating amoebas in science class last year. They literally swim up to your brain up through your nose and *eat* you from the inside out."

Dillon froze and his hand flew to his nose and plugged it tight. "Is that true, Mom?" he asked nasally.

"It kills 97% of the people it infects," Chance relayed the statistic with glee and then pointed to a warning sign in the distance. "Wow, look at that! The water is so hot here, it can burn your skin clean off your body."

"Chance," Holly warned. "Seriously, dude, stop freaking Dillon out." Proud of the rise he got from his brother, but deciding to give it a break, Chance wandered out further into the stream.

Dillon stood paralyzed until Holly bridged the gap between them and gently pulled his hand away from his face. "It's a one in a million thing, buddy, incredibly rare. You can't let fear stop you from having awesome experiences. Just keep your head out of the water and follow the directions on the signs, and you'll be fine."

"Promise?"

"Pinky promise." She held out her hand and linked her pinky with his.

"Lock it up." He touched her thumb with his and then walked toward his brother. His shoulders that were around his ears finally began to descend to their normal resting place.

Holly gasped as the ice-cold water rushed around her ankles and then up to her knees. Mixing and swirling together, some places were hot and others were cold. "The trick is to Goldilocks it," she recommended to the boys, it was a Deacon reference that flushed her core. "You have to find the sweet spot between the cold and the hot."

The boys waded in further, and Dillon hurried to catch up with Chance's longer stride. Holly found a nice flat rock to perch on and let the warm water tickle her left side and the cold water invigorate her right. Then she rolled to the other side and let the warm water comfort her shivering side and the cold cool down her overheated thigh. Closing her eyes, she tipped her chin up into the sun like a lizard on a warm rock. The warmth radiated from her cheeks to her throat and down her arms. Finally finding the perfect sweet spot in the boiling river, she relaxed onto the rock and scanned for the boys in the crowd that had gathered in the water. Her eyes landed on them among a group of kids on the bank. Twenty minutes later, when her thumbs were beginning to wrinkle and become prunes, she waved to the boys and started picking her way back to their clothing and towels on the bank.

She threw a towel to each of them, wrapped another around herself, pulled a worn sweatshirt over her head, and tugged yoga pants over her damp suit. "Did you guys like that?"

"Yeah, it was cool. What's next?"

"I think we're only about an hour from Old Faithful. Maybe we can stop on the way and see a couple geysers?"

It took another hour to hike back to the car where she passed out sandwiches and drinks and then crawled into the driver's seat. Holly then began following the signs toward Old Faithful. She stopped and pulled into the lot at Mammoth Hot Springs.

Chance opened the door, and a rotten egg stench hit his nostrils immediately. "Did you fart?" he asked Dillon, waving his hand in front of his face.

"The one who smelt it dealt it," Dillon joked as he plugged his nose.

Holly rolled her eyes. "No one farted, you guys. It's Sulphur. See that steam? It's released into the air and has a pungent, skunky smell." Her nose crinkled, then she continued. "Push through the pain, boys. I promise the view will be worth it."

They stood at the base of an enormous rock formation that included a wooden walkway and observation deck. The rock formations were white and gray, an unusual prehistoric sight that looked more like the surface of another planet. Water trickled and steam rose up from the stone in heavy plumes. On one side, long brown horizontal ledges were tickled by steam, dripping with water, and stacked up a hundred feet high like a haphazard staircase. On the other side, predominantly white terraced travertine looked like snow as steam continually rose from the ledges. A solitary tree dotted the formation, brave enough to attempt to survive under such hostile conditions. Holly stopped to enjoy the view at a yellow sign that screamed burn warnings, hoping her boys would heed the warning.

"Whoa," Dillon said, awe in his voice at the sight in front of him as he dropped his hand. He stared up at the massive rock and mineral formation with huge eyes.

"Right? Skooch together, you guys. Let me take a picture," she begged the boys, attempting to press them closer together by pinching her fingers in the air in front of her. They eventually gave in, jostling each other in front of the massive formation.

"One, two, three." Holly then clicked away. The photo after the forced one was always her favorite, when their faces relaxed and the real smiles chased away the fake ones. "Let's go explore," Holly told them, starting down the boardwalk as the boys trailed behind. It took thirty minutes to navigate the wooden boardwalk with the crowds. The boys ran on ahead like boys are conditioned to do, the hunter and gatherer instincts still driving them even after decades of video game sloth should have reversed the motivation. Holly stopped to take photos every few seconds, marveling open-mouthed at the beauty of this unexpected mineral formation. She felt tiny and insignificant in the best way, knowing that millions of people before her had witnessed its raw beauty, and millions more would come after her and be equally captivated by it.

After a solid hour of navigating the boardwalk and stopping to read the educational signs the boys were too jumpy to enjoy, she caught up with them on the backside of Mammoth

Hot Springs. Here, it looked like a cream-colored mountain, the great shelves of the front no longer on display. Occasional billowy clouds of white steam pulsed upwards and wafted around the rocks as she lingered and viewed the impeccable view through a frame of evergreens. Holly was struck by the incredible beauty of it all; it was a humbling moment that forced her to pause.

Thank you.

She breathed in the dank air that was oddly crisp with the scent of pine needles at the same time.

"Old Faithful?" she asked the boys when they finally wandered over.

"Yeah," they agreed, neither knowing what they were agreeing to. The drive there was a frustrating stop and go, allowing for wandering bison who always had the right of way. The engine idled as they were stuck in a long train of cars slowing down for something that Holly eventually figured out was a bear. She was learning that bear sightings in Yellowstone made the crowds slow to a stop and rubber neck like no other. It was a Where's Waldo moment when a crowd of cars was gathered in one place. You had to scan and search for the cause of the commotion. Usually, it was a tiny speckle of fur picking its way between evergreens and around boulders. Groups of bison were far more common, and cars would slow down for them, too, but they didn't command the crowds like an actual bear sighting did. Holly was forced to acknowledge there was a hierarchy of importance of wildlife in the park, as there was in life. Elk, Bison, Bear. You slowed down for elk, but you always stopped for bears.

Holly pulled into the parking lot at the lodge at Old Faithful, snagging the last parking place. "Let's go see if they have ice cream," she told the boys, who yanked open the sliding door to the van and tumbled out of it like it was on fire, half-walking, half-running to the entrance. Once inside the gift shop, they stood in line for soft serve. Thickly coiled chocolate ice cream cones just under a foot tall and weighing nearly a pound were placed in their hands and were worth the nine dollars they were charging for them. She filled her purse with napkins and then they settled on metal bleachers in front of Old Faithful to wait for the next eruption.

Precisely fourteen minutes later, the geothermal theatrics began. First came powerful thundering in the distance, followed by a loud hissing sound accompanied by billowy clouds of steam. Then the first deluge of water burst forth from the mouth hidden in the ground. Higher and higher it shot, over a hundred feet in the air, and a gentle wind pulled the water in a veil of misty droplets behind as it evaporated back into the atmosphere. Oohs and ahhs came from the crowd as mouths dropped open and couples leaned in to savor a spectacle rarely seen in nature. The raw power of the bursting, frothing water held each viewer captive. Holly was transfixed on the faces of her boys, enjoying their reactions more than the actual geyser. Leaned in closer together, Dillon was a tiny twin of Chance, their mouths were equally agape and eyes like huge saucers. Holly felt a little tug on her heartstrings, being able to enjoy this moment with them. It chased away her worries and doubts. For the next two and a half minutes, she watched the awe and wonder play across their faces and felt peace fill her soul. It was a memory she would hold dear in her heart forever.

TWELVE

The sky was darkening later that evening when Holly pulled the van up to the house. She called out for Murph, who had taken to hanging out in a pillowed crate she tucked into a corner on the porch. Usually, the familiar sound of the van skidding on the rocks down the driveway sent him running to the front door. His sensitive ears were able to discern the particular sound the gravel made by her tires. He would greet them immediately, tail wagging and jumping up on his hind legs, trying to thrust his body into their arms. His ever-earnest bid for attention was an endearing quality that solidified their bond even more, but tonight, there was no Murph jumping at her legs and it was instantly unsettling.

"Guys," she said sternly to the sleepy boys in the back of the van. "Help me find Murph." She shouted into the darkness, "Murph! Come here, boy. Mama's home." Leaving the headlights on for light, they fanned out, walking into the taller grasses and rocks.

"Murphie Man!" Holly shouted, jingling her keys. "Want to go for a ride?" The tinkling sound of the keys echoed out onto the prairie. Tired from the long day spent exploring the park, she wanted him to come running as quickly as possible. She'd give him a peanut butter spoon to soften the blow of the lie and a few belly rubs after her long shower. The sun lowered even more, connecting with the horizon. Orange rays shot out over the mountains in the distance, and Holly's stomach was filled with dread knowing there were only a few minutes of daylight left. It would be infinitely harder and more dangerous to search for him in the dark.

"You want a treat?" she begged, willing her wiggling white ball of fur to appear. The word 'treat' always got his attention and sent him running. She heard Chance and Dillon shouting further in the distance.

"Come on, buddy." Her voice was now strained with the first notes of panic creeping in.

I should have locked him inside the house. Her default self-blaming mechanism reared its ugly head, kicking in again.

"Mom!" Chance's deepening voice cracked at the end. "Come here, hurry!" Her ears strained to locate where his voice was coming from.

"Where are you?" she shouted, unable to quell the panic that was raising her voice an octave.

"We're in the barn!"

Holly ran toward the old barn on the property that was storing her furniture and other random relics from her old life in New Hope.

Murph was laying in the dirt. Whimpering when he saw her, his tail twitched in happiness for a moment. His fur was reddened in his stomach and back leg. Holly collapsed onto her knees and tried to assess his injuries as Dillon began to cry behind her.

"We need to get him to a vet." Holly searched google for the nearest animal hospital and was relieved to see one not too far away. She scooped up the trembling dog and held him close to her chest. "Get me that old blanket." Dillon sprang into action, grateful to have something to do, a way to contribute. "Chance, you need to drive us so I can keep pressure on Murph's wounds."

She hopped into the back of the van with Dillon as darkness fell, holding Murph swaddled in the blanket like a baby. The white stars winked in the distance as Chance drove following the GPS instructions. His foot was heavy on the pedal, and Holly didn't even reprimand him for speeding, grateful that speed limits in the west were just a suggestion. She pressed a towel to Murph's back leg, and her heart broke when the red bled through it. Murmuring soft, calming noises, she said to Dillon, who was desperate for another task to contribute, "Stroke his ears, honey. You know he loves that."

Dillon nodded solemnly and began to tug on his ears with one hand and swipe away the tears with the other. Holly briefly wondered how much longer before his quest into manhood would require him to camouflage his emotions. How many more months would it take for him to learn to hide them in the hard line of his lips and the strong set of shoulders that Chance was currently exhibiting. Her boys had already lost so much. Murph was as much a part of their family as she was. In the silence, in tune with the hammering of her heart, she begged the dog to live.

Don't you dare leave us now, Murph.

She knew his injuries were significant. His eyes were glassy and his blinking was slowing down. "You're such a good boy," she whispered, knowing it was his favorite thing to hear. His soulful brown eyes swung back to hers. "We're almost there, buddy. Hang on."

Ten of the longest, most painful minutes spooled out as

Chance drove them to the animal hospital. Finally, he pulled into the empty parking lot and they rushed into the waiting room.

"Help us!" She cried out. "My dog is dying."

The word hit Dillon hardest, and he began to sob. "He's dying? No, Murph, no! You can't die."

Chance ran up to the empty reception area and banged on the window at the desk with his fist. "Help us! We need help!" His voice cracked, and he shouted louder, "Please, help us!"

A gray door opened, and her terrified eyes registered the veterinarian immediately. It was a man she recognized. A man she knew would save her dog.

THIRTEEN

Dillon rushed to the big man in relief. "Deacon. You have to help Murph. He's dying."

Deacon's warm capable eyes met hers, and he said calmly, "Follow me." He swept open the door, and Holly ducked under his arm and into the examination room. It was a humble outdated office with fluorescent lights and advertisements for Frontline and Heart Gard on the walls. A cabinet was tucked into the corner, housing supplies and a stainless steel sink, where Deacon stopped to quickly wash his hands.

"Let's set him on a table and see what we're dealing with before we rush to conclusions," he said. Holly was able to take her first breath as she laid him down and gently unwrapped the blanket. Her heart dropped when she saw crimson staining the lion's share of it.

"He's lost so much blood," she mumbled as tears filled her eyes, and she rubbed the soft spot between his eyes that were glassy and sad. Leaning in, she kissed the top of his head and murmured, "Who's my good boy? You are." Even in his current battered and bloodied state, his tail registered the slightest wag.

"That's a good sign," Deacon said as he began to assess the dog's injuries. "Grab a chair and stay close."

She pulled up a rolling stool and sat down on it, snuggling her face into Murph's fur, his face the only part of his anatomy that wasn't covered in dirt and blood. She rubbed the top of his head and whispered to him as Deacon's nimble fingers tenderly tested the wounds.

"Looks like he had a fight with a coyote and lost," Deacon assessed. He used a bottle of saline to clean the wounds. "We'll give him some stitches and a little something to make him drowsy so he won't feel a thing." He pulled on latex gloves, pulled out a syringe, and injected the medicine into the dog. Chance studied him as he pulled out his instruments and administered the anesthesia. Deacon began to explain, "After we clean the wounds, we can stitch him up."

"Can you give me a hand?" he asked Chance. "I'm going to have to give him a little haircut around the wound. Wash your hands and keep pressure on it to contain the blood flow." Chance quickly washed up then pressed the wound together, the red staining his fingers as the buzzing noise on the electric razor began. A few minutes later, Deacon handed him a bottle of saline. "Irrigate the wound, and I will add some antibiotics."

"You can give a dog stitches?"

"You can," Deacon confirmed as he pulled out a needle and a long black thread.

"What is that?" Dillon asked.

"It's actually made from sheep guts. When they heal, they will fully dissolve." He turned to Holly and Dillon. "You might not want to watch this part."

"It's okay," Dillon said as he continued to stroke the dog's soft fur. Murph was lying still on the table. "He looks like he's sleeping."

"He is. He can't feel a thing." Deacon began to suture the wound, sewing neat little stitches that were a contrasting ebony against the dog's freshly exposed pink skin. "You did the right thing bringing him in right away. If you would have waited until morning…" His voice trailed off and made Holly's eyes well up. "Anyway, we can fix him right up. I promise Murph is going to live to tell the tale and even have some pretty badass scars to show for it."

In relief, Dillon perked up, watching Deacon deftly suture the wounds. Leaning in, he worked quickly, and an hour later, the wounds were a roadmap of deep back lines across pink patches of skin and short haphazard tufts of hair. Finally finished, Deacon stood to his full height and stretched, then removed his latex gloves.

"All finished," he said and shot the dirty gloves into the trash can five feet away. "Nothing but net!" he exclaimed with a smile to diffuse the lingering tension in the room, but it didn't work. He reached out to gently shove Dillon's shoulder. "You can relax now. He's okay."

Holly's shoulders finally dropped, and she twisted her neck to dispel the stiffness now that the imminent threat of losing Murph had dissipated.

"I'll need to keep him here overnight, to make sure he doesn't have a reaction to the anesthesia, but tomorrow afternoon, I can bring him back to your place." Deacon opened a cabinet and pulled out a protective cone, then flung it across the room to Chance.

"He's going to need to wear one of these for a while."

"The cone of shame?"

"He's going to be itchy where the stitches are. It's the only way to stop him from licking himself."

"Can I get one for this guy?" Chance joked and hiked a thumb at Dillon. "He seems to have the same problem."

"I do not!" replied Dillon, the tips of his ears pinking in embarrassment.

"Hey, guys, I need to talk to your mom for a minute. You can grab a soda from the break room and hang out in the waiting room if you want." They followed him out to the soda, and the room was instantly silent.

Holly rubbed her tired eyes then swiped through her hair with her fingers. She was exhausted. Looking down at the reddish-brown stains on her t-shirt and shorts, she wheeled closer to the sleeping dog and rubbed the curly hair on his long ears with the pads of her thumb. Noticing her fingernails were grimy with dirt and dried blood, she stood and washed her hands at the sink. She felt a breeze as the door opened again and quickly turned around. Deacon filled the doorway, assessing her now.

"Everything is going to be okay. You can take a breath now."

"Thank you," she mumbled words that felt empty as she tried to explain. "We spent the day in Yellowstone, and when we got back…" Her voice cracked and she crumpled, wrapping her arms around her torso. Deacon crossed the room in one step and pulled her into his arms, hugging her tight. She couldn't stop herself from snuggling into his embrace, finding the perfect place to rest her head on the thick muscle protecting his heart. The slow rhythmic thump of his heartbeat cocooned her senses. She unwrapped her arms to nestle closer to him and then circled them around his trunk, pressing her head closer into his chest. The slight softness in his midsection calmed the body image insecurities that roiled up in her mind.

"I can't believe you're here," Holly murmured into his chest. "You must think I'm incredibly self-absorbed. How did I not know you were a vet?"

"People tend to wear lots of hats around here," Deacon answered. "It's not your fault. I'm the kind of guy who likes to keep my cards close to my chest. Keep people on a need-to-know basis."

Her heart fell, understanding fully that, in his mind, she had been classified as a person who didn't need to know. The truth made her shy and pull away from the power of his embrace that warmed her from the tips of her toes to the last hair on her head.

She swallowed and looked away.

"It's dangerous for a dog like Murph to be left unattended. There's lots of things in Montana that can kill him. Snakes, coyotes, wild dogs. Bears."

"I didn't even think," Holly admitted. "God, if we lost him, it would kill the boys. He's like their brother. Sometimes he's my favorite child," she tried to joke.

A warm smile crossed his face. "I'm not here to beat you up. But maybe he needs a friend. Something a little more intimidating than a giant cotton ball on legs? You *are* living alone and inviting strangers to stay at the property regularly."

"You might have a point."

"How about a pit bull?"

"You can't be serious. One of those would kill Murph."

"Look at you, buying into blatant misconceptions," he pushed. "I never saw you as the kind of person to do that."

"I'm not."

"Pit bulls actually make great service dogs. They are loyal and strong, and when trained properly, will protect and love you like no other animal."

"I don't know." She hesitated, her voice unsure. "Aren't they aggressive and banned in some states? I think I read something online about one that bit an infant's face and scarred him for life." She paused and then tried to deflect her uncertainty with humor. "I seem to be scarring my kids for life all on my own. Not sure I need the help."

"How about you come meet a couple I know before you make up your mind? Dogs are like people. They give back what they get. If you give them love, they return it back to you ten-fold. But it's true; if they are met with anger and aggression, they become angry and aggressive."

"Maybe," Holly admitted. "It's obvious that Murph can't hold his own in the Wild West. If your professional opinion believes it will help, I'll at least consider it."

A warm smile deepened the lines on his face, and Holly felt her heart flutter. "I would feel a lot better about you being alone out there if you had a real dog," he admitted without fear or worry of her reaction. The admission made Holly's heart swoon.

She looked over at Murph's still sleeping body. His fur shaved down to the pink skin made him appear half of his normal size. "Did you hear that boy? Deak said you're not a real dog."

"Dogs are pack animals. We just have to figure out the right one to add to your pack."

"I'll think about it."

"You look exhausted," Deacon said. "Go take your boys home. I'm going to clean up around here and keep an eye on him. He's in good hands."

Her eyes darted to his meaty, capable hands. Hands that saved her dog, hands that fixed her leaky plumbing. Hands that seconds ago pulled her to him. She was falling in love with those hands, seeing for the first time that a man could have capable hands and that she could put her trust in them.

FOURTEEN

The next morning, Holly was sipping her coffee on the front porch when her heart leapt at the now-familiar sight of Deak's truck coming down the lane.

Holly jumped up to open the door and shouted into the cabin, "Deak is here! Murph is home, guys!" The boys scrambled to find shoes and ran out to stand on the front porch, anxious to see him.

A few minutes later, Deacon hopped out of his truck and walked around to the passenger side door to pick up a freshly coned Murph. His fur was ragged and patchy, shaved to half an inch in most areas, revealing large swaths of bright pink peeking out where he had been shaved to the skin. Cradling the dog in his arms, he walked most of the way to the porch, then set him down gently in the grass. Holly flew down the stairs to her little dog and crouched down as Murph hobbled over to her, his whole body quivering with delight to be with his people again.

"Oh! Look at you, poor baby." Holly bent over to gently scratch his nearly hairless chin. "He looks so pathetic with this thing on." Dillon and Chance gathered around Murph, drowning him in attention.

"He'll hate it, but it will stop him from licking his sutures. In about a week, we should be able to remove it," Deacon answered, then handed her an orange bottle filled with antibiotics. "Give him one of these twice a day with food until they are gone."

She tucked it into her pocket and stood. "How can we thank you for this?" Holly asked sincerely, looking into his eyes.

"No need." A flicker of movement caught the corner of her eye, pulling her focus from him. Two muscled dogs were rough housing in the back of Deak's pickup. She pointed to them.

"What's going on over there? Are you running a dog delivery service now?"

Deak laughed and his white teeth flashed a brilliant contrast to his suntanned skin. "Actually, those are my girls. A couple rescues that weren't smart enough to make the cut."

"The cut for what?"

"To become service dogs."

Her brow crinkled in surprise as he continued. "I run a pit bull rescue. Last Chance Ranch."

"Why do you call it Last Chance Ranch?" Dillon asked, ever curious.

"Well, because pit bulls are the most euthanized dogs in every shelter across the country."

"What does euthanized mean?"

"It means put to sleep, dummy," Chance answered, then mumbled a quick apology. "Sorry, Dilly."

The apology surprised Holly. Usually, he was mercilessly teasing and insulting his little brother. It came with the territory, but Holly was beginning to notice a different side to Chance when Deak was around.

"We rehabilitate them, save them from the kill shelters, and either find them a forever home or put them to work. Some of my dogs have gone on to be service dogs for disabled veterans."

"But they are such an aggressive breed," Holly cautioned.

"Man, if I had a nickel for every time I've heard that," Deak said. "Have you ever been around a properly trained pit bull before?"

"No," Holly admitted.

"Then all I ask is that you keep an open mind. They are strong and loyal and smart and have no concept of personal space." He laughed. "Want to meet them?"

"Sure?" Holly said the word, sounding more like a question than she wanted it to. She bent down and picked up Murph, cradling him in her arms protectively.

"You don't have to do that. Daisy and Tink love him already."

He walked to the truck, opened the tailgate, and whistled, and the two dogs jumped down and then immediately sat on their haunches next to him, sniffing the air. Daisy was a gorgeous deep charcoal grey with steel-blue eyes and a thick pink tongue that hung out of her mouth sideways. Her chest was massive and thick with ropey muscles. Tink was caramel-colored with an upside-down triangle of white on her face and warm brown eyes, and she was smaller than Daisy. Holly could already tell that Daisy ruled the roost by the way Tink laid on the ground, always keeping her head lower.

"Heel," he demanded in a low voice, and the dogs walked toward her slowly. He stopped, and they immediately both sat and waited. "Good girls," he praised and patted their heads before continuing to where Holly was standing with the boys.

"Now those are *dogs*!" Chance exclaimed and rushed over to pet them with Dillon.

"You can put him down. I promise it's okay," Deak said, and Holly hesitated then placed Murph's paws gingerly on the ground. She knelt next to him, careful to provide a buffer between the pit bulls and Murph. She reached out tentatively to pet Daisy's meaty head. Her short fur was surprisingly velvety to the touch. Dillon scratched her ears, and she began to lick his face with her wide tongue. Murph walked over to them and laid down in the space closest to Tink. She sniffed him and then folded her body around his as Murph's coned head came to rest on her massive torso.

"Ooh! Murph has a girl… friend!" Dillon sang out, watching them canoodling on the ground together.

"Looks like he does," Deacon said as he scratched Tink's exposed belly, then playfully slapped her chest muscles. "These two are big ole sweeties. Might lick you to death, but that's the only thing you have to worry about." He watched Daisy make quick work of mopping Dillon's face with her tongue while he giggled.

"Feels like sandpaper."

"I've been looking for some help actually," Deacon suggested. "Would either of you two be interested in making a little extra money? Cleaning kennels and socializing the dogs? They need a lot of training before they go to their forever homes. Maybe once a week, if that fits in with the work you have to do for your mama."

The boys' eyes lit up. "Can we?" they begged in unison. "Please, Mom. Please!" Dillon laced his fingers together dramatically and knelt on the ground, begging for her permission.

"You guys realize this involves poop, right?" she joked, and Deacon laughed.

"Wow. You're making my life sound so glamorous." He turned to the boys. "But I have to admit, your mom pretty much nailed it."

"If we do a good job, can you teach us how to train them?" Chance asked.

"Well, you have to walk before you can run," he cautioned. "Do you know what is the most important quality in a trainer?"

"No."

"Consistency," he answered. "A dog needs to know without a doubt who calls the shots and what will happen if they don't follow a command."

"It's the same with teenagers," Holly added, anticipating Chance's eye roll, but he kept it in check.

"Saturday afternoons? 3-7?"

"C'mon on, Mom! Please!" Dillon begged.

"Okay," she relented, "but no complaining when I need you in the mornings for cleaning the cabins when we really get busy."

"I got a jo-ob! I got a jo-ob," Dillon sang out, doing a little cabbage patch victory dance.

The next Saturday, Holly punched the address Deacon had given her into the GPS.

"I could have driven him to Deak's myself," Chance offered.

"I know," Holly admitted. "Next time you can. I just wanted to get a better lay of the land and get my bearings around here." It was a lie, or maybe half-truth was more accurate. She was curious to know more about Deacon, and she knew from experience that you could tell a lot about a person by the way they lived. If they left dishes in the sink, or let their lawn be overgrown, or if their garage was organized and the bathroom so clean you could eat off the floor.

Her final turn was marked by an enormous carved cedar log with the stylized face of a pit bull and the words "Last Chance Ranch" engraved into the caramel-colored wood. The massive trunk was thickly chiseled, sanded, and stained to withstand the elements. A split rail fence ran on either side of the blacktop lane. Pine trees and mountain views hid a rambling two-story white clapboard house with bright blue shutters. A flower garden flush with blooms of white daisies burst from the sea of grass on either side of the walk leading up to the house.

Flowers?

She didn't expect that. Her heart dropped. Women planted flowers, and men put up with their useless beauty because men loved women. Internally, a sea of questions consumed her.

He did say there was no one waiting at home for him, didn't he? I'm sure I heard him say that. Holly doubted the information, trying to remember the exact words he used, and found herself praying it was true. Hopefully, the woman who had planted the daisies had moved on and the sunny blooms were all that remained of her.

Next to the house was a huge modern pole building complete with a series of ten dog kennels, all of them occupied by barking dogs.

The lawn was meticulously groomed, and a large fenced area was set up with agility beams and equipment. She parked and couldn't stop a grin from spreading across her face when Deak appeared on the porch. Tink and Daisy flanked either side of the trunks of his legs. His thick forearms were crossed against his chest, and his auburn hair ruffled in the wind.

She crossed over to him, and Dillon and Chance ran over to the dogs. Tink immediately flopped back on her belly, and Dillon scratched her tummy while her pink tongue lollygagged out of her mouth onto the ground, giving her more of a crazed hyena look.

Daisy took the opportunity to lick Chance's face like it was her job while he squeezed his eyes shut and shouted mock protests.

"I'll bring them home when we're done," Deak offered. She was itching to see more of his world, to be invited inside so she could snoop around his things. He was so quiet and kept his cards close to his chest that she was scouring his surroundings for any clues.

"That would be great. I'd really appreciate that." Her eyes drifted and settled on a sun-bleached garden gnome tucked into the daisies. She pointed at the flowers. "Is that why you call her Daisy?"

"Yeah, we'll go with that," he said, leaving her wondering what he was leaving out. "Did you want the nickel tour?"

She nodded, glad to have a reason to linger at his home, to learn more about this man who baffled her and was unlike any man she had ever met.

His long legs made fast work of crossing the distance from the house to the pole building. Holly had to practically skip to keep up with him. The boys and dogs fell in step behind her.

"I'll need you guys to clean out the kennels. Feed and water the dogs. After that's done, we will work on socializing them."

There were three long dog runs next to the agility area. Holly sniffed the air, expecting to smell animal waste, but there was none. The facility was clean and bright and well-maintained. Holly's eyes recorded every detail, taking it all in and seeing there was so much more to Deacon than she ever dreamed.

"Did I pass inspection?"

Holly smiled up at him, embarrassed that her motives were so paper-thin. "Yep. You passed."

"Good. So, you feel safe enough to trust me with your babies?" Deak grinned at her.

"Hope you know what you're getting yourself into with these two."

"I think I can handle it." And she had no doubt there wasn't much this man couldn't handle.

"Get out of here, Mom. We have work to do!" Dillon enthused.

"Well, alright, I'll let you boys get to it." Holly dawdled on her way back to the van, cataloging all the visual clues of Deacon's life. It wasn't at all what she expected and left her desperate for more.

SIXTEEN

At dusk, Murph barked at a car driving down the lane he didn't recognize.

"What in the world?" Holly said, slinging the dish towel over her shoulder as she pulled back the curtain to look out the window. She wasn't expecting anyone, and a flutter of panic that she forgot a guest forced her to quickly log in and check her listing. She exhaled with relief when she saw it was blank and then looked out the window again.

Walking up the lane, wearing a faded Jimi Hendrix t-shirt and wrinkled cargo shorts was the last person she thought she'd ever see in Montana.

Mick.

Who drives sixteen hours to visit their kids without so much as a courtesy phone call? Mick, that's who.

Anger bubbled up as she opened the squeaky door and walked out onto the porch. She sat in a chair, waiting for him to approach.

"What are *you* doing here?"

"Jeeze, Hols, you really know how to make a guy feel welcome." The joke landed on deaf ears.

"Seriously, what are you doing here?" she asked again.

"Needed a change of scenery, so I decided to…" He launched into a cheesy air guitar solo and sang out, "head out west where I belong." He laughed weakly, and she noticed how thin he had gotten, looking like he was surviving on cigarettes and coffee. He coughed self-consciously and waited for Holly to give him permission to sit down. She uncrossed her arms from her chest and waved one exasperated hand at an empty chair.

"What the hell happened to him?" Mick jerked his head over toward Murph, who was curled protectively at Holly's feet.

"He got into a fight with a coyote and lost," Holly answered. "Quit changing the subject. Why are you here?"

Right as the words left her mouth and before he got a chance to answer, she heard gravel spitting as Deak's pickup rambled down the long lane then parked in front of them.

Great. Perfect timing.

The truck door jerked open, and Dillon screeched out. "Dad?" Her youngest son ran up the stairs to hug him.

"Missed ya, sport," Mick said meekly as he ruffled Dillon's hair. "Decided I'd get in the car and head out here."

Seconds later, Chance came running up and launched himself into Mick's arms, knocking Mick back against the logs of the cabin. A jolt of jealousy stung Holly's core. No matter what Mick did or didn't do, he would always hang the moon in their eyes. A tiny selfish part of her yearned to tell them the truth, to enlighten them as to why the back-to-school clothing budget had been slashed and she had taken to cooking meatless dinners lately. The relief she would feel from the words leaving her tongue and revealing the truth would only last for the briefest moment. It would only serve to make her feel better and hurt the boys. She knew it wouldn't do any good, and it wasn't fair to them, so she remained quiet.

Deacon was the last one stepping up onto the porch, and Holly stood to introduce them. "Mick, this is Deacon."

He thrust out his hand and engulfed Mick's smaller one with his own. Holly noticed he was almost a foot taller than Mick, who seemed to shrink in his presence.

"Well, that's a hell of a hand shake you got there," Mick admitted, shaking his hand out to get feeling back to his fingertips. "But you gotta be careful with my digits, man. I'm a musician."

A small smirk flashed on Deacon's face that didn't escape Holly.

"Dad! We have so much to tell you! We've gone white water rafting and hiking, and Murph got hurt." Dillon's chatterbox explanation came out jumbled up, fast, and furious. Almost as if he was afraid Mick would disappear again, so he had to fill him in on every event of the last two months before that happened.

"Wow, that's a lot to unpack," Mick said. "Can't wait to hear all about it, champ."

"How long are you staying?" Chance asked, hopeful. "We can take you to Yellowstone, right, Mom?"

"Sure." Holly forced her face into a relaxed expression, not wanting her true feelings to hurt the boys who missed their dad. "Where's your hotel?"

Mick's tired eyes met hers. "I've been sleeping in the backseat of the Buick," he admitted. "You'd be surprised how comfortable it is. Reminds me of the good ole days on the road touring with the band."

Chance was confused. "No, that's dumb, Dad."

"I know! You can stay here!" Dillon offered. "Mom lets people stay here all the time."

Holly rankled, barely able to keep her rage under control. The idea of Mick freeloading in one of her cabins made her blood boil. "Can you guys go get washed up and set the table for dinner? Looks like there will be four of us tonight. I need to talk to your dad for a minute."

Your dad. It was a purposeful distancing term that was one step above worthless cretin. He wasn't even her ex-husband anymore; he had been demoted to baby daddy, and if he didn't start pulling his weight financially, she was ready to strip him of that title, too.

"Go on," Mick said to Chance and Dillon. "We'll have plenty of time to catch up."

The boys reluctantly went back into the house.

"That's my cue to leave, too. It was nice to meet you." Deacon cast a quick glance at Holly before heading back to his truck. They were silent as they watched him go.

"Mick, you've got some nerve. Skipping out on support payments, then showing up here on a whim, and using the kids to manipulate me into letting you stay?"

"I didn't think."

"You never do." She stood, needing to pace. Disgust for him built up in her belly. "I guess you can stay, but I can only offer you the barn. It's one step above camping, but you can shower at my house, eat with us, and spend time with the boys. I'm sorry, but it's the best I can do."

His eyes slid from hers to the two empty cabins standing on her property. His mouth opened like he was going to say something. He paused for the briefest second, then started in, "But, Hol…"

"Seriously?" Her voice was pinched, reading his mind already. Sixteen years of experience made the task as easy as breathing. "You've got to be kidding me! No way," she interrupted him before he could get his entire request out. "Since child support checks from you lately are becoming few and far between, I have to keep the cabins open for last-minute rentals."

"I understand," he mumbled, his head hung low.

"Do you?" she asked. "Because I don't think you do."

"You seem to never tire of making me feel shitty. That's why things never worked out with us."

"No." Holly couldn't keep quiet any longer. "*Things* didn't work with us because you had an active addiction that you refused to face combined with a weak work ethic. " The words emboldened her. It was a new way of thinking that still sometimes felt foreign. It was easy to backslide into who she had been for the first forty years of her life. There was a constant process of recalibrating. She was vigilant with the words she chose and the thoughts that filled her mind now, measuring if they were lining up with the life she wanted to live or actively fighting against it.

Put in his place, Mick seemed to shrivel and become smaller. "I will make that work. Thank you. I do appreciate getting to spend some time with the boys."

"That's the *only* reason I am trying to help you out. I am doing it for them. They love you and want to spend time with you, but there are some ground rules. No drugs. No alcohol. I see it one time and you're gone."

SEVENTEEN

The next day, she packed a picnic lunch in a basket and handed it to Chance. "Don't you want to come with us?" he asked with a twinge of hope in his voice so deep it made Holly's heart pang. He was desperate to see his parents spending time together like they used to, eager for one more family memory.

"I can't, buddy. I've got to get the Elk Ridge Cabin ready for guests tonight. You guys go on and have fun showing your dad the park." Taking cues from Reddit and rental groups, she learned naming the cabins made for a more unique experience. So, Chance christened one of them Elk Ridge, and Dillon named the other Bear Valley.

She cleaned the cabin and set out a welcome tray of Montana goodies—pastel taffy wrapped in wax paper and the spicy bison jerky she bought every week from Ruth, a Sudoku puzzle book, and a bottle of drinkable yet inexpensive wine. Over the last month, she had assembled a binder for each cabin with things to see and do. In it, she listed Cal's white-water rafting company, the address to Ruth's store, and a few other local gems she had found on her own.

She put in her earbuds and listened to *CoDependant No More*. She almost knew it by heart, having listened to it nearly twenty times in the last year. It was a deliberate action to fill her head with healthy words, each one a weapon in her arsenal to fight Mick's inevitable encroachment on her new healthier habits. Holly knew having him around was a trigger for her to fall into her old ways, and she was determined not to do that this time. To go back would erase all the progress she'd made. There was no backsliding, and if she had to listen to this audiobook every day until he left, she would do it.

In the zone, she pulled the sheets off the bed and snapped fresh white ones back onto it. High thread-count sheets and a fluffy white down comforter were a splurge, but Holly was trying to position and stage her listing like a luxury hotel, knowing that bed linens made a huge difference. She scrubbed the bathroom spotless as lemon-scented bleach stung her nostrils. On her hands and knees, she cleaned the floor with rubber gloves pulled up to her elbows to protect her from long-lost stray hairs. In the sink, wrapped around the drain, and scattered behind the doors, hair was a pet peeve she'd adopted in college, when her roommate left copious amounts of it everywhere and could never be bothered to clean up after herself. Other people's hair was something that always grossed her out and triggered her gag reflex.

Two hours later, she was satisfied with the cleanliness of the cabin. You could eat off the floor, the kitchen was immaculate, and the windows sparkled. She opened them to let in the fresh Montana air.

Holly made herself a salad, added a slice of buttered bread and a glass of lemonade, and ate on her porch. She peeled off a chunk of crust and tossed it over to Murph. It landed inside his cone, and she laughed while he shook his head in confusion. Smelling the delicious bread, but not being able to find it. Finally giving up, he plopped back down on the floor with a dramatic sigh, causing the crust to dislodge and fall down next to his nose where he chomped at it eagerly.

Glancing at her watch, knowing it was going to be a while before Mick and the boys came home, Holly drove into town and walked into the general store. She knew they would come home from the park hungry, and she wanted to be prepared.

"Well, hello there, Holly Simon," Ruth sang out. She always used her first and last name. Holly wondered why. Were there oodles of Hollys in her life making the distinction necessary?

"I wanted to thank you for that last-minute rental recommendation you gave me last week," Holly said.

"You're welcome, dear. Glad it all worked out."

Holly piled a tin scoop full of taffy into the steel scale that was suspended from the ceiling and wrote down the amount on the tag attached with a twist tie. She stacked hamburger, cheese, and taco shells into her basket.

"Deacon said your little dog suffered a coyote attack." Ruth leaned forward, her thick hands rubbing the middle of her back as she stood at the register.

"He did, but Deak fixed him up. How come you didn't tell me he was a veterinarian?"

"Well, he hates it when I talk him up. I promised him I would quit that, but it's impossible when you're proud of the man your son turned out to be."

Warmth flooded Holly's chest, hearing Ruth talk about Deacon like he was a little boy. "I hope I get a chance to say that someday about my boys."

"I think you will." Ruth reached to a shelf where a hand-made label identified a jar of raw honey. She placed it inside the paper bag of Holly's groceries she'd just scanned. "Just a little something sweet for you. It's great on English muffins."

"You are spoiling me," Holly gushed, making the older woman smile.

"Every mom deserves a little spoiling now and then. It's the hardest job in the world and even more difficult when you do it on your own," Ruth went on as she folded the brown paper bags.

"Thank you so much. I could use a little treat after an unexpected visitor showed up today."

Ruth glanced up, interested, waiting for Holly to continue.

"The boys' father got a wild hair and showed up on my doorstep unannounced yesterday."

"Did he now?" Ruth mused. "In my experience, a man doesn't drive halfway across the country unless he is in love or needs something."

Holly laughed at the absurdity of the idea of Mick driving across the country for love. "He's definitely firmly in the second category."

"Be careful, sweetheart." Ruth handed her the groceries. "A man shouldn't always take."

———

Later that night, the boys came running from the car and burst onto the porch, a ball of charged energy. They whooped and hollered as Mick strolled behind without a care in the world, his hands in his pockets. Holly had just enjoyed a stunning Montana sunset with Murph curled at her feet on the porch and could already tell the rest of the night wasn't going to be as peaceful.

"What's got you guys so worked up?"

"Dad touched a bison," Dillon announced with stars in his eyes.

"What?" Holly was confused. No one in their right mind would ever get close enough to touch a bison. On an almost monthly basis, there was a newspaper article about a tourist trying to get a selfie with a bear cub and getting mauled, or getting too close to the edge and falling down a ravine. Articles that she read out loud to the boys to warn them of the dangers in the park that had apparently fallen on deaf ears.

"Actually, he *spanked it*, Mom. Like a boss," Chance interrupted. "Slapped his haunches, and it shot off like he hit it with a cattle prod." Chance growled and chest-bumped Mick in a testosterone-injected gesture that made Holly furious.

Holly's eyes started to bug. She swallowed the building rage as she watched Chance high-five his dad and carry on like it was some sort of heroic act.

"You should have seen it, Mom. Dad's a savage!" Chance continued. "The bison reared up and caused a stampede. Traffic was backed up for miles."

"And where were you guys when all of this was happening?" Every syllable she uttered was strained as she tried to keep her anger in check.

"Don't worry, Dad told us to hang back a few feet."

"A few feet?" Holly repeated in shock. "Every year, someone dies in the park from pulling some stunt like that. Wild animals are unpredictable."

"Relax, Hols, we were just cutting loose. Nothing happened."

"That's not the point," Holly hissed. "What if it had turned and charged you or the boys? Do you know how challenging it is to get medevac'd out of Yellowstone? Some parts of the park don't even have cell coverage."

"At least it wasn't a bear, Mom," Chance joked weakly. "You always tell us not to poke the bear."

She rolled her eyes. "Boys, go get washed up for dinner." They stole fleeting apologetic glances back toward their father, who shrugged his shoulders and settled down on a rocking chair for the lecture he knew was coming.

"That was reckless and dangerous."

"Sometimes you just need to do something to get your blood pumping," he explained. "Something to make you feel alive."

"Do not involve the boys on your mid-life crisis-driven quest for excitement." She rubbed her hand along the smooth wood of the arm of the chair she was sitting in to ground her emotions. "I knew this was a mistake," she admitted first to herself and then to him.

"When did you become so hostile and salty? You used to be fun."

Holly laughed bitterly. "It took about sixteen years, don't you remember? You were there the entire time."

"Go ahead and blame me for that, too. Just add it to the pile of my punishable offenses," he waxed on dramatically.

"Stop it. You don't get to do that. You don't get to make me feel like a bad person for holding you to a normal healthy standard."

"Are we done here?" He stood and stomped out his cigarette butt.

"Pick it up and put it in the barn," she ordered. "Dinner's ready."

They ate in silence, a painful reminder of what dinners used to feel like when they lived under the same roof. Holly forced a smile and asked Dillon, "Who wants to play High and Low?" It was a nightly dinner activity they used to do together. Each person had to go around the table and say their high and low events for the day. It forced them to interact and was a takeaway from the continuing education she was required to complete to keep her teaching license.

"I'll go first," Dillon offered eagerly. "My high was watching how fast the bison ran to catch up with his bison buddies." Holly clamped her lips together to keep her criticism inside. "And my low was having to skip ice cream at Old Faithful."

Chance pushed the Spanish rice around his plate with a fork. "My high is having Dad here, and my low is knowing he'll have to go soon."

"Mick," Holly directed, "your turn."

"My high is being with my boys." He smiled a genuine smile. "And my low was getting read the riot act for having a little fun."

It was taking everything in her not to respond in anger. Mick was pressing all of her buttons, and she was furious.

A few more days. You can endure this for a few more days for your boys. Look at how happy they are, gathered around the table, sharing a meal as a family.

"Mom?" Dillon's voice broke through her impromptu self-pep-talk.

"My high was seeing Ruth today. She sent me home with some goodies."

And my low was having to parent my ex-husband again. She wanted to say it, but she swallowed the words knowing nothing good would come from them.

"And I didn't have a low. It was a great day." She smiled at them and finished her taco in a few bites, then began to clear the plates. She noticed Mick's hand trembling when he reached for his water glass and met his eyes. He looked away first and pulled his hand under the table to hide it.

Holly filled the sink with soapy water and began to scrub

the dishes. The boys went to the loft to play video games, and when she turned back around to ask Mick a question, she discovered that he'd let himself out, eager to escape. It was a relief; she was finding it hard to relax in her own home when he was around.

EIGHTEEN

The next morning started early for Holly, and she sat outside enjoying her first cup of coffee, waiting for the sun to come up. When the first rays broke the horizon, spilling soft yellow light into the deep navy of night, her eyes fixated on the barn. She squinted at a shape she couldn't make out.

"What in…" She set her cup down and walked to the barn as Murph followed in his cone. The wet grass was cold and damp on her toes, tickling her feet through her sandals. Leaning back on a lawn chair, a rumpled Mick was passed out, snoring away with an empty bottle of vodka laying on its side in the grass. His mouth hung open as she watched his chest rise and fall, cloaked in his dirty t-shirt. Instantly enraged, Holly shook him.

"Mick!" she spat out, shaking his arm roughly to wake him up. Leaning closer, she hissed, "Get up!" The metabolized vodka was seared in every pore of his skin. His breath was sour and hot on her cheek. She wrinkled her nose in disgust and shoved him harder. "Wake up!"

He slowly came to life in the chair with a groan. "Jesus," he muttered, taking a full minute to get his bearings.

"Go sleep it off in the barn before the kids see you," she hissed.

Holly whipped her head over her shoulder, searching for any sign of the boys, and was relieved they had stayed up late gaming the night before. She pulled him to his feet, and they stumbled forward as Holly struggled under his weight. He slung an arm around her shoulders and began to laugh a dry, low sound that put Holly on edge even more.

"Nothing about this is funny. I will let you sleep it off and then you're leaving, got it? I will not let you undo all the work I have done to give the boys a healthy life."

Mick stopped and stood up straight, seeming to sober up instantly. "You've changed, Hols."

"You're right, Mick. I have. That's the difference between me and you. You never will." Her words deflated him, and she was left dragging him into the barn, struggling under the effort as he began to shake. Holly shuffled forward, grateful when he was finally hidden inside the barn. She dropped him roughly onto his back on the overstuffed sofa that had officially taken up residence there the day it didn't fit in the house. Mick immediately turned onto his side and began to retch into the dirt. Holly turned away from the smell of it, beginning to dry heave herself. Taking a step back into fresher air, she stood with her hands on her hips, sickened at what he had become and knowing she was going to have to break Chance and Dillon's hearts again in a few hours.

"You always were a better man than me," Mick uttered, then let loose a morose chuckle as he wiped the back of his hand across his mouth.

"It wasn't hard," Holly stated as she pulled the wrinkled quilt from the end of the sofa and laid it over him. His eyes met hers, and he began to cry as she tucked him in. It was a pathetic wail like an animal keening. He was broken, and in spite of herself, she pressed her palm to his forehead. She shushed him. "There is nothing you can do now. Go back to sleep." He began to blubber, and she waited for him to calm down, afraid of the scene he could make and the impact it would have on her boys. She smoothed the skin on his forehead to calm him down, and in a few minutes, he passed out.

His mouth was open wide, his tongue jiggling as he began to snore. The anger dissipated and she saw him for what he was. Pathetic, strung out, addicted. His skin was sickly and gray, his hair quickly following suit. It had thinned considerably since she saw him last. A shell of what he once was, he was so far away from the man she once adored, loving him felt like it happened in another lifetime. The woman that fell for Mick Simon's charm didn't even exist anymore. Now, she saw him clearly and grieved for the young woman she used to be. The one who fell for his charisma and charm. The one who was so ready to please and to prove her worth as a partner to him at any cost. That girl was dead now.

Sometime during the next morning, when she was dropping off the boys at Deacon's, he disappeared without a goodbye, and Holly was relieved he had at least enough respect for her to hold up his end of their bargain.

<h1 style="text-align:center">NINETEEN</h1>

ugust was a blur of activity, punctuated by the delivery of Stacey's gift baskets and late-night Skype sessions. Holly began to fall into her rhythm as an Airbnb host. She started to include little extras like rides to and from the airport and to the Zipline, offering to drive guests to Cal's white water rafting company, and to a ranch that Deacon recommended when a guest requested horseback riding. She learned her lesson with Kendall's group and fully vetted every single guest, and she never made the mistake of renting to college kids at the last minute again. She was gaining a slew of five-star reviews and knew that within a year she would close in on her goal of Superhost status. Holly scoured the internet for a second-hand hot tub after finding out her listings could bring in so much more if a hot tub was included on her list of amenities. And best of all, as an added bonus, when the cabins were vacant, she could soak in it.

Calls from Mick were sporadic, some late at night long after he had gotten deep into the bottle of vodka he craved. Most of the time, Holly would have to turn him away because he was obliterated. Slurring his words, begging to talk to his kids, his anger focused on Holly, who he accused of standing in his way of being a father. He was sinking deeper into a pit of depression, and it was hard to watch his unraveling. She was relieved when the calls slowed to once every month because, after every call, the boys would spiral downward for a few days in sympathy with their father. It was getting harder and harder to push past her anger. Phone calls from Mick would spin them out and send them reeling, and the only one who could reach them in that state was Deacon.

There was a pilgrimage to Bozeman for school supplies, clothing, and shoes. There were the weekly AA meetings Chance was attending with Kent with only minimal complaining. Kent was becoming a reliable, steady force in Chance's life, adopting the much younger sponsee almost like an uncle. They talked every day on the phone, and Holly saw a shift happening in Chance. He was calmer and becoming stronger and more self-assured. He was maturing and starting to think differently about almost everything. He was also filling out and getting taller, due to his recently discovered love of apple pie ala mode. Every month he made Holly measure his height with a pencil tick on the hallway door to see if there was any change.

The boys entered their new school system, and so far, Holly was cautiously optimistic. Dillon came home with tales from biology class that usually involved weird random facts. "Did you know that spiders are nearsighted, and the jumping ones can jump up to fifty times their own length?" He was obsessed with nature and had taken to looking for birds on their hikes with an old pair of binoculars Ruth had given Holly.

Holly's doubts began to disappear. Every day, she felt

better about the drastic life change she'd made. Leaving New Hope was becoming one of the best decisions of her life. They were all starting to settle in, to take a breath and relax into their new routines. And after all the fear and drama in New Hope, it was a welcome reprieve.

Every brick she formed from her own hard work became part of the foundation of their new sense of home. It gave her stability and security, two things that had always been elusive in her life. When she was younger, she thought a man would give her those, and the revelation that she could create them on her own motivated her to keep going on a path that was infinitely harder but much more stable and satisfying.

Deacon started regularly coming to dinner on Wednesday nights. What started out as a thank you quickly evolved into a weekly tradition. After he helped her wash and dry the dishes, they would talk for hours on the porch. Long evenings flew by watching sunsets together as the sky first washed itself in pastels and then deepened into the darker hues as night settled in and the stars began to wink. She could talk to him about anything. As usual, she was wide open, answering his questions about Mick and her life in New Hope, her dad, and her own difficult childhood. She didn't hold back, but he did. He was hard to read, never offering much, but always asking questions about her and redirecting when she tried to turn the tables. She got the sense there was something he kept locked inside, and no matter how hard she worked to unlock it, the door remained shut.

When he came over, he allowed himself only one beer. Holly never questioned him about it, and she wasn't sure if he was doing it for Chance's benefit or hers, but either way, she admired his self-control. It was another character quality that set him apart from Mick.

At the end of the night, he would eventually stand and

stretch his huge arms over his head, and she would sometimes catch a glimpse of his soft underbelly.

There was a little pudge with a matting of hairs, and if she was brutally honest with herself, it made her feel even more attracted to him that he wasn't rocking a six-pack under there. He wasn't an unattainable Greek god who measured macros and lived in the gym. Deacon was a real man, flawed like she was, and that only increased her attraction.

Some mornings, she'd wake up tingling with desire and wonder what it would be like to walk her fingers across the sheets and find him lying there next to her, skin on skin. She found herself wondering if the ginger-colored hair snaked up his chest? Would it tickle her face if she laid down on it? What did his lips taste like?

She learned he was afraid of clowns since he read "It" when he was twelve. He liked his biscuits with butter *and* honey. He was a meat and potatoes kind of man and didn't leave much room for any kind of green leafy vegetable on his heaping plates. His voice never raised an octave *ever*. You could tell him the house was on fire, the dog was shot, or you crashed his pickup into a tree, and you would be met with the same. "Well, I guess it could always be worse."

He religiously checked her doors and windows to make sure they were locked. One late summer afternoon, he had taken her to the shooting range. She tried to calm the hammering of her heart when he wrapped his arms around her to show her how to focus on the target. "Take a breath, exhale, and then gently squeeze." When he said it, her heart squeezed tighter, bursting in her chest. On her ninth shot, she hit the bullseye. Holly was shocked and amazed. When Deacon rolled her target back and she saw three satisfying holes in a grouping near the center mass, her heart swelled from his pride at her accomplishment. The high-five he gave her sent a bolt of lightning to her core.

But there was an invisible line, a barrier that neither of them was eager to cross. Holly stayed on her side because of the boys. If she dated Deacon and they crashed and burned like every other relationship in her life, the real victims would be her sons. She felt a pull toward him that was undeniable, but she couldn't explore it because the price was too high.

It's good having Deacon in my life. It's good to have a friend like him.

She reasoned with herself when after an extra glass of wine during their Wednesday night chats the idea of pushing the boundary more into uncharted territory reared its head. He was like no one she had ever met. Solid. Steady. Honest. She felt herself relax in his presence and become comfortable. After a life of chaos with Mick, ease was something new. A new feeling she was going to have to get used to.

He usually brought his dogs, and they would lay curled at his feet. Tink and Murph cuddled up, circling their bodies toward each other, fitting together like two pieces of a puzzle. She grew to love his overprotective, drooling monsters.

One day, she cut the fat and gristle off their steaks and tried to scoop it into a bowl.

"Whoa!" He quickly extracted the bowl from her hand and scooped it into the trash can. "You can't feed them that."

Shocked, Holly waited for him to explain.

"Those idiots would gobble it up, but then you're just asking for GI problems. Use this instead." He put a sweet potato in her hand and showed her how to dehydrate them into treats that were healthy for the dogs, which they devoured. Being a rural emergency vet, he kept crazy hours, and he gave her a key to his house and the rescue so she and the boys could help him out when he was running late or got called in unexpectedly. Holly was delighted to reciprocate after feeling the friendship began so one-sided. She had to admit the dog breed she'd harshly judged previously had found a special place in her heart. Each dog had its own personality, and it was always a bittersweet moment when one of them graduated from the program and was placed with its new master as a service dog.

The rhythm of living in a place that celebrated the changing of the seasons seeped into her soul, forcing her to slow down, to savor and enjoy things more. She found it easy to live more simply. Spending weeks going through everything she owned, Holly got a weird thrill every time she scaled back. She got rid of clothing she hated, or that had holes or looked bad on her. Holly walked and hiked, and at the end of the summer was shocked to learn her clothing had begun to hang in places, and when she finally stepped on a scale, discovered she was twenty pounds lighter. It gave her another burst of confidence, and she found some great second-hand maxi dresses and long fleece-lined leggings that would keep her warm in the frigid winters that were coming. When Montana would turn into the treacherous cold wasteland she kept hearing so much about.

And deep in September, she awoke after sleeping a full eight and a half hours. After realizing it, she laughed out loud and clamped a hand to her mouth to stifle the giggle and then stopped herself. The peace and joy she desired had finally found their way into her life and tingled from her heart to her limbs. A sense of complete contentedness flushed her with warmth. Goodness was flooding in, and it bowled her over, bringing tears to her eyes when she counted her blessings every night as she drifted off to sleep. This was the exact right place she was destined to be at the exact right time.

Every morning as she stretched and stood with her feet on

the floor, when the boys had already gone to school and the house was quiet, she thanked God. This life she had fought for, had risked everything to begin, was falling into place, and a feeling of complete gratitude filled her soul. It was good to feel good again.

TWENTY

October in Yellowstone was a sight to see. Shades of crimson, bright yellow, and orange dotted the forest views that went on for miles. The jaw-dropping summer vistas were made even more breathtaking with showy autumn displays, and on drizzly fall days, the colors seemed to pop even more. The wetness of the nearly black mountains contrasted with the white birches and maples with their bright golds and reds. Roaring campfires kept campers warm and infused the air with a scent that Holly found intoxicating.

The stunning foliage drew even more people to the parks and resulted in last-minute getaway bookings that kept Holly busy right up until the middle of October, when the leaves had dried up and were ripped away by the late fall winds.

Bookings had increased, and Holly was squirreling away money as much as possible. Cal, Deacon, and Ruth put the fear of God in her; she didn't know what to expect of a Montana winter. Holly pinched pennies where she could and did her best to quell the worry that came with her fear of the unknown. She would figure out a way. She had successfully kept her boys alive so far, and she knew if she had to dig deep, she would. Holly had never been afraid of hard work.

Deacon took them on long drives through the park, where they would picnic and hike, and Holly loved how easy he was to be around. The boys followed him around like lost puppies, coming home from their weekend work shifts with stories to tell and exhausted from the physical work at the rescue, a job they never complained about.

After two months of biding his time cleaning out kennels, Chance finally earned the privilege to help with the training of Tank, the newest beefy rescue Deacon brought into the brood, who was going to be a service dog for a former Marine who'd lost his legs in Afghanistan. It was going to take at least a year to get him trained for the skills he would need to help his new master, and Chance was running over to the rescue two and three days a week to check in on Tank and help Deacon.

Holly hung back, afraid of how attached her boys were getting to Deacon. She had her own feelings about him but tried to push them away. It was messy having feelings for Deacon when her boys were so involved in his life. If they took a chance and it ended badly, the boys would lose someone they truly cared about.

No, it was better to remain only friends.

She continued to push her feelings away, trying to ignore them, trying to rationalize them and talk herself out of it, and most days she was successful—successful-ish.

TWENTY-ONE

One early morning in late October, Holly was taking a shower when she heard a knock at the door. Suds ran down her body as she rushed to finish and wrap a robe around her body.

"Mom!" Dillon shouted through the door. "The police are here."

"What?" Hearing murmured voices she didn't recognize, her heart plunged to the floor and her breathing labored. In a panic, she threw on a pair of sweatpants and a t-shirt, her hair dampening the collar of her shirt.

Chance was home, wasn't he? Sleeping safe in his bed? I should have checked.

The wounds were too raw, dredging up the past when she had already run a thousand miles away from it.

The officer was talking to Dillon when she opened the door, and she met his eyes.

"Ma'am." He tipped the brim of his hat toward her.

"Where's your brother?" Holly asked the only question that was on her mind.

"He's still sleeping."

Holly exhaled a deep sigh of relief and looked back at the officer, confused as to why he was standing in her living room. "Can I help you?"

"Are you Holly Simon?" he asked.

"Yes." The formality of his question frightened her. She reached for Dillon and pulled him to her protectively, his ears hanging on every word. "Do you mind if we talk on the porch?" Holly tipped her head toward Dillon, and the officer nodded and followed her to the front porch.

"I'm sorry to be the bearer of bad news, but I am here to notify next of kin. Mick Simon passed away last night. They are still investigating, but it looks like an accidental overdose."

"No… Wait, what?" Holly's hand flew to her mouth, and she collapsed onto a chair as the officer began to riddle off facts from a notebook in his hand while her brain struggled to collect them.

"The police were called to his house for a welfare check and found him unresponsive. Finding opioids near his body, they administered Narcan. His pulse was thready and weak, so he was taken by ambulance to the hospital and intubated, but his organs had already begun to shut down. Do you know any reason why he would want to take his own life?"

"Whoa… I mean..." Holly stammered, struggling to put a full sentence together. "I know he was struggling financially and seemed a little lost when he came out to visit the boys at the end of the summer, but he's not the type of guy to do that. An accidental overdose is much more likely."

"The coroner will complete the autopsy and have more answers in a couple days." Shutting his notebook, he continued, "I'm sorry for your loss. Is there anyone I can call for you?" the officer asked.

"No," Holly admitted, "it's just me." In a daze, she

watched him nod and then walk away. Her eyes stayed glued to the cruiser as he got into it and disappeared down the lane in a cloud of dust. Holly sank back into the chair, the weight of truth pressing her down. Gone. She couldn't believe it. She was stunned. A man she had spent almost two decades with, the father of her children. Gone forever, snuffed out by his own weakness. A tragic ending to a life barely lived. Tears welled in her eyes as the truth began to settle in.

How was she going to tell the boys?

Tears trickled down her cheeks.

What a waste. Oh, Mick, how could you break our children's hearts again?

She sat stunned in the chair, trying to absorb the news, when the creak of the porch door opening made her jump.

"Dillon wouldn't shut up about the police being here," a still sleepy Chance said as an interested Dillon followed behind him. "What's going on?"

"Come here, guys." She pulled a stool and a chair closer and patted the seats, waiting for the boys to sit. Racking her brain for the right words to say, she struggled to find ones to soften the devastating blow she knew Mick's passing would have on their lives.

"You're scaring us, Mom." Chance was wary.

She wiped her tears and leaned forward, taking one of their hands in her own. "Your dad is… in the hospital." She couldn't bring herself to say the word dead. It seemed too final.

Dillon's face crumpled into confusion. "He's okay, though, right?"

Holly squeezed. "Unfortunately, he didn't wake up, honey. He passed away."

Dillon shook his head violently. "No."

"But he was just here," Chance argued, then anger filled

his eyes "I don't believe you." His jaw set in a hardline. "You're lying. It can't be." His voice cracked, and he yanked his hand back and stood up fast. The stool toppled and hit the ground behind him. "No, Mom. No."

"I'm so sorry, honey. It's the truth." She began to cry. She reached out for Chance, but he pushed her away.

"No!" Dillon took off running into the field as if he could outrun the truth.

Chance turned to follow, but Holly grasped his forearm. "Let him go," Holly whispered. "Just give him a minute."

"What happened?" Chance asked as he fell back down in Dillon's empty chair, wringing his hands. "Tell me. I need to know."

Holly swallowed the lump in her throat. "Are you sure?"

"Please," he begged.

"They think it was an accidental overdose or..."

"Or what? Suicide?" Chance guessed. "No way! He would never do that. He would never leave me and Dilly."

Holly remembered the state he was in just a month ago when she'd talked to him last. He was incoherent and sobbing, and she'd hung up on him, telling him to sober up. Fresh guilt welled up in her gut. As much as she wanted to believe it was an accident, she wasn't entirely convinced. But knowing the truth wasn't going to make her children feel better. It would be far worse if it was discovered that he made the choice to leave.

"You're right," she agreed. "He would never leave you guys on purpose. He loved you both so much."

She wrapped an arm around his shoulders and pulled him closer to her as his body began to shake. "I'm so sorry, sweet-heart." She hugged him as he began to sob, his body taut and trembling. He mumbled muffled words and fragments of sentences she didn't fully understand, and Holly smoothed his hair and made soothing sounds. His heartbreak echoed her own, but with triple the intensity. Good or bad, Mick was his dad, the only dad he would ever have, and now he was gone forever. The finality of the fact shook him.

"Let's go find Dilly." Chance nodded and found his feet. They walked in silence in the field toward the barn where they found Dillon on the sofa Mick occupied during his last visit. His face was dirty and tear-stained, his arms crossed protectively around his torso.

"Are you okay?" She knelt down and put her arms around his angry, unyielding body.

"That's a dumb question. No offense, Mom. It just is."

"I guess you're right."

"How do they know it's him?" Dillon asked, still grasping at straws.

"They know, sweetheart." She smoothed his hair back from his forehead. "This is a lot to absorb. Why don't you guys go inside and get something to eat? I've got some phone calls to make."

They followed her directions obediently, a sad parade to the front door as Murph trailed behind them.

The phone rang in her hand. It was the only person she wanted to talk to.

"I was just going to call you," Holly answered then choked on the last word. "You've heard?"

"I did. Oh, honey, what can I do?" Stacey murmured softly.

"I don't even know." Holly sighed. "I have to make arrangements and get tickets for us. It's going to cost a fortune."

"You're staying here," Stacey insisted. "Do the boys know?"

"It was brutal, Stace."

"I bet."

"The guy was a mess, but he was their father. I still have all this unresolved anger and frustration with him, but I have to set it aside for the boys. They are devastated."

"That is going to be difficult," she agreed. "I'm so sorry this happened."

"He was in rough shape when he came out, but I never in a million years thought it would be the last time we'd see him. I said some pretty horrible things to him."

"Don't do that."

"What?"

"Feel guilty." Stacey continued, "It is truly a tragedy that his life devolved enough for this to happen, but you can't feel guilty about his decisions."

"You're right," Holly answered. "Won't do any good anyway. He will still be gone."

"That's true," Stacey answered.

"I'll let you know what the arrangements are."

"Stay strong. Love you, girl."

TWENTY-TWO

The silence was the worst part. Like a cloud, grief hovered over them all, and there was a numbness that made every movement thicken and become exhausting. She was driving the kids and Murph over to Deacon's, to explain and ask for help.

He was working in the yard when she pulled up. He cut off the mower and walked toward her with a surprised look on his face.

"Didn't think I'd see you today." He immediately registered the shift in all of them. "What's going on?"

"Why don't you guys take Murph and go hang out with Daisy and Tink while I talk to Deak?"

"There's some pancakes inside if you're hungry," Deacon offered.

Holly's eyes darted to his and then away. She didn't trust herself and was so fractured, seeing her sons in such agony she thought his sweet gesture might shatter her into dust.

His eyebrows lifted, and he sat down on the porch swing and patted the seat next to him. She sat down, her knee hitting him mid-thigh. She looked out onto his land, unable to meet his eyes.

"Mick overdosed last night. He's gone." The words came out like a whisper.

"No shit?" He sighed and put his hand on her thigh, giving it a gentle squeeze.

"I can't believe it." She twisted toward him slightly. "We are flying back in a couple days, and I need someone to watch my place and Murph."

"Of course. Anything you need, I'm here." His fingers tucked under her chin and pulled her eyes to his. "Are *you* okay?"

"It's the boys I'm worried about. They are devastated." Holly explained, "And Chance, I always worry when there is stress or bad news because it puts him at risk for relapse. I'll have to watch him like a hawk."

"That's true, but I need to know if *you* are okay." His genuine concern reflected in his eyes as he examined hers.

"I'm okay."

"Liar."

A small smile tugged at the corners of Holly's mouth as she stood up.

"Come here," he said and pulled her into a hug. Her head rested on his chest, and she felt his chin sit on the top of her head. He smelled like sweat and soap and freshly cut grass, a smell so incredibly masculine and normal it crushed her. She finally broke, her pieces scattering then surging back together with the power of his embrace. "I know you have to be strong for them, but it's just you and me right here."

She shook with an intensity that scared and embarrassed her, revealing herself in a way that felt unsettling and foreign. After several long minutes, she pulled away with a shy smile and swiped at her cheeks with her hands. "Thank you," she whispered. It was all she could think to say, but the words felt weak and empty.

"You're welcome." He tucked a wayward curl behind her ear, a gesture that melted her. "You take care of the boys, and by the time you get back, Murph will be part of the pack. Hell, he might never want to go home." She smiled a sad smile, then corralled the boys back into the van.

Another silent drive home, she gathered their suitcases and booked tickets. She checked in with Mick's fractured family that never made her feel welcome or took time to get to know the boys. That night, she stood outside the closed door to the boys' room, hearing soft sobbing and murmured words through the door. She pressed her ear to it, longing to go in. After a few minutes, she knocked softly with the back of her knuckles and then opened the door.

"I love you guys," she said into the darkness. Her eyes adjusted, and she heard Dillon sniffling, his back to her on the bottom bunk. Chance was bouncing a tennis ball onto the ceiling. It made a soft, rhythmic *thunk* each time it connected with the wall. "Good night," she whispered and gently closed the door behind them. Freshly fatherless. It was going to take a long time for all of them to accept this new normal.

<h1 style="text-align:center">TWENTY-THREE</h1>

Grief dampens and blocks, shutting off most body processes except those necessary for survival. Shell-shocked and numb, they survived the next four days hunkered down in the house. Joined together in a silent hell, she made food the boys picked at and she barely tasted. They watched movies and waited for the days to pass to fly back to New Hope to lay Mick to rest.

Never say never. She told herself, remembering how vehemently she protested the idea of ever returning to New Hope.

Well played, Mick. Well played.

It was hard to hate him anymore. As the days passed, her hatred began to transform into pity. Finally, with the funeral arrangements set, she dropped off Murph with Deacon and then started her journey back to Indiana. Holly couldn't remember buying the tickets, driving to the airport, or boarding the flight, but hours later, she was stunned to hear the pilot say, "Welcome to New Hope, Indiana. We know you have choices when you travel by air, and we want to thank you for flying with us." She sat in her seat, frozen, as frustrated travelers stood cramped in the aisles, desperate for the hatch to be opened so they could spill out away from the stale air and head toward their final destinations.

"Are you ready?" she asked the boys when the deplaning had finally advanced to her row.

They stood and stretched and opened the overhead compartments to pull their carry-ons out and began to drag them. Holly's phone buzzed with an incoming text from Stacey. She glanced at it and then put it away, led them through the gates, down the escalator, and made her way to baggage claim. Chance and Dillon were quiet, dark circles marring both their eyes, and they followed like zombie ducklings behind her.

Surveying the crowd gathered at baggage claim, she saw Stacey's head pop up and then zip around the clusters of people waiting for their luggage. Stacey let out a little squeal when Holly finally crossed the security threshold and tackled her with a hug. Holly squeezed her eyes shut, but the tears flowed anyway.

"You give good hugs," Holly praised her friend. "You have no idea how much I needed one."

"It's my superpower." She laughed and pulled the boys into her arms, then fell in step next to Dillon. "Sarah can't wait to see you." Dillon perked up. "She's got the Xbox ready and waiting and has already downloaded Zombies vs. Doggies." Grateful for the distraction, Holly watched Stacey chat with him as they walked toward the parking lot. It did wonders to cheer up Dillon.

Holly slowed down and walked beside Chance. "You're so quiet," she observed. "Everything okay?"

"A stupid video game isn't going to have the same effect on me," he explained. Holly nodded as he continued. "It's so weird to be back here."

"It is," Holly agreed. "But it's just for a few days, and then we'll be back home."

"Home? Nothing feels like home anymore, definitely not this hell-hole, and Montana still feels like we're on vacation. It's like we're nomads."

"Hell-hole is a little dramatic, but I can see why you'd say that." She paused and then added, "For me, home is wherever you guys are."

His brow crinkled as he considered her statement. "So, it's not so much a place as a feeling."

"Exactly."

"I guess it's easier not forming attachments to places. I mean, in a few years, I'll be moving out or going to college."

A sliver of fear unfurled in Holly's heart, but he was right; time was fleeting. "As long as I'm alive, you'll always have a home." She saw Chance stiffen at her word choice. "I'm sorry, honey. You know what I mean."

He nodded and looked away to hide the tears that were gathering in the corners of his eyes. She wrapped an arm around his shoulders and pulled him in closer. "This will be a rough couple of days to get through. I know you loved him, and as flawed as he was, he loved you, too. So much. You should never doubt that."

"I know he loved us, but we always came second," Chance said, wiping his eyes. "It sucks being a consolation prize. I'm angry," he admitted, "and then I feel guilty for being angry."

"You have every right to be angry," Holly confirmed. "It's a natural part of the grieving process. There are five stages, and anger is number two."

"What are the next ones?" he asked.

"Bargaining, depression, and acceptance."

"Wow. That sounds like a great time. Can't wait." Sarcasm coated his words.

"Yeah," Holly sympathized. "You hurt because you loved. It's just going to take time to process it. Some days, you will feel normal and almost happy, and some days, you will struggle to survive."

"You aren't helping," he cautioned.

She sighed. "There isn't a way to fast-track it, buddy. The only way out is through. I have to be honest with you, I am scared this can put you at risk for relapse."

"Me too," he admitted. "But you have to trust me and trust the process. As long as I'm going to meetings and staying sober, you have nothing to worry about."

"When did you get so wise?" The statement brought a flicker of a proud smile across his face, and Holly watched as he picked up the pace to catch up with Stacey and Dillon. She slowed her roll and watched them glide through the airport. Her two man-cubs, growing up. Life had intervened and forced them to mature far earlier than she ever hoped they would. She couldn't protect them, and that reality stung.

TWENTY-FOUR

The morning of the funeral, Chance tugged at the constricting collar of his dress shirt. In the late October Indian summer heat, Holly saw beads of sweat beginning to dampen around his hairline.

"Why do we have to dress up?" Dillon whined. "I hate these shoes."

"To show respect." Holly stopped at that; it was short and sweet. Holly was determined today to put aside her feelings about Mick the husband so she could support her boys grieving Mick the father.

The little country church was an hour outside of New Hope, and the same one she and Mick had gotten married in sixteen years ago. Faithfully restored and lovingly maintained, it was white clapboard with a huge stained-glass window. Flanked by a gravel parking lot, it was tiny enough that it had an attached rural cemetery with rows of headstones behind wrought iron gates. Inside, it never left the 70s with its drab olive-green carpeting and dark paneled sanctuary.

The crowd of mourners at the church was sad and sparse. Holly led the boys down the center aisle to where the casket lay open and showy sprays of red flowers were draped dramatically over the shiny oak burl coffin. Each step she took closer to it was oddly reminiscent of the trip she made down the same aisle of the same church on their wedding day. Afraid, Dillon clung to her hand as she gently guided them closer.

"Marilyn." Holly greeted her estranged mother-in-law evenly, who was dressed head to toe in black and dabbing a black lacy handkerchief to her eyes. Time had transformed the old woman into a chubby shrew.

"Hi, Grandma," Chance said in a heavy obligatory tone just out of her grasp. Dillon wasn't so lucky and cringed from being embraced too tightly, crushed into the chest of his grandmother, a woman who was practically a stranger.

"Only the good die young," Marilyn declared with a sob and more dabbing of the eyes. Holly didn't even register the absurdity of her statement, completely focused on the boys, who seemed to shrink the closer they got to the coffin.

"That doesn't look like Dad at all," Dillon exclaimed with false hope after his first furtive glance into the coffin.

"It's him, Dilly," Chance confirmed. He pulled a guitar pick out of his pants pocket, bent down, and slipped it into the casket. A heavy lone tear rolled down his cheek, and he brushed it away. They both stared at their father, unable to move. Mick was stiff and dressed in a suit, at least from the waist up. Holly had a sneaking suspicion that Marilyn only paid for the jacket and blew the rest of the budget on flowers. His hair was gray, woven with strands of white. His skin was thick and pasty, almost appearing painted on. His mouth formed a tight line, and his arms were crisscrossed over his chest.

"Doesn't he look good?" Marilyn cooed as she reached down to straighten the collar of his jacket.

Holly nodded, unable to outright lie to the woman who had hated her since the day they met. Marilyn was clingy, resentful, and inserted herself into their relationship where she didn't belong. Always a momma's boy, Mick struggled to choose a side, but eventually chose Holly and his sons.

"And these boys, left without a father…" Marilyn cried and swiped at the tears in her eyes. Holly struggled to keep her eyes from rolling at the dramatics. Chance and Dillon crept away from their grandmother, just out of reach from her grasping, desperate fingers.

"Can we go?" Chance whispered in Holly's ear.

"Yes," Holly decided, "let's get some air before the service."

———

The pew was wooden and heavy, in perfect congruence with how she felt. Holly was surprised how many memories rushed to the surface, dredged up by the end of a life she had entwined with hers for so many years. Like an episode of "This is your life." She ran through their greatest hits. The night they met, when it felt like magic. The first heady days of their fast and furious courtship. When they spent hours on the phone until she'd wake up with it in her hand, hear him snoring lightly on the other end, and think it was adorable. Their wedding day, a small private ceremony at the church when she was secretly already in her first trimester with Chance and was craving chocolate milk and kimchi constantly. Then four months later, when he sat next to her growing belly and played *Here Comes the Sun.*

There was Chance's birth, then Dillon's. Each year, Mick seemed to fade away and disappear a little more until he became a ghost in their lives. Each year, his dream of making it big in the music industry fell further away, just out of his grasp. Crushed under the brutal truth that he was nearly geriatric in an industry famous for churning out picture-perfect models whose actual musical talent was a secondary consideration. Each year, he became less hopeful and more bitter and distant. Pulling away because of his personal failures and losing himself while he numbed the pain with booze and then prescription drugs. It was a slow descent, and she had witnessed most of it firsthand.

Sitting in the pew, listening to the minister speaking about a man he didn't really know, next to a larger than life-size portrait of his smiling face, Holly wondered what their life would have been like if he had really gotten the chance to live his dream. Would they have even met in the first place, or would he have had a trophy wife in the Hollywood Hills?

Seeing the casket closed and then being carried to its final resting place under the blue funeral home canopy next to a freshly dug grave made Holly feel like she was suffocating. Dillon sobbed as it was lowered into the ground, his hand shaking when he dropped his rose onto it. Chance bit his lip and dropped his into the hole next. Behind him, Holly lingered with her rose as tears coursed down her cheeks.

I hope you find some peace. I forgive you. You are finally free. We will miss you.

She sat back down on the folding chairs next to her sons as more family and friends of Mick's shuffled forward and dropped red roses onto his casket. It hit her that life was an endless forward motion. You either try to steer your life and work to make your dreams come true, or you give up and let it take you down whatever twisted road it wants. Either way, your clock is ticking down to the end. She swiped tears for the man she used to love. Seeing Chance stiffening his lip, his jaw trembling in an effort to control his emotions, broke

Holly's heart. She reached out to squeeze his hand and was surprised but grateful that he actually let hers rest there. Dillon sobbed softly next to her. Heartbroken, his nose whistled and was congested from crying. She wrapped her other arm around him, pulling him closer. His breath caught in his chest as he tried to take a deeper breath and then began wailing again.

She felt a hand on her shoulder and a gentle squeeze. Reaching back, she put her hand on top of Stacey's. They had stayed up late into the night talking. Holly didn't have to pretend or put on a brave face. She could finally let her guard down. It was Stacey's words that brought her the most comfort.

"It's okay to grieve for him. I know Mick was worthless as a partner, but you loved him once, enough to bring those two handsome men into the world, and if he did absolutely nothing else right, it was still worth it."

Holly nodded and wiped away a tear. "It's the boys I'm most worried about. They loved him so much."

"It's going to take some time," Stacey agreed. "But they have other strong men in their lives now—Kent and Deacon."

"I know, and they are lucky in that respect."

"No one will ever replace their dad," Stacey explained, "but death has a way of mellowing your memories of people. The sweeter times stay, and the awful ones fade."

Holly nodded. "You must be right. I can feel my anger dissipating. It's hard to feel hate and empathy for the same person at the same time. The heart doesn't work that way. Mick was a mess, but he sure did love our boys, and for that, he will be missed."

They sat in comfortable silence, staring at the fire in Stacey's fireplace. Holly's tears wouldn't stop flowing.

"I'm a terrible person for saying this, and I know it's not

the time or place to discuss it, but at least you won't have to worry about fighting him for child support anymore. You can collect his social security for the boys."

"What?" Holly asked, the new information snapping her out of the fog.

"My sister-in-law went through a similar thing. It will help you provide for the boys until they are eighteen."

"The thought never even crossed my mind." But this surprising fact didn't bring her the relief she thought it would. As flawed as he was, he was her children's only father, and now he was gone. The finality is what will kill you. She always thought that one day Mick would grow up. He would mature. He would finally get it… but now he never would.

TWENTY-FIVE

The plane ride home was silent, each of her sons lost in a sea of their own private grief. Reflective and quieter, it was like they had aged overnight. Dillon was sleeping in the seat next to her, his head bobbing up and down in sync with the slight turbulence from the plane. She glanced over at Chance, who was awake and deep in thought.

"How are you doing with all of this?"

"I still can't believe it," he started, then bit his lip as he looked away as his eyes filled with tears. "I tried to get him to go to a meeting with me once. Did I ever tell you that?"

"No," Holly answered. "I wish you would have. It was incredibly brave of you."

"Maybe if I would have pushed harder for him to go, this would have never happened."

"Oh, honey. You cannot carry that around with you. It's too heavy."

He wiped a tear off his cheek with his fingers, whisking it away. "I know in my *head* that it was not my problem. I know I didn't create his addiction and so I couldn't fix it. But in my *heart*, I wish I had done more. I wish I had tried harder, set bigger boundaries. Maybe it would have made a difference."

She leaned closer to him. "I love your heart for thinking that way, but there was absolutely nothing you could have done to change the outcome. All you can do is use his example to hold yourself to a higher standard and maintain your own sobriety." He nodded in agreement and leaned his head back onto the headrest, closing his eyes. Holly hated seeing him so conflicted.

They touched down and found the van, dragging their carry-on luggage behind them, and almost an hour later pulled into their driveway. When she was back in New Hope, she was amazed that it didn't feel like home any longer. She was putting down roots in her new community, and after the funeral, she was even more motivated to give her sons a solid foundation.

When they finally arrived home, Deak was sitting on a rocking chair on the porch with their pack of three. Murph was freshly released from the cone of shame, but his wonky patchy hair left him looking homely. Daisy and Tink ran to the boys the second their doors opened, their thick stubby tails wagging eagerly. Dillon laid on the ground and let Tink lick his entire face for a solid three minutes.

How did Deak know this was exactly what the boys needed?

She watched the love fest for a minute, then Holly gathered their luggage from the trunk and sent the boys and dogs inside to relax.

"Well, you're a sight for sore eyes," Holly said with a tired grin as he stood and took her suitcase from her hands, depositing it by the door. He pulled her into a hug that made her heart flutter. She indulged in it, savoring the warmth of his body through his flannel shirt. Resting her head on his chest, she felt instantly grounded and calm.

"I thought y'all could use some cheering up of the canine persuasion."

"Smart man." She answered then pulled away from his warmth, an act that took real effort.

"How was it?" he asked as they sat down facing each other.

"Sad. Such a waste."

He nodded and waited for more details. When Holly didn't give any more, he continued, "So, I was thinking it will be important to keep Chance busy. I called Kent for some advice, and he said this is a dangerous time for Chance. It will be easy for him to slip back into bad habits. Chance has a definite interest and a natural knack for training dogs, and I want to offer him more responsibility at the rescue if that is okay with you."

"As long as it doesn't interfere with school or his weekly meetings, I think it's a great idea."

"Good."

"I need to thank you."

"For what?" he asked.

"For always being someone I could count on. You've been an amazing support and a great friend. I don't know what I'd do without you."

"Friend, huh?" he asked as his eyes bored into hers. "That's funny because I was hoping we could turn it into something more than that." His words flushed her with warmth, and the corners of her mouth turned up in response.

"You did?" Her voice cracked at the end, full of hope and insecurity.

"I've had some time to think since you've been gone."

"You have?" She chose her words deliberately, afraid to get too far ahead of herself. Reluctant to give away the truth of her own feelings.

"I have." He paused and looked down at his hands, wringing them together like he was grappling with something. She leaned closer to him and reached out a hand to squeeze his forearm.

"It's been a long time since I've felt anything like this," he started to explain, then stopped himself, unable to look in her eyes.

"What is it?" Holly asked. "Whatever you're struggling with, you can tell me."

He exhaled a deep breath, then brought his eyes back to hers. "I was engaged a long time ago."

Holly's eyes widened, and she leaned forward, waiting, not wanting to push him for details he wasn't ready to give.

"Her name was Ashley. I met her when I was eight. She was a tomboy, always hanging out with my group of friends. We spent our summers barefoot and filthy, and we'd be outside from sun up to sun down. Ashley wasn't like other girls; she was fearless. One day when I was fourteen, she dared me to kiss her, and the rest was history. We spent nearly every day together."

The memory made him smile. "I had it bad for the girl. You know that mushy, puppy kinda love they talk about? That was me, following her around like she hung the moon, but right after we turned sixteen, Ashley got sick." His voice lowered. "And a few weeks later, her diagnosis was confirmed. Childhood leukemia."

Holly sighed, imagining a boy the same age as Chance learning his girlfriend had cancer. "That had to have crushed you both," she empathized. "I can't imagine."

He sighed deeply, remembering. "It did." After a long pause, he continued. "We fought it, and it actually brought us closer together in a weird way. A couple years later, she gained a remission status, and we were thrilled. We had just turned eighteen and started to make plans for a real future together. Plans that weren't just words anymore, but a real possibility. We got engaged and moved in together, and for a nice long time, things were perfect."

His eyes misted over as Holly waited for him to go on. "But then the cancer came back, but this time with a vengeance. She started throwing up again, and I knew. Didn't need a doctor to tell me. Didn't need any more tests. I just knew." He sighed. "She fought harder, but her body was worn down from years of chemo and radiation. She tried every-thing—meditation, superfoods, vitamin cocktails—and refused to marry me until she was back in remission. She didn't want to make me a twenty-year-old widower."

Holly swallowed the lump in her throat. "God, that's so young."

"She was twenty-six when she died," he said bluntly. "When she got worse and had to get hospice care, she forced me to move her back to her parents' home. She didn't want me to have to continue to live in a house where she died. Turns out, she was right, like she was about most things. I wouldn't have been able to handle it." His voice broke, and Holly wrapped her arm around his shoulders, drawing him closer, waiting for him to gather enough strength to continue. Deacon was finally letting her in, and she felt the utter gravity of the moment and didn't want to rush him or scare him silent again.

"Those last moments, all of us were gathered at her parents' house in her bedroom. I remember it so vividly. Her head was covered in a downy fuzz since she'd stopped chemo treatments. I stroked her forehead and held her hand, unable to leave her side. Watched her shrink and disappear before my eyes. Day by day, cancer was stealing the woman I loved away from me." After a long pause, he started again. "She had moments of clarity where she laughed and teased me and said goodbye to all of us. Her bedroom was full of people she loved bound together by our love for her. About a week later there was a shift. Ashley was in so much pain, they began to administer more morphine, and that pretty much laid her out." His words were nothing more than a whisper.

"She fell asleep one day and never woke up." He pinched the top of his nose then continued. "Her breathing slowed until she was unconscious, but she would shake and make these horrible sounds. Like an animal in pain. She was suffering and it crushed me. Here I was, sitting at her bedside, selfishly praying for her to wake up and give me one more moment of lucidity, but she was already gone. After fighting this disease with her for so many years and thinking we were winning, it was time to admit defeat. So, I leaned close to her temple and whispered, 'It's okay to go on ahead without me, sweetheart. Should have known you'd figure out a way to win this race, too.' God, the girl was crazy competitive." He laughed at the memory, swiping tears from his eyes. "She sighed once and then she was gone."

Deacon forced his hands to lace together as Holly focused on his thumb, afraid to make a sound.

"What I'll never forget is the silence. Being present for the most sacred moment of a person's life—when they pass from living in a body to living in a soul is a privilege. I will always be grateful I got to help her transition there." His voice tightened as another tear fell down his cheek, and Holly gently swiped it away with the tips of her fingers. Deacon reached up and rubbed his eyes with the palms of his hands and sniffled.

"Losing her spun me out, and one night after having a few too many, I got behind the wheel. It was dark and raining, and I had no business being on the road in the first place. A deer darted out, and I swerved to miss it coming up over the top of a hill. In the oncoming lane, a minivan with a family of five was on their way home from their Yellowstone vacation." He hesitated as Holly held her breath, waiting anxiously. "I nailed the driver's side and sent the father to the hospital. His foot was crushed, all the bones in it completely pulverized. He will never walk again without pain. He won't be able to play tag with his kids or run a marathon."

Deacon pulled his hands away and pressed them to his face. Seeing him hiding, and the overwhelming guilt that filled him, Holly leaned closer.

"Hey," she whispered. "That's a lot to shoulder. It could have happened to anyone. You know as well as I do that deer dart out at the worst time."

"I just wonder if I would have had a quicker reaction time if I hadn't been drinking. The officer on the scene was one of my dad's childhood friends, so he delayed the test, and by the time I blew into the breathalyzer at the station hours later, I was just under the legal limit."

Holly held the quiet space for him. Pulling his thick shoulders toward her, she began to rub his back in soft circles.

"I donated six thousand dollars to his GoFundMe page anonymously. It was all the money Ashley and I had saved for our wedding," he mumbled into the space in her neck. "It wasn't enough, but it was all I had. I started the rescue, and I was bound and determined to make a life that would make amends for the one I lost and the ones I hurt. I put my head down and focused completely on the rescue."

"Oh, Deacon. I am so sorry."

She laid her head on his shoulder and sat with him in the quiet, not needing to fill the space with words that had already held so many. She stroked his arm, nestling into him. After several long moments, he pulled away, meeting her eyes again.

"And I would have gotten away with it, too, if it wasn't for you and your meddling kids," he joked with a forced smile, making Holly recall her favorite line from Scooby-Doo. A deep sadness was etched so deeply in every word that even his attempt at humor couldn't conceal it. "You dropped into my life, and I started feeling things again. It's like I had been sleeping or hibernating like the bears do in the winter, and then you came along and woke me up. I found myself using any excuse I could find to come by and help you out. My truck kept turning down your drive, no matter how much I tried to fight it."

His confession made bursts of joy bubble up in Holly's heart as he reached out to hold her hand. Looking down, he traced his thumb over the back of her hand, a simple gesture that had Holly feeling undone and her heartbeat accelerating.

Almost a full minute passed while he memorized the lines and curves of her hand. His touch, barely a whisper, had a profound impact. "And over the last few days when you've been gone, I discovered something."

"What's that?" Holly questioned softly.

Deacon smiled and pulled her closer to him. "I discovered I might have a soft spot for you, Holly Simon."

"Might?" she teased.

"Fine, woman, you got me." He flushed pink and leaned forward on his forearms, wringing his hands. "You can actually thank Ruth for my recent revelation. Apparently, I was moping around last week, looking more pathetic than Murph in his cone of shame. When I showed up every day at dinner time, she picked up on it and said, 'When are you going to admit you have a thing for Holly?'"

Holly laughed.

"She's a smart woman," he admitted. "But don't you dare ever tell her I said that."

She grinned as hope rushed to the surface. "Is it true?" Holly asked, her voice barely a whisper, but she had to know.

"It is," he confirmed and brought her hand to his lips, delivering a soft kiss. "And I was wondering if you might feel the same way." His gaze was direct, and she found herself getting drawn even deeper into his warm eyes. She pulled her hands away, scrambling to brace herself for the fall. The pure vulnerability radiating from him was opening up pieces of herself she had long thought were dead.

"I think I do."

"Think?" he tossed back with a wink.

"Okay, fine, I do," Holly admitted, flushing every shade of pink known to man. "But what happens if we take the risk and it doesn't work out? This is a vulnerable time for Chance and Dillon. You're the first solid, healthy man they have spent time around."

"Then we go right back to the friend zone," he replied. "I promise you I will always have a soft spot for your boys. No matter what happens between us, I'm not going anywhere."

She tipped her head to the side, considering his proposal.

"So, we have a deal?" He extended one hand to her, and she placed her hand in his, then let out a little surprised gasp when he pulled her from her chair onto his lap. "I've been wanting to do this a long time." She felt his warm fingers lace into her hair and his thumbs brush her cheekbones, pulling her in for a kiss. His lips were smooth and sure, and she closed her eyes, falling into him, unafraid and ready to take a risk. Because with Deacon, it seemed like the most natural thing in the world.

TWENTY-SIX

Holly and Deacon reverted back to acting like teenagers, sneaking kisses and making out in the barn, waiting until the boys went to bed and then engaging in heavy petting on the sofa. Their ears strained for the creaking of the door to the boys' bedroom. Deacon would reluctantly leave to go home every night, getting Holly so worked up she had a hard time settling down enough to sleep. Her lips stayed swollen and chapped from brushing against his stubble. She was deliciously smitten and looking forward to what the next day would bring.

Holly was afraid to move too fast, to pop the bubble of gushy romantic feelings that cocooned them. She loved everything about Deacon. The white strands of hair that were woven in with the auburn ones. The way he rubbed her shoulders while she stood at the sink washing dishes when the boys weren't around to see. His strong hands that held hers under a blanket and his deep sense of purpose. Deacon was solid, he never wavered, and his steady pursuit of her made her head spin.

She was shy, too. It had been a very long time since a man

had seen her body naked, and that fear held her back from becoming physical with him. She was critical of her softened and flattened breasts that hung lower than she wanted them to, her stretch marks, and slight arm wings that flapped back at her when she waved. Gravity didn't discriminate.

Holly finally confided her fears in Stacey during one of their weekly Skype sessions, and two days later, a package arrived with a lacy lavender bralette and a pair of matching satin short shorts. They camouflaged a multitude of middle-aged sins, and she eagerly tried them on with the bathroom door locked. She had to stand on the toilet, twisting and contorting to see her reflection, cursing the tiny mirror that was hung above the sink. When she finally got a glimpse, she had to admit she felt pretty and feminine, maybe even bordering on sexy.

A few days later, after the boys had gone to bed, instead of snuggling on the couch, she tugged on his hand and led him the short distance down the hallway to her bedroom. His puzzled expression registered into sexy surprise when she shut the door behind him quietly and told him to close his eyes.

She ran into the closet, shut the door, and pulled on her lingerie. She tugged the hair tie out of her hair, letting her sun-streaked curls rain down her back. Holly took a deep breath and gave herself a mental pep-talk.

You can do this. Keep the lights off and run straight from here to the bed. It's only ten feet.

A few minutes later, she opened the door and darted across the room to the bed, then pulled back the quilt.

"Can I open my eyes?" he asked, groping the space between them for her hand.

Might as well get this part over with. Why was it so hard to stand bare in front of the man you loved?

"Yes," she finally breathed out, frozen with fear as he opened his eyes. She sucked in her stomach and waited.

He smiled and held out a hand to her. "Come over here."

Holly bit her lip and moved toward him, her legs wobbly and her heart hammering. She stood in front of him, trembling and shy, crossing her legs to quell the tension growing in her belly.

"Look at me," he urged as he took her hand and pulled her closer to him for a warm, wet kiss. She had to stand on her tiptoes to kiss him. Her hands met his waist and then moved up his back, craving skin-on-skin contact. His kiss deepened as his tongue met hers, sending electric shocks to her center.

Her fingers walked down the length of his torso and slid in front, lingering for a moment at his belt buckle. He sighed into her next kiss, and she took it as an invitation. "Wait." He pulled her hand back, and her heart dropped. "Let me look at you." He took a step back and drank her in. "God, you're beautiful. Do you know that?"

She shook her head no, tearing her eyes away from his powerful gaze. She flushed warm; being the sole focus of his attention was uncomfortable. He drew her closer as the pads of his thumbs brushed against her cheeks.

"Where'd you go?" he whispered as he tipped her chin up, leaning so close she could feel his breath on her face. "You are the most beautiful woman I have ever seen," he murmured as his lips met hers again. Holly sighed. He was beginning to break down her fears and her insecurities, kiss by kiss. With every caress, it was becoming more believable.

"You are, and I'm going to tell you every day until you start to believe me."

She pulled his hand closer to her mouth and sucked on his thumb, a sexy tidbit she learned swiping through the online edition of *Cosmo* last week. Feeling out of touch and insecure about her bedroom skills, her recent search history was filled with titillating rabbit holes she was embarrassed she went down. It was research. Research she was grateful she gleaned when he moaned and his voice deepened with desire. Deacon's warm eyes darkened, and he playfully brushed her nipple that hardened through the lace from his touch.

She tipped her head to look up at him, an ocean of feelings churning through her. The hum of desire crescendoed in her belly from his touch and the words he carefully chose. It had been such a long time since she'd been with a man; she prayed it was like riding a bike. Holly drifted closer to his warmth and opened herself up to him fully in a way she had never opened before. Blooming under the warm light of his love.

This is so simple. Being with Deacon is so easy. Why did I never grasp this concept before?

He peeled her lingerie off one garment at a time, taking time to kiss and stroke every inch of her body. Savoring every curve, he pulled her hands away from the stretch marks she tried to conceal.

"You don't have to hide anything from me," he whispered into her neck, making goosebumps break out from her throat to her fingertips. With every word and every touch, she felt her inhibitions melting away. She didn't want to hide anymore. She didn't want to protect herself anymore. She wanted to be free and open and to give herself fully to him.

It was a great risk with an even greater reward. She thought the idea of it would terrify her more. That it would make her freeze, or force her to pause, but taking the leap with Deacon was easy. He held out his hand and wrapped it around hers, and they took it together.

TWENTY-SEVEN

After falling into a deep sleep and forgetting to set an alarm, hours passed as the new day started. Slivers of light crept into the bedroom, and Holly stretched her arms over her head as a satisfied smile bloomed on her face. Deacon was dead to the world, and she snuggled into his back, enjoying the warmth his body generated. Sleepy and content, she almost fell back asleep, but the second her eyes glanced at the clock on her nightstand, panic jarred her back into reality.

"Crap!" Holly stood and began to get dressed hurriedly.

"Come back to bed, darlin'," Deacon drawled, his voice deep and jagged from sleep.

"We have to get you out of here now. The boys…" she whispered as she yanked off the blankets and stumbled around the dark room, looking for his clothes.

"Careful there, Ms. Simon, you're starting to make a guy feel like he's a dirty secret," he teased as he pulled himself up to a standing position from their warm bed and reached for his jeans on the floor.

When they were finally dressed, Holly slowly opened the

bedroom door to find Dillon standing outside it. Chance was already up, too, standing in the kitchen eating a bowl of cereal.

Holly's cheeks pinked up, and she ducked her head in embarrassment. Changing the subject and desperate to distract them, she quickly offered, "Anyone want some eggs?"

"No thanks, Mom," Chance said with a knowing smirk, clearly enjoying his mother's mortification. "Um… You missed a button." He pointed at her shirt that was gaping open at the belly. Horrified, Holly scrambled to fix it.

Seeing his mom squirm made Chance laugh. "Relax, Mom. We've known something's been going on with you two for a while now."

"Did ya' now?" Deacon smiled, amused as he filled the coffee maker with water and pulled Holly's favorite mug and flavor of coffee pod out of the cabinet.

"Deak's been here almost every day since we got back from New Hope," Chance offered as evidence. "You guys aren't exactly good at hiding things."

"What? No way!" Holly exclaimed in fake shock. A bored Dillon walked over for a hug and then left to eat a bowl of cereal. She gratefully accepted the cup of fresh coffee that Deacon handed to her, and he pulled her in and kissed her forehead.

"Relax, darlin'. You're making a bigger deal out of this than they are."

"Have you met me? I make a big deal out of everything," Holly admitted, then after two long sips of vanilla bean morning blend, she felt herself soften and her shoulders drop to their natural resting place as her defenses melted away. From the sink, she watched the easy way Deacon had with the boys. He teased them as they ate bowls of cereal, ruffling their feathers. The sarcasm was thick and rife between them with typical testosterone-fueled banter. When he stood and announced they all had to leave for work at the rescue, the boys quickly jumped up to help him clean up the kitchen. Then they gave her hugs and left together in his truck.

All alone in the quiet of her kitchen, she let out a giddy squeal and danced around in her socks, punching the air in victory, feeling on top of the world. Desperate to share the news with her best friend, she Skyped Stacey.

"Whoa! Woman! What's got you smiling like that? Was it….?" Stacey asked with an eyebrow waggle.

"Oh my God, Stace! Deak's amazing. You know how much I hate that word. It's so overused, but there truly is no other word I can use to sum up one of the best nights of my life."

"Ooh, girl! You trollop! You sealed the deal! Spill it!"

"It's been a long time," she started.

Stacey nodded. "You locked that kitty up, padlocked it, and threw away the key."

Holly laughed. "I was almost afraid a moth or two might fly out."

Stacey snickered. "I know! I was so worried! Use it or lose it, sister!"

They giggled, and then Holly continued in a salacious tone with a shoulder shimmy, "Well, I definitely used it last night!"

Stacey applauded as she giggled. "Yeah, you did!" After a moment, her voice softened, "But seriously, I'm so proud of you for putting yourself out there."

"It's weird, Stace. I turned that part of myself off years ago. Shut the sexy factory completely down. I had no idea it could be like this," Holly gushed, and her fingers brushed against her lips that still smelled like him. "It was magic."

Stacey leaned in and smiled. "You deserve some magic."

Holly took another sip of her coffee, trying to accept her friend's words. Another huge grin spread across her face.

"I take it my little lacey care package came in handy?"

"It did! I felt so sexy in it!" Holly exclaimed. "You saved a life."

"Then it served its purpose," Stacey answered. "But it better be balled up and thrown on the floor right now."

"You know it!" Holly declared and high-fived Stacey through the Skype screen as they laughed together.

"God, I was so afraid for him to see all my flaws. I'm over forty. I've breastfed two children. The girls are *not* where they started out."

"It doesn't matter." Stacey waved away her worry. "When the right man loves you, he falls in love with *all* of you, not just the frosting."

Holly nodded as Stacey continued. "He looks deeper and can see what you bring to his life. Men like Deacon don't play games. They know when it's right and will do whatever it takes to keep you around."

"I always heard you say those things, and I have to tell you I thought you were full of shit. Or maybe you were just one of the lucky ones who found a unicorn. A man that is a real partner, one that is not afraid to commit and build a real relationship. But as usual, you were right."

"You know, I'll never get tired of hearing you say that," Stacey teased, then shifted back. "Look at you now! All aglow. Deacon has lit you up from the inside out, and that is exactly what a good man does! And it was only possible because you cleaned your house last year and made space for him to find you."

Holly nodded, listening to her words. She had to agree.

"He told me I was beautiful and he was going to keep telling me that until I believed him," Holly said softly.

"You *are* beautiful," Stacey repeated. "And now you finally have a man in your life who will force you to see it."

"I've never been this happy," she confided as another giddy rush zinged through her core.

"It's about freaking time!" Stacey joked. They chatted a few more minutes, and when Holly got off the phone, she felt euphoric. Warmth flooded her from the hair on her head to the tips of her toes. The contrast of the pain of the last year made her joy even more complete. It made her appreciate it more. Holly was blissfully in love, and there wasn't a better feeling in the world.

TWENTY-EIGHT

Winter changed Yellowstone into the most magical winter wonderland Holly had ever seen. Blankets of snow covered the pine trees and transformed the mountains into bright, gleaming peaks. She found pairs of used snowshoes for herself and the boys, and they spent hours traipsing across the tops of brilliant white snowdrifts, adding their own tracks to the smaller raccoon paws and the big moose prints that covered the frosty landscapes. The lakes began to freeze, and she scoured the internet for used ice skates, sleds, and winter tubes, bound and determined they were going to enjoy all the seasons in their new home.

Holly accumulated outwear for all of them, and Deacon packed an emergency kit for the van. Filled with granola bars and water bottles, blankets, and a first aid kit, he stuffed a box of wooden matches, flares, and a battery-operated radio in a plastic tub in the back. He also added a shovel and sand in case she got stuck in the snow or ran into someone who needed help.

"Don't you think this is a little excessive?"

"Not at all," Deacon said. "The winters here can kill you,

and we can't have that. I seem to have gotten a little attached to you."

"A little?" she questioned with a smirk.

"Okay, fine. I'm attached," he admitted freely, but she couldn't quite make herself say the words back.

Winters in Yellowstone were jaw-droppingly beautiful but also punishing and treacherous. In Holly's mind, the charming winding roads with steep drop-offs and non-existent shoulders became terrifying death traps in winter. She white-knuckled the steering wheel, and even with snow socks on her tires, she didn't feel totally confident driving anywhere. Luckily, there wasn't as much to get out and do, so she stayed home more and adopted a slower rhythm for wintertime life in Montana.

Even with Kent's experience, their drive to the twice-weekly AA meetings kept her awake and alert, with her phone in her hand in case they got stranded. She didn't feel comfortable until Chance was home and tucked into his bed.

To keep warm, Holly endlessly stoked a roaring fire in her cabin and hauled loads of firewood to her renters, who were fewer and farther between. The snow brought the skiers, snowmobilers, and hunters to Yellowstone—mostly groups of men or father-son trips hungry for outdoor adventures. Holly had just gotten used to the summer population, where the town swelled with tourists over five times its original size. When huge tour buses packed with Asian tourists caravanned into town and loaded up on souvenirs and made in Montana treats. In the winters, the tour buses stayed away. There were whole days that shops on Main Street were shuttered, and the snow-covered streets were sparse and desolate.

Life slowed to a crawling pace Holly was surprised to learn she loved. The high-adrenaline period of their time in New Hope was fading to a distant memory as she focused on simpler things. It was a welcome respite from the stress that had previously infiltrated her life. She felt her heart healing, being mended by the effort and attention Deacon lavished on it. He spoiled her and the boys, coming to the house almost daily with Daisy and Tink, who loved the snow and charged through it recklessly in pursuit of a ball or a piece of leftover meat from their dinner. The dogs would do almost anything for bacon. After an exhausting few hours in the snow, they circled then dropped to the floor to snooze and fart around the wood stove that Deacon continued to stoke until he would leave around midnight.

November brought Thanksgiving, Holly's favorite holiday because it wasn't an orgy of greed like Christmas. It was about food and family.

Holly set the table with candles and linens that the boys ribbed her about. "I didn't know we were *tablecloth* people," Chance teased her when he saw her pulling out all the stops to impress Ruth. It was the first time she had formally invited the woman for a meal at her house, and Holly was nervous. She bustled around the kitchen, basting the deep brown turkey and making a velvety pumpkin cheesecake for dessert. She wiped her sweaty palms on her apron and then sprinkled the homemade yeast buns with dill weed before slipping them into the oven when Ruth and Deacon arrived.

"Smells incredible in here, darlin'," Deacon declared and pulled her into a warm hug, then pressed his lips to her forehead as Ruth watched their interaction with a soft smile on her face.

Holly's face flushed pink, then she finally choked out, "Happy Thanksgiving."

"Is there anything I can do to help?" Ruth asked as she set a pecan pie on the countertop and washed and arranged pomegranates into an olive-green bowl. "Aren't they pretty?" she asked. "They reminded me of you."

"Aww. That's so sweet," Holly answered. "Thank you. I think we're just waiting on bread now and for Deak to slice the turkey." She pointed to the foil-wrapped bird. "It's almost done resting."

Deacon washed his hands and sliced the turkey, and Holly plated up all the food and placed it around the table.

"Guys!" she called upstairs. "It's time to eat!"

There was a thunderous rumble as they ran down the spiral staircase and came to a skidding stop just short of the table.

"Wash up, you filthy animals!" Deak teased them, and they scrambled to the sink to comply.

Chance then proceeded to tuck his cloth napkin into the neck of his t-shirt while Ruth watched, amused. They passed platters of buttered beans and thick caramel-colored gravy. Stainless steel spoons floated in billowing clouds of mashed potatoes.

"Do you want to say grace?" Ruth asked and then placed both her open palms face up on the table as Dillon swallowed the bite currently in his mouth, looking embarrassed. Holly took Ruth's hand and gave it a squeeze. The boys reached around the table awkwardly, holding hands with Deacon, a sight that made Holly grin.

"Thank you, Lord, for this food we share, for the company of family, and for bringing us together. Amen," Ruth said with her eyes closed, giving Holly's hand a squeeze when she finished.

"Don't be shy. Let's dig in," Holly encouraged as she passed the turkey. Silverware clattered on pristine white plates, and Ruth sipped at the wine in her glass as conversation flowed about the upcoming Christmas concert and the dog Chance was training. Ruth took a genuine interest in the boys, asking lots of questions, and their answers were a fountain of excited words that jumbled out fast and furious between bites. From his spot at the head of the table, Deacon caught her eye and grinned.

They shoved in forkfuls of stuffing and spoonsful of jiggly cranberry jelly until their bellies were bursting.

"I'm so stuffed," Dillon exclaimed, pushing back from the table.

"Well, I would hope so," Holly answered. "You ate your weight in bread."

Deacon got to his feet. "Alright, knuckleheads. Your mama slaved over this meal that we just decimated. Let's give her a rest and take care of the dishes."

The start of grumbling was cut short with one look from Deacon. They began to scrape the dishes, adding tiny tidbits of turkey into the dogs' bowls.

"I like seeing what you and my son are building here," Ruth said, her eyes warm and open.

"I do, too," Holly admitted with a sweet smile. "He's one in a million."

"He says the same thing about you."

The compliment made Holly burst with pride. "There's nothing better than getting together for the holidays with the people you love most in the world."

Ruth nodded in agreement.

"I can't remember when I enjoyed a meal as much. You're an incredible cook."

"I love people with food. It's a gift *and* a curse," Holly admitted with a smile as she patted her soft mid-section.

"Well, I think it's delightful." Ruth sat back in her chair.

"So, I take it that's a yes for Christmas?" Holly asked, eager to please.

"That's a yes!" Ruth reached over to squeeze her forearm. "Thank you for sharing your boys with me. I wouldn't miss it."

"My mom wasn't the warmest woman," Holly admitted, "but I feel like I'm getting a second chance having you in my life."

Ruth's smile deepened. "I never had a daughter, and I feel exactly the same way."

It was such a moment of profound joy that Holly felt an internal shift as the pieces of her broken childhood heart knit closer together.

"Can I ask you something?" Holly asked, treading lightly.

"Sure, dear."

"What was Deak's dad like? He never talks about him."

Ruth leaned back, crossed her arms across her chest, and considered her words. "He was hard on him. The man lived to work and did so right up until the day he died. Deacon got his work ethic but not much else."

Holly's heart hurt as she imagined Deacon as a little boy, knowing how boys were driven to earn their father's approval.

"It's been just me and him for a long time after Ashley died." Her voice trailed off. "I never thought I'd see him smile again, so I have you to thank for that."

Holly felt a prickle of insecurity and fear rear up. She wondered if Deacon would love her like he loved Ashley, or if she would always be a consolation prize.

This isn't a competition. You are being ridiculous. Stop trying to jeopardize the best thing that has ever happened to you. It's time to start believing you are worthy of love.

Holly was starting to understand that when you loved someone, there was always fear. If they were a bad partner, you had one set of fears—worries about money and their commitment to you. If they were a good one, you were afraid of losing them or the possibility of them falling out of love with you. It was amazing how fast her mind whipsawed from one extreme to the other. Sad, really. It wasn't easy for Holly to just relax and believe. It was a constant recalibration to the new standards of her healthier mind, talking herself through her past traumas so they didn't spill onto her new life and ruin it. She was learning love didn't grow in a vacuum. You couldn't hold it so close you suffocated it.

When they first started dating, her fears and insecurities made her do stupid things, like push Deacon away and test him. She checked up on his whereabouts by 'randomly' dropping in and interrogating the boys when they came home from the rescue. Deacon passed every test with flying colors, and when he caught on to what she was doing, he called her out on it while they were lying in bed during a few blissful afterglow moments before the boys came home from school.

"When are you going to relax and let yourself believe that I love you?"

Holly bit her lip, ashamed at what she was doing, and finally saw she didn't need to test him anymore. "You're such a good man." She paused and then, before she lost the courage to continue, blurted, "I love you, too." Nestling her body into his, her heart was bursting. She couldn't remember the last time she felt this happy. She pulled back and reached her hand to Deacon's scruffy cheek, brushing her thumb against the roughness of it. She kissed him and then leaned her forehead to meet his. Wrapped up there in her bed with the man she loved, it was a heady, wonderful moment she didn't think she'd ever get to experience.

Strengthened by his steadfast love, Holly read and journaled and worked through her insecurities one at a time. Unwilling to let them run rampant in her life anymore, she was determined to heal herself. It was hard, soul-crushing work to unearth the real reasons she doubted his love. Worthiness was something she struggled with her entire life; it was deeply entrenched in her psyche. Deacon was slow and methodical. He proved his love and commitment to her every day. With each text and hug, with each word of encouragement for her and her sons, he was healing them all.

November morphed into December, and darkness came earlier. Deacon installed thick chains on her tires and found her an ATV to use as a snowplow. He actively searched out ways to make her life better and easier, like plowing her driveway when it snowed and bringing her groceries when the roads were slick. Holly knew she hit the jackpot with Deacon, and her fears began to fade away.

Overnights were impossible. Even though Holly never wanted Deacon to leave their nice warm bed, he couldn't take the risk. Whiteout conditions could happen at any time in the winter, and his commitment to his dogs pulled him out of her bed and back into the cold. When he was on call, he'd often leave Daisy and Tink with her, and she'd find the dogs curled up in a sea of blankets in the mornings with Dillon and Chance, hogging the bed like pit bulls are prone to do.

She'd never admit it, but Holly was actually grateful for the forced time away and space. It slowed the progression of their relationship to a healthier pace that she wasn't sure she would have been able to enforce on her own. It gave her kids a chance to get used to the idea of their mom being in a relationship, and it gave her heart a chance to relax into what was happening between them. A deepening sense of complete love, a true best friend, and soulmate connection that she used to think was unattainable. The sappy romance books she fervently read as a twenty-something weren't right either. The truest feeling was an enveloping sense of safety and security. She finally found a peaceful place for her heart to rest.

They baked and decorated Christmas cookies. Deacon helped them hunt for the right tree on his land, and Chance and Dillon took turns wielding the ax to chop it down. Holly was a sucker for traditions, and her heart burst with joy at each new one they added to the mix. Stringing popcorn garlands while drinking mulled cider around the wood stove and watching *It's a Wonderful Life*. The tree lighting festival in the Garden Brook town square. Deacon even created polar bear dares for Chance and Dillon. A rite of passage that sent them screaming and hollering into the cold to prove their manhood by running and rolling into the banks of freshly fallen snow wearing only their boxers.

After another six inches of fresh snow fell, he took them all sledding down Murder Mountain. Holly hadn't been sledding since she was a child. They all took turns piling onto the long toboggan-style sled that was a relic from Deacon's childhood. After a dizzying zip down a hill that practically defied gravity, they would trudge back up and flop down for another ride as white plumes of her breath and the sound of her children's laughter filled the air around her.

Christmas was a blur of wrapping paper and another family dinner with Ruth. She became a regular during their Wednesday night dinners and had become such a fixture at their house Dillon asked if he could call her Grandma, a sweet, unexpected gesture that made Ruth tear up and nod yes. Holly was shocked when she heard Chance voluntarily join in. Ruth filled a void in the boys' hearts Holly didn't even know was missing. She doted on them and enjoyed having them around, engaging them in conversation about random topics from global warming to the life cycle of a rattlesnake. She genuinely wanted to know every thought that entered their heads, and her ability to listen to the mundane with sincere interest made them instantly smitten with her.

When a blizzard would come—and in Montana, Holly learned they sometimes came one on top of the other—the boys scrambled to help Deacon shovel 'Grandma's' snow, and she rewarded them with licorice and egg creams. Dillon spent hours at Ruth's house learning how to cook, and on New Year's Day, he proudly presented the family with a beef rib roast he made himself that melted in their mouths. No one was prouder of him than Ruth, standing next to him in her starched white apron.

They were living inside a Norman Rockwell painting, enjoying the simple pleasures. Life was good and safe in Garden Brook, or so it seemed.

TWENTY-NINE

One early morning in the middle of February, a noise jolted Holly awake. Confused at first, she stirred from a deep sleep in a blackened room, trying to get her bearings. Straining for sounds, she tucked the quilt under her feet in a feeble attempt to hide and listened.

Nothing. The house was still and quiet. She counted to sixty twice before settling back down and drifting off, when she heard glass shatter.

Oh My God! Someone's in the house.

Bolting upright in bed, she tried to steady her hammering heart in the darkness as adrenaline pumped through her. Quickly, she dialed 911 and left her cell phone out in the open. Unable to speak, she let it ring, knowing the dispatcher would have to send help. Her breath quickened as she stood and silently picked her way across the floor to her bedroom door, avoiding the boards that creaked. She squinted her eyes, trying to make out shapes in the darkness, her heart pounding the entire time.

From the doorway, she glanced over at the boys' bedroom, and relief flooded in when she saw their door was still shut. Hands shaking, she quickly scanned her bedroom for a weapon, and after ruling out all the other options, finally settled for the sharpest thing she could find—an umbrella.

Great, I'll give him seven years of bad luck. Maybe poke out an eye if I'm lucky.

In the stillness, she heard the deadbolt shift in the lock and the front door creak as it opened. Fear zipped up her spine as she pressed her body against the wall, trying to take up as little space as possible. She exhaled through her pursed lips, trying not to draw attention to herself, but every sense was amplified. Her panicked breathing was loud; Holly swore she could hear her eyes blink. She craned her neck around the corner and jumped when she saw movement and shadows lengthening across the floor as the intruder walked into her kitchen. Her heart began to race and left her lightheaded as she tried not to hyperventilate and force air out of her flaring nostrils.

Shoes crunched as they crushed the glass, then she heard drawers scraping open and silverware jingling.

It sounds like he's searching for something. The most valuable thing in the kitchen is my Keurig.

Paralyzed with fear, she took another step closer, and as she leaned through the doorway, she caught her first glimpse. It was a skinny teenager with long dark hair, rifling through the cupboards, pulling items out one by one, and shoving them into a bulging backpack. Long-limbed, swimming in his dirty jacket, he looked older than Dillon but younger than Chance.

Murph whined at her ankle. "Shh!" She tried to get the dog to quiet and lie down, but it was too late. The boy jumped and spun around, and Holly was shocked to see him wielding an old shotgun, pointed right at her chest.

He's just a child, she reasoned but then corrected herself. *But he's a child with a gun.*

She held her shaky hands up in front of her and lowered her voice to a soothing, even tone. "Hey there," she said gently, trying to win him over. Her survivalist brain served up a past memory from an active shooter drill at school.

If you're ever faced with an active shooter, throw things at him. It will destroy his accuracy. Throw something, anything. It can literally be the difference between life and death.

"I promise, I'm not here to hurt you," Holly continued. "How about you put that thing away?" She tried to smile at him. "I'm just going to turn on the light so we can talk. Is that okay?"

His expression was wary and pinched, but after a long silence, he finally nodded.

With both her hands still raised, she reached over slowly and flipped on the light switch, illuminating the entire kitchen.

He looked like a cornered animal. His dirty hair hung greasy, the fringe sweeping across his dark eyes. He stared down the barrel of the shaking gun with his left eye squeezed shut and his skinny forefinger resting on the trigger. It was a patch of white skin swallowed almost whole by the sleeve of his enormous jacket. She caught a glimpse of a dirty t-shirt, and his fingernails were bitten down to the skin and ringed by grime underneath. He was rail-thin, not much more than seventy-five pounds soaking wet.

The most accurate word to describe the boy was neglected. "Are you hungry?" she asked him with her hands still raised.

His forehead crinkled in confusion. "What?" he asked with the gun still pointed at her.

"I was going to make some pancakes this morning

anyway," she continued. "If you put that thing down, we can get started. Have you ever had peanut butter on pancakes?" She chattered on, "It's delish." She pulled one shaking hand to her lips and gave a chef's kiss.

He wavered and began to lower the weapon. In the silence, she could hear the clock ticking on the wall, which ratcheted up her anxiety as it sounded like a bomb. Then she heard his stomach growl.

"Looks like your stomach thinks it's a good idea." She took a tentative step closer to him. "How about you hand that thing over?" she asked. "We can pretend this never happened, and I'll make us some pancakes so we can get to know each other better." His thin shoulders sagged as he relinquished the weapon. She exhaled when the shotgun was finally in her hands. A few seconds later, in the distance, sirens began to trill.

Hearing them, he looked up at her, the betrayal burning. His blue eyes were huge and panicked, filling his face like empty saucers as he scanned the room for an escape route.

"It's okay," Holly said in her most soothing voice, her own panic lessening the louder the sirens wailed. "I didn't know if you were a friend or a foe. I'll just tell them I made a mistake."

"Why?" he asked.

"I think we got off on the wrong foot." She offered him a hand. "I'm Holly, and you are?"

He considered it for a second, and she wondered if he was going to tell her the truth. She had no way of verifying anything he said. She looked down at his feet. His shoes were filthy, and his big toe peeked out of a hole on the front. The soles were duct-taped on.

"Shane," he finally said.

"I might have a pair of shoes around here that would fit you a little better than those," she offered.

His shoulders tightened defensively. This was a proud kid who was used to being disappointed and fighting his way through life.

Holly heard the sound of spitting gravel on the driveway. An officer got out of a cruiser, and with a rush of relief, she saw Deacon's truck pull into the spot next to his. "The bathroom is over there. Quick. Go wash up and don't come out until I tell you it's safe."

Wary, he eyeballed her, but trapped and having no other options, he darted to the bathroom and shut the door behind him.

Holly crossed the room quickly, stopping at the hall closet to tuck the shotgun inside, and then opened the door with an apologetic smile. "I'm so sorry," she gushed. "False alarm. Everything is under control here. A bird must have broken the window. Guess I should cut back on the window washing." She tried to make her joke stick with a weak laugh. Deak's radar went up, and he narrowed his eyes to study her with a puzzled expression but remained quiet.

"No problem, ma'am."

Deacon turned to the officer. "Sorry to drag you out here in the middle of the night, Duane. Let's get together for a beer next week?"

The officer nodded. "Sounds like a plan." Then he turned back to Holly. "It's been a quiet night at the station. No harm, no foul."

"Thanks again," Holly said as she walked him to the door and shut it behind him. Then she pulled a broom out of the closet and swept up the glass shards. Deacon waited silently for an explanation, but she wasn't even sure where to begin or how he was going to react.

"You have about two seconds to…" Deacon started in.

Holly held up one finger. "Just give me one second.…" Then she crossed the floor to the bathroom door and said, "It's okay, you can come out now."

The wood door slowly creaked open, and Shane stepped out sheepishly, his glance darting from Holly to Deacon. Deacon's eyebrows shot up in surprise.

"Both of you sit down," he barked, and Holly and Shane were equally startled at the directness in his tone. He pulled out two chairs and growled, "Now!" Shane scrambled to the chair, intimidated by Deacon's tone and size. Holly quickly followed suit. It was the first time he'd raised his voice, and she knew she had some explaining to do.

"Want to introduce me to your friend?" He asked Holly.

"Deacon, this is Shane."

"Shane, do you mind telling me what you are doing this late at night at my girlfriend's home?" The word girlfriend made her center tingle, and she pressed her lips together to keep the joy of hearing the word from escaping. Deacon's voice was deadly serious. The boy tittered in the chair.

"Where are your parents?" His eyes were narrowed as he peppered the boy with questions, demanding answers that Shane refused to give.

Shane snorted and crossed his arms across his chest in an act of defiance, unwilling to answer the question.

"Where are you from?"

"A little here, a little there."

Deacon dropped one meaty hand on the boy's shoulder and leaned in, but Shane wouldn't back down. "I can play this game all night, but I suggest you start talking." Silence filled the space like a giant inhabiting the room. Frustrated, Deacon stood and paced to the sink. Then he abruptly switched gears and dipped back down inches from Shane's face. "I have Duane on speed dial. He can be back here in five minutes. And you heard him. He has nothing better to do tonight."

Holly stood and pulled him away. "Come on, honey. Is this third degree really necessary?"

"If *he* won't talk, then it's your turn." He took a step back, putting physical distance between them, and leaned against the countertop. His arms crossed over his chest as he waited for her to speak.

With a heavy sigh, Holly walked over to the closet and pulled out the gun. She handed it over to Deak, who immediately checked the barrel and found it empty.

"It wasn't even loaded?" Holly asked, surprised.

Shane just shrugged his shoulders.

Deacon slammed the chamber back and set the gun down on the countertop. Holly could feel his anger building.

"Can you give us a minute?" she asked Shane.

"I got nowhere else to be," he muttered bitterly.

She pulled Deacon into her bedroom and shut the door. He sat on the edge of her bed while she paced the room, biting on her bottom lip, trying to process what happened now that the threat was over.

"I think he's a runaway. He broke in looking for food. Did you look at him? You could break him in half."

Deacon's jaw was tight. "When I heard your address on the scanner…" He scratched at his jawline with his fingers and then ran them through his hair. Holly walked over to him and sat on his thigh, wrapping her arms around his shoulders.

"He's a stray. I know a certain someone who has a weakness for those." She smiled at him, trying to diffuse his anger, and kissed his cheek. "You know, the misunderstood, the unfairly judged, the lost causes?"

He shook his head no, but cracked a small smile in spite

of himself, then his expression quickly sobered. "He had a *gun*."

"An *unloaded* gun," she corrected. She felt his arms pulling her closer and his resistance starting to weaken. "There's a big difference."

He rolled his eyes exasperated. "What am I going to do with you?"

"Love me. After all, that's what you do for your *girlfriend*."

He pinked up. "You are *something*." He pulled her in for a kiss, and she relaxed into his chest.

"Mom!" Dillon shouted through the door, and she jumped up and stepped out into the living room with Deak following close behind. Completely confused, a still sleepy Dillon stared Shane down. "I thought I heard sirens." He balled his hands into fists and rubbed at his eyes.

"Hey, buddy." Deacon tried to break the ice. "We're having a little pancake party. You in?"

"Well, duh," Dillon said with a smile. In his world, pancakes were always a good idea.

Holly found some clothing Chance had outgrown that was sitting in a box to donate. While Deacon and Dillon got all the pancake ingredients out of the cupboards, she walked over to Shane, who was watching them tease each other from afar like he was watching an exhibit at a zoo. A rare and wonderful sight. She set her hand on his shoulder, and he flinched at the contact.

"Didn't mean to scare you," Holly apologized, then handed him the pile of clothing and a fresh towel. "Did you want to go take a shower?" She didn't want to embarrass him, but he had seriously crossed over into puberty and desperately needed deodorant. He lifted his arms to take the backpack off, and his shirt hiked up, revealing a network of bruises and old injuries. He quickly yanked the bottom of the shirt down to hide himself from her prying eyes as a red stress rash walked up his scrawny neck. "How did you get those? Is someone hurting you? I'm a teacher, and I can help you."

"I'm just clumsy," he dismissed, swiping his hair from his eyes.

"Can I call your parents?" she asked, glancing at the clock. It was 2:11 am. "It's pretty late."

"I'll think I'll take that shower now," he said gruffly, changing the subject, then followed her into the bathroom where she pulled out a stick of deodorant and an extra toothbrush for him to use. Ten minutes later, he emerged squeaky clean, his hair still damp and curling up now that the weight of caked-on dirt was gone.

"Looking good, my man!" Holly raised her hand for a high-five. "Up top!"

Stunned for a minute, he looked behind his shoulder to see who she was talking to. Finally understanding the comment was meant for him, he raised his hand up cautiously. A quick smile flashed across his features, transforming him back into a child for a moment.

"Mom! You're such a dork!" Dillon cried from his pancake-flipping perch next to Deacon.

Holly knew giving him a task would help him relax, so she handed the plates to Shane. "How about you set the table for me. Silverware is in the drawer next to Dillon." He accepted the assignment and began to set the table. She studied his movements, watching him second-guess himself, and then quickly correct, working to please her, a defense mechanism he adopted for survival. Holly had been trained; she knew what to look for. She knew the signs of a child at risk. He had them all. Dirty clothing, lack of personal hygiene, skinny and malnourished. Visible bruises. It was heartbreaking.

"Great job!" He visibly puffed up with pride at her praise. "Can you grab the OJ in the fridge?" she asked as she gathered glasses and began to set them around the table. He filled them quickly and waited, standing off to the side, separating himself and looking like he wanted to disappear into the wall behind him.

"I think we're ready," Deacon said, carrying a massive platter filled with steaming golden pancakes that were thick and fluffy. He set them down in the middle of the table and then returned with another platter of bacon. Holly sat down and then patted to a spot next to her. "Shane, come sit by me." She disarmed him with a huge smile, and he pulled out a chair and sat next to her. She pulled a pancake off the plate and passed it to Shane. "Dig in. Eat as much as you want." She swiped a butter knife through the jar of peanut butter while Shane watched. "Pay close attention. You are going to want to commit this method to memory." Then she picked up the syrup and let it drizzle in horizontal stripes over the peanut butter. "I'm not kidding, Shane, this combination will change your life." Warming up, he peanut-buttered his pancake and then drizzled it with syrup. Tearing into it with his fork, he took a bite so huge it puffed his cheeks out like a chipmunk. A stray drop of syrup dribbled down his chin, and he groaned in delight.

"It's good, right?" Holly said, her eyebrows waggling, nodding enthusiastically.

"Better than good." Shane continued to stuff himself full with two more pancakes, a half dozen strips of bacon, a glass of ice-cold milk, and another full glass of orange juice. He winced.

"Not a fan of orange juice?" Holly asked.

"Cold drinks make my teeth hurt," he admitted.

Another tally to add to the signs of neglect noticed by Holly's practiced mandatory reporter eye. Outrage bubbled to the surface.

"Where are you putting all that?" Deacon asked him. "You must be hollow inside."

Shane grinned, then leaned back and rubbed his belly. "I'm so full."

"Help me clear the table?" Deacon asked, and Shane jumped up and gathered the sticky plates. Holly caught Deacon's eye and mouthed "Thank you." She pulled Dillon in for a maple-infused kiss and rubbed the top of his head. "Why don't you try to go back to sleep for a couple hours?"

Dillon yawned and then sauntered off to the bedroom. Holly listened to Deacon draw out responses from Shane as they worked on the dishes together. He was opening up, and Holly felt a pull to help this boy.

"Where are you from?" she asked.

"Here and there," he offered.

"Where are your parents?"

He hesitated, wary of what telling the truth would mean. She felt his walls going up and could see the gears turning in his head, wondering if he could trust her.

"I've been camping in the woods," he finally admitted.

"All by yourself?" she asked him, shocked that a boy could survive the bitterly cold Montana winters alone. "How old are you?"

"Thirteen," he answered. "But I can take care of myself."

"Breaking into people's houses for food? I don't think that qualifies as taking care of yourself," Deacon countered quietly, and Shane's head hung in shame.

"I'd rather be hungry than…" His voice trailed off.

"Than be with people who hurt you?" Holly answered for him.

He nodded and tears filled his eyes, then a panic rushed up. "I can't go back. Please. I can't go back there." His teary eyes pleaded as he begged. Holly's eyes met Deacon's over his head and locked. Deacon nodded in agreement.

"Let me make up the sofa for you. Get some rest and we'll figure everything out in the morning."

Shane swiped at his tears with the back of his hand. Within twenty minutes, he was snoring on the sofa. His face was relaxed during sleep, far from the pinched caged look Holly noticed earlier. He was so young and fragile and vulnerable, and one thing was sure. He needed their help. Their paths crossed for a reason, and she just had to figure out why.

THIRTY

After getting Shane settled, sleep was elusive as they lay on Holly's bed. For the first several minutes, they stared at the ceiling, each lost in their own private thoughts about the events of the evening. Recognizing they weren't going to get any rest, they rolled toward each other and began whispering in the dark. Holly studied the blue moonlight that flooded in through the window, illuminating the planes of Deacon's face, and whispered, "He's just a kid. Chance has got three years on him, and I know for a fact he'd never survive in the woods by himself for any length of time."

Deacon corrected her, "Hmm, I don't know. I think Chance might surprise you. He's definitely maturing."

Her heart melted from the praise he lavished on her son. "Can I tell you something?"

"Of course." He reached out to lace his fingers through hers.

"I never thought a man could love children that weren't biologically his own."

"Then you don't know me at all, Holly Simon." He pressed her hand to his lips. "I'd never let a little thing like

DNA stand in the way. I know I will never replace their father, but I want your boys to know they are important to me, because you are important to me."

"Chance loves his work at the rescue, and you should hear the things he says about you."

Deacon smiled softly, then traced the long line down her jawline, his eyes locked on hers. "Darlin', you need to relax. You don't have to sell me on this. I know you, Dillon, and Chance are a package deal. One of my biggest regrets in life was never having children, and look at me now, knee-deep in teenagers. I got to skip the dirty diaper stage completely and get right to the thick of it." He cracked a smile that made her heart ache.

Holly nodded as her eyes began to swim with happy tears. "You've been there for them more than Mick ever was."

"This is just the beginning, sweetheart." His thumb brushed the first tear away. "I want to do so much more for you and for them."

"How did I get so lucky?" She closed her eyes and leaned closer, feeling his lips brush across hers and his fingers lace into her hair. After several minutes, her thoughts circled back to Shane and she sighed.

"What are we going to do about Shane?"

"That's a tough one," Deacon agreed, and the silence hung heavy between them.

"Do you think you could poke around without arousing suspicion? Ask some questions and find out if he's telling us the truth? I get this overwhelming sense of loss coming from him, and he doesn't trust anyone. He's too young to start life jaded and afraid. It's so sad."

"Yeah, I've known Duane for a long time. I'm sure I can meet him for a beer and can get some intel, but it will all have to be off the record. Let me see what I can find out."

"He's being abused," Holly blurted then shuddered, remembering the evidence she'd seen with her own eyes.

"We don't know that for sure."

"Actually, we do. His shirt shifted up accidentally, and I caught a glimpse of some bruises and deep scars on his torso, and that's just what you can see on the outside. Who knows what kind of cruelty that poor kid has been exposed to?"

Deacon shook his head in disgust. "If running away and wild camping in the middle of a Montana winter was a better option than living at home, I don't think he's had an easy road at all."

"He hasn't. We *have* to help him," she begged, gripping his shirt with her fists, her eyes imploring him.

"I know, honey. What do you think we should do?"

"I don't know." She glanced around the room like she could find the right word hiding in the shadows of her bedroom. "But I can't in good conscience force him back into the cold or send him back home if what he's saying checks out."

Deacon sighed then nodded in agreement as Holly continued.

"Did you see his shoes? They are barely held together with duct tape. I mean, we have plenty of room here. Maybe he can stay for a few days until we figure all this out?"

He grimaced. "You don't know what you're getting yourself into. Are you sure about that?"

"He ended up here for a reason." Holly sighed. "I can't turn my back on a child in need. I just can't."

"Let me do some digging. We'll get some information and then make a decision moving forward," Deacon said and reached out to squeeze her hand. "Together."

The single word eased Holly's heart.

"Just do me a favor, darlin'?"

"Of course," Holly answered.

"Don't make any promises to him right now. We don't want to be more people who have let this kid down."

"That's good advice." She stifled a yawn.

"Get some rest," Deacon said and pulled her onto his chest then kissed her forehead. Holly snuggled into his warm body and drifted off, marveling at how safe and protected she felt. Did Shane even know what those words meant? Holly had her doubts. She drifted off curled up in Deacon's arms, part of her content and happy while the other part sifted and searched, desperate to find a way to help Shane.

———

A few hours later, rays of yellow sunlight filtered into the bedroom, bouncing off the snowbanks. Holly's eyes popped open, and she glanced over at the empty side of the bed. Her fingers reached out in search of his warmth but were cooled by the sheets that had been unoccupied for a long time. Getting to her feet, she stumbled into the living room in search of caffeine and heard voices coming down from the loft. All the boys were up, and Shane's blankets were neatly folded in a pile on top of the coffee table.

Deacon gave her a warm smile and stood up to hug her. Holly drifted into his arms and squeezed his solid warm middle. Resting her head near his heart, she inhaled his vanilla and cedar scent.

"I made some fresh coffee," he offered. "Go sit down and I'll bring you a cup." He brought back a steaming cup of dark roast coffee, and Holly squeezed her hands around it, warming her fingers and mulling over their options for the thousandth time.

"I wanted to make sure you were up before I left, then I was going to see if I could get some answers," Deacon said.

"Has he asked to go home yet?"

"Doesn't sound like he ever wants to leave." Deacon pointed up to where the boys were smack-talking each other, and she was amazed how quickly Shane was folding into their lives.

"Can he do that?" Holly asked. "Just not go home? Surely, someone will come looking for him."

"It's hard to say. In his situation, there might not be anyone who cares." Deacon rose and put his hat on. "If it's okay with you, I'm going to go home to feed the dogs then stop in and see Duane."

Holly nodded and took another long sip with her elbows propped on the wood table.

Deacon leaned down and kissed her cheek. "Be back after while. Call me if you need anything." There was a cool burst of air as he opened the door and sauntered out into the brisk morning.

A few minutes later, Chance drifted down the stairs and sat down at the table next to her. "What happened last night? Dilly said the police were here?"

"You can sleep through anything." Holly ruffled his wavy hair. "I see you've met Shane?"

"Yeah. He was pretty quiet at first, but he seems to be coming out of his shell."

Holly heard a laugh she didn't recognize and had to agree.

Chance reached forward and poured a bowl of cornflakes from the box on the table, spooning a heaping spoonful of sugar on top before swirling it around and shoveling it to his mouth.

"Guys! Time to get dressed," Holly called up the stairs, finally deciding the best plan of attack was to act like nothing was out of the ordinary. "We need to start chores. We have new guests arriving today."

Upstairs, Dillon groaned and started explaining to Shane, "Sometimes we have strangers come and rent the cabins. Everything has to be spotless according to Mom."

The staircase rumbled as they ran down it. "We'd love your help, Shane. Chance, why don't you do the shoveling, and the boys will help me clean the cabin."

"That's right, freaks. Mom asked an actual man to do the real work." He puffed up and flexed his biceps as Holly rolled her eyes and laughed at him.

"Here." She handed Shane an old pair of boots. "Why don't you try these on?" Looking down at his threadbare socks, she said, "Wait," and walked to the laundry room, pulled out a pair of clean socks, and handed them to him. "I think you deserve a pair without built-in air conditioning."

Shane's eyes were giant brown pools in his face as he silently pulled the dirty socks off his feet and placed them in the trash can that Holly held out for him. Thin and full of holes, the soles were nearly black. Holly whisked them away to save Shane the embarrassment.

"All set?" She turned to him with a big smile, and he nodded. "Alright. Let's boogie, boys." She handed the caddy of cleaning supplies to Shane, and clean sheets to Dillon, who fell into step, trudging through the snow behind him.

"Mom's so lame," Dillon said, trying to look cool in front of the older boy. "No one says boogie anymore."

"I'm *vintage,*" Holly said. "The seventies are coming back around, mister. You wish you could be as cool as we were."

Dillon rolled his eyes with a smirk, used to Holly's ribbing. Shane listened to the exchange quietly, his eyes scanning his environment for possible threats.

Holly unlocked the cabin and said to Shane, "Why don't you stick with me? Dillon, start taking the sheets off the bed." When Dillon disappeared into the bedroom, she turned to Shane.

"Were you able to get some sleep last night?"

"Yeah," he admitted and stood there awkwardly, shifting uncomfortably. "A nice warm bed and a belly full of pancakes. It didn't take long."

She handed him a rag and a bottle of Pledge. "Can you start dusting the furniture for me?"

"Sure." Busy for a few minutes, it was silent in the cabin before he asked.

"You're going to make me leave soon, aren't you?" His voice pulled taut and timid, reflecting the fear that consumed him. He froze and lowered his eyes, waiting for the disappointment to come.

"I'm not sure," Holly answered. "We are kind of in uncharted territory right now."

"What does that mean?"

"It means I don't know what we're supposed to do in this situation," Holly replied honestly. Satisfied with her response, Shane went back to work.

"In my house, the most important rule is that we always tell the truth. Do you think you can follow that rule?" Holly asked. She needed more information from Shane to compare it to Deacon's.

He thought about it for a moment and then nodded.

"Where are your parents?"

"Mom died when I was little. Dad just got out of prison, so we went to live with Uncle Carl."

"Where does Uncle Carl live?" Holly asked, needing to pry and hating herself for it.

Instantly spooked, his fear-filled eyes swung over to meet

hers. He set down his cleaning supplies and moved toward the door. "I'll get my stuff and leave."

"Hey. Not so fast, mister," Holly said, taking tentative steps toward Shane. "Let's talk about this. Where will you go?"

"I don't know."

"Well, that doesn't sound like a good plan at all. Let's take a breath, okay?" Holly exhaled fully and waited for him to copy her. "I'm a teacher, and part of my training helps me look out for kids who are neglected and abused."

Shane's shoulders stiffened and his eyebrows shot up. He glanced at the door again like a startled deer.

"That's a good thing." She walked closer and sat down on the sofa in the living room, patting the seat next to hers. "Come here. You have nothing to be afraid of."

Still wary, he sat down on the edge of the sofa, perched and ready to run as he began to chew on the inside of his cheek.

"I think someone is hurting you, and that is why you ran away."

Shane's eyes blinked repeatedly and refused to meet hers.

"It's not okay, Shane." She reached out to steady him and put a reassuring hand on his shoulder, and he flinched. "What's been happening to you is wrong, and it's against the law."

He chuckled and shook his head. "No one cares about kids like me."

"You're wrong. I do. But I need to know the truth."

He hesitated, wringing his hands, trying to figure out what to say. Finally, his shoulders sagged and his words came out in a torrent, all sharp edges. "You want to hear about the time I was so hungry I ate a can of dog food because it was the only food in the house? Or the time they locked me in the closet for days, and when they got back, they beat me for the mess I made in the corner when I had to go to the bathroom? Or do you want to hear about the time they had me steal cold medicine from every pharmacy in town because I was a minor and didn't have a record, and if I got caught, it was juvie instead of jail?"

He stood, his anger growing and expanding, morphing into another being in the room with his hands balled at his sides. "Or do you want to hear what it's like going to school when you haven't had a bath in a month because the water was turned off? And then when you try to bathe in the pond near your house, your uncle takes the only jeans you have and throws them in the burn pile so you have to walk back home naked?"

"Or did you want to hear about the time a teacher takes an interest in you and files a report to send child protective services over to your house? You finally think help is here. Finally, the pain will stop. Except your uncle is an actor and lays it on thick with some shitty sob story about how he just needed a little more time and that it was important to keep his precious nephew home because nothing was more important than family." His words multiplied in frequency and volume as he paced like a caged animal. His voice broke, and his thin frame trembled with rage. "I waited for an opening, and I ran away. I am *never* going back there." His face was stone, and his lips were set in a hard line. "If you send me back there, I'll kill him." He oscillated from one extreme to the other like teenagers do, strong and invincible one moment, small and weak the next.

Holly swiped at the tears in her eyes, imagining the terror he lived through. Hearing him put it into words that she had to digest made her sick to her stomach.

"I'll kill him. I will." His rage seethed into the room from the outrageous manly claim, then cracked, and a sliver of the broken little boy he was dribbled out as he implored her, "Don't make me go back there. Please," he begged. "I'll do anything. I'll do all your chores. Shovel the snow. Mow the yard. I can stay in the barn. You can pretend you don't even know I'm here."

Holly stood up next to him, then reached out and pulled the heartbroken boy into her arms. He clung to her, shaking like a leaf. Over the top of his head, Holly locked eyes with a shocked and frozen Dillon standing behind Shane who had heard everything.

Embarrassed by his weakness, Shane pushed her away at first, fighting against the comfort she wanted to give him, but she held tighter. Emotionally exhausted, he broke, falling into her arms and sobbing. She whispered soothing sounds into his hair. "I'm sorry that happened to you. You deserve better." After five long minutes, he pulled back and wiped at his face with the back of his hands, his face pink and swollen from the tears.

"My mom won't let anything bad happen to you," Dillon piped up, eager to soften Shane's feelings. "Right, Mom?"

"It's not that easy, Dillon," Holly said, trying to squelch the one quality that Shane was desperate to find. Hope. "We will do everything we can to help, but we have to do this the right way. I can't keep a child here that is not legally mine."

"Why?" Dillon asked the question that Shane couldn't. Shane's eyes were locked on hers, waiting for a response. "Someone is hurting him."

"There are laws," Holly tried to explain.

"Fuck the laws," Shane said bitterly.

Dillon's eyes bugged out of his head, and he held a hand to his face and whispered to Shane, "Mom doesn't like us to use bad language in her presence."

"That's true," Holly agreed. "But he has a right to be frustrated. It's a broken system, but I promise you, Shane, we are going to find a way to help you."

He snorted in disbelief. "Sure."

"She will!" Dillon enthused on Holly's behalf. "When my mom says she's going to do something, she *always* comes through."

Holly's heart panged, hearing Dillon's childish optimism and earnest faith in her ability to fix the situation.

I really hope I can.

To distract them, she turned back to the cabin. "Let's finish up here, guys, and I'll make us some lunch."

Shane worked quickly with the tasks he was given to finish the dusting and clean out the fridge. He was so focused on trying to please her, Holly had to turn away. Holly was lost in her own thoughts, desperate to save him, but knowing that the system was overtaxed and full of loopholes. Even caring social workers were ground down to dust in a few years under the weight of heavy caseloads and bureaucratic red tape. The biggest casualties of this war were always the children. Every day, living in fear and intimidation from family members who viewed them as a cash cow, milking the system for their benefits. Oftentimes inflicting wounds that scarred their souls so deep, it fundamentally changed who they would become. For many lost children, it was the catalyst that would choke their options and drive them down into the rabbit holes of addiction and alcoholism to escape the pain. It was a scenario that Holly knew intimately, and she didn't want that for any child, but most of all Shane, who snatched a piece of her heart when she wasn't looking. She had to find a way to protect him or she would never forgive herself.

THIRTY-ONE

Later that night Deacon returned with answers. "He can't go back there." Holly anxiously glanced around for little ears and held a finger to her lips to shush him as he pulled off his boots and set them on the ground.

Holly grabbed his hand, pulled him into her bedroom, and shut the door. "I know." She sighed sadly. "He had an outburst when we were cleaning the cabins. It's worse than we thought, but I don't know what we can do legally to help him."

"Do you know anything about how to become a temporary foster parent?" Deacon asked.

"Not a thing," she admitted.

"I'd try to do it myself, but as a single man, it's going to be an uphill battle. Duane said we have a much better chance at being successful if Shane is integrated into a family."

Holly's eyes loomed large in her face, and she gulped hard.

"I know what you're thinking," Deacon started to answer before she could formulate the words herself. "It's too fast." He began to pace, and it made Holly anxious.

She bit her lip and bobbed her head in agreement.

"And in any other circumstance, I would be inclined to agree." Deacon stared into her eyes. "But sometimes you just have to jump and build your wings on the way down."

Holly hesitated. "I know it's selfish, but I've been trying to get the boys settled here, and they are still grieving the loss of their father. Dillon and Chance have always been my first priority." Deacon sighed and sat down at the foot of her bed, resting his head in his hands.

"I understand how you feel, but it's *meth*, Holly," Deacon admitted. "If we turn our back on this kid, he never even has a chance."

"Meth? Sweet Jesus." Holly dropped onto the bed next to Deacon, the weight of the word dragging her down. Terror unfurled in her belly.

"Agriculture makes Montana a prime target. It's a top ten list we never wanted to be on." Deacon looked down at his fingers laced together. Several long moments of silence hung heavy as they tried to grapple with the truth.

"I've been over and over our options in my mind. It's all I can think about. I am overextended trying to support the kids and settle them into our lives here as it is. I wasn't ready to take on another challenge yet."

He reached out and engulfed his huge hand in hers, squeezing it gently.

"I understand your fears, and they are valid. But this is bigger than both of us. His mom OD'd, his dad just got out of prison, and his Uncle Carl has been in and out of jail for the last five years." Deacon recounted the info Duane gave him in confidence and confirmed Shane's story to Holly. "We have to do s*omething*."

"I know." Holly stared at the floor. "I know," she repeated. "But I'm afraid."

"It's okay to be afraid." Deacon pulled her close. "Sometimes you have to get close enough to feel the fear but do it anyway." She settled into the warmth of his body, letting it calm her heart. "What are you most afraid of?" he asked.

"It's a lot of pressure to put on a new relationship," Holly blurted out. "This is a real commitment."

"It is." Deacon's voice soothed her fear. "But I know we can handle it."

"How do you know that?" Holly asked, hoping it was true but needing confirmation from him anyway.

"I just do." His voice softened. "I know who you are, Holly Simon, and I love you. I know we can do this. Shane needs us." He paused and then continued, "I can guarantee no one is going to come looking for that kid." Deacon wrapped an arm around her shoulders and pulled her in to kiss her temple. "Look, I know this is a lot to take on, but we have to help him."

Holly let out a long hot breath and decided, "Okay. Let's do this."

"Are you sure?"

"No, but you're right. If we don't help this kid, no one will." Her mind raced. "I just don't know where to start, but I *do* know the system is slow. It will take us months to get approved. We have to submit to a background check, attend classes. There's so much red tape to cut through." Holly was instantly overwhelmed.

"I know," Deacon conceded. "Duane gave me some contacts that can help us navigate the process. They can show us what we need to do to become foster parents. He said one of the most important steps we need to take is to document the abuse and go on record. I am going to take him to the clinic and get him checked out."

Holly's nostrils flared as she exhaled her pinched breath

through her nose. The weight of the decision was heavy on her heart. "We can't do that. I have a feeling there will be a lot of questions when he's examined. Questions we can't answer. The doctors are required to report suspected cases of abuse and call them in to the Department of Human Services. They will launch a full investigation, and God knows where he'll end up, but it won't be with us."

Deacon turned the problem over in his mind. "You're right."

The road ahead wasn't easy, and Holly was apprehensive, knowing they would have to fudge the details and not be entirely forthcoming with the truth on their application. But what other choice did they have?

"So, what's next?"

"We need to get the ball rolling to become emergency foster parents. It's his best shot at a normal life. I've been thinking about the logistics of this all the way home." He grabbed her hand. "I'm not comfortable with you being here alone with the boys. If his family ever comes looking for him…"

Holly's eyes widened. "It's what you're *not* saying that is scaring the hell out of me."

"I need to be around, to keep an eye on things and make sure you and the boys are safe, but I can't leave the dogs."

Holly gulped and nodded.

"We're a team, and it will be a lot easier to be involved in the entire process if we live in the same house. So, I was thinking, what if you moved in with me? I have plenty of room, and you could put the main house up on Airbnb to host larger families and generate a bigger income."

Holly was stunned. It was the plan that made the most sense, but she still had her doubts. "Do you think we're making a mistake by rushing into this?"

"Not at all," Deacon said. "In a perfect world, we would have waited a few more months before having this conversation, but as we both know, the world is far from perfect. All this is doing is making me move the timeline up a little."

Holly's mouth was dry. "But what does it *mean*?"

"Whatever we want it to. Come here." He pulled her to his chest, and she felt her anxiety melting.

"Are you sure about this?" Holly asked. "Going from zero to three boys is pretty extreme."

"Of course, I'm sure. I wouldn't have even mentioned it if I wasn't. Besides, I always wanted a big family."

"Wish granted," she teased with a bitter laugh. "Bad joke, I know." She pulled back to look into his warm eyes, then peppered him with another question.

"What is Ruth going to say?"

"I'd guess congratulations and then ask me when I was going to make an honest woman out of you."

Holly laughed; the man did know his mama. "I *do* want to get married again someday."

"You do?"

"I want to prove to myself that I can make it work with the right partner."

"Well, then someday we will." He kissed her forehead. The fear and insecurities she had were dissipating. It was a good plan, and she could trust him to help her carry it out.

"Do you want to tell the boys or should I?" she asked.

"I have an idea. Let me take the lead." Relieved, Holly relaxed into him, knowing their plan seemed to be the best way to protect Shane.

Life sometimes rushed at you, forcing events, and when that occurred, Holly shriveled and usually remained paralyzed, but this time she felt more certain. Huge, sweeping life changes were rocketing toward them both, and instead of feeling filled with doubts and insecurities, wondering if she could shoulder the burden alone, she felt peace. This time, she had a strong man beside her who was willing to do whatever it took. That knowledge filled her with such a sense of peace that instead of looking toward the future with uncertainty and fear, she saw it ripen with new possibilities and growth.

THIRTY-TWO

The next day, true to his word, Deacon planned an afternoon hike for all of them in Yellowstone.

Holly was scouring the house for a pair of boots for Shane when Chance popped up behind her holding the pair he just outgrew. "Hey, Mama, are you looking for these?"

"How did you know?"

"Deak asked me to look around for any old boots Shane could borrow today. They aren't new, but they're in good shape."

"I'm sure he'll appreciate them," Holly answered.

"Deak showed me the pair of shoes he was wearing when he landed here. Did you see them, all duct-taped together with paper-thin soles? I didn't want to say anything to embarrass him, but how did he stay outside in the winter in those and not lose three toes to frostbite?"

"That's a good question." Holly bent down and pulled Shane's coat from the dryer, then scrounged up an extra set of mittens and a stocking hat. None of it matched, but it was warm. "Shane hasn't been given very many good things in life so far."

"Is that why he's so quiet?"

She nodded. "You can't blame him for being untrusting. Kids are all born with the same factory settings, but then life changes them. Your family of origin writes on the slate of who you are and who you will become—good or bad. He's survived some pretty horrific circumstances."

"Dillon told me a few things he overheard. Are they true?"

"Unfortunately." Holly knew the boys were going to talk. "Both his parents were addicts."

Chance listened, letting it all soak in. "I guess I'm lucky that one of mine wasn't, or I could have ended up like Shane."

"Yeah, lucky you," she said softly. It was still a bitter pill to swallow knowing she chose an addict to father her children.

"I *was* lucky, Mom," he emphasized. "I see that now."

Tears prickled at Holly's lashes, and she pulled him into her arms. "I love you, Chancey, and I am so proud of how far you've come." She hugged him tight, his body thicker and more muscled now that his journey through the fantasy land of childhood was coming to a conclusion and he was nearing adulthood. "Just be patient with him. It takes time to build trust."

"I know, Mom. It's like when we get a new dog at the rescue. They are usually very skittish and wary of new people. It takes a while for them to warm up to you, settle in, and find their place in the pack."

"Exactly. He just needs time," she agreed.

"How long is he staying?"

"Well, that's what I wanted to talk to you about." She took a step back and looked into his eyes. "Shane needs someone to step up for him, and I think that someone is us."

She let the statement sink in, watching Chance's expression closely, trying to decode his true feelings. "But I need to know you're okay with this decision. If you don't think it's the right one, then I will try to find him a suitable placement."

"Where?" he asked.

"With a foster family."

"No," he said firmly. "You're right. He deserves a real family. With a *real* mom."

His conviction made warmth trickle from her heart to her fingers.

"He does. If you and Dilly give us your blessing, Deacon and I are going to apply to become his foster parents."

"Wow."

"I know. It's a huge step," Holly added, "and it won't be easy. We'll all have to adjust, Shane more than any of us. But, if we get approved, you'd become a big brother again. Are you ready for that?"

He smiled. "Yep."

"Okay then." Holly gave her oldest son a smile and handed him the pile of outerwear she'd created for Shane. "Can you give these to Shane and ask Dilly to come down?"

"Sure." He headed up the stairs to the loft, shouting, "Hey, loser! Mom needs to see you now."

Holly rolled her eyes at his insult.

Some things never change. Brothers will always be brothers. I hope Shane gets to feel that connection. It would be so good for him.

Unfazed by the slam, Dillon ran down the stairs in stocking feet and then jumped off the third step from the bottom, landing with a splat in front of Holly. "Yeah?"

"Come here, you." Holly opened up her arms, and he rushed in for a hug. "So, I want to talk to you about something serious."

Not used to being informed about important family business, Dillon was instantly intrigued.

"What do you think about Shane coming to live with us for a while?"

"How long's a while?"

"I don't know," she answered. "Does it matter?'

"But doesn't he need to go home?" Dillon was confused.

"I'm sure this feels like the world's longest sleepover, honey, but Shane doesn't have anyone waiting for him at home like you do. In fact, I don't think he even has a home. That's why he was camping and was so hungry he ended up here."

"What? No home?" Dillon tried to understand it, but the concept was too big. "What about his mom? Where is she at?"

"She's in heaven, like your dad."

His face crumpled, finally understanding the loss.

"Will he be my brother?" Dillon asked. "Will you love him as much as you love us?"

"It's different, sweetheart. You and Chance will always be my first priorities. But we met Deacon, and he's become kind of like family, don't you think? And I believe we have enough love left in this family for Shane, too. Your heart expands with every new person you bring into it. You aren't given one amount of love to last your whole life to ration out; you create more every day."

"So, love just grows and grows and grows?"

"Exactly." She smiled at his wide eyes.

He considered her words, and after a few long moments wrestling with this new information, he smiled. "I think I'd like another brother. And don't tell Chance this, but Shane is nicer to me than he is most of the time."

Holly laughed. "Chance loves you in his own way. When you're older, it will all make sense."

"Ughhhh! You say that all the time!"

"I say it because it's true." Holly ruffled his hair. "Now, we told Deak we were going to be dressed and ready for our hike at eleven, and that's only five minutes away, so you need to go put on your boots and snow pants."

———

A few minutes later, Holly tossed her keys into Deacon's outstretched palm on the front porch and crawled into the passenger seat. The boys walked out carrying backpacks filled with water and snacks. Dressed in coats and boots, ready for their winter hike, their breath plumes of white smoke escaping from their mouths as the cold pinked their cheeks.

"Mama packed us a real picnic and lots of treats, so we should be all set," Deacon said with a smile as he hauled a huge cooler from the bed of his truck to the van. Uncharacteristically chatty, Deacon rambled on in the seat next to her as he drove. Holly stole glances at him. His fingers anxiously drummed on the steering wheel, a nervous trait she recognized in herself, but seeing it taking over her capable mountain man unnerved her. Lost in her thoughts, she was relieved when they drove through the gates at Yellowstone twenty minutes later.

Inside the park, he drove down the zebra-striped roads where black asphalt peeked out from icy and snow-covered tracks, remnants of storms from the previous week. He slowed when the sparse traffic paused for herds of bison and moose as they threaded through the roads of the park. Some of the routes were closed for the winter, but he was a man on a mission and finally parked the van just off the road on a small pullout. He handed backpacks of supplies to the boys and strapped an enormous one on himself.

They struggled up the steep rocks for the first half-mile, and the boys ran on ahead. Rounding the corner thick with evergreen trees, Holly gasped at the view. There was a perfect mirrored reflection of snow-capped mountains and pine trees on the dark lake. Huge swaths of snow-covered ice made most of the lake a frozen tundra, but ice-cold water still flowed in places. The air was crisp and clean, and Holly closed her eyes, feeling her soul recenter from the peaceful quiet around her.

"Wow." Holly stood in front of the pristine panoramic lake view, soaking in the pure beauty of it. She stood to face the mountains, her hands balled in red yarn mittens, resting on her hips that were covered in navy blue snow pants.

Snowflakes began to fall. Fat and thick, they descended slowly from the sky and landed on her eyelashes. The flakes meandered gently down, floating on the breeze until they piled up on top of the drifts. She glanced over in time to see Dillon running around in circles with his mouth wide open to catch snowflakes as they descended. Shane watched for him a moment from the sidelines.

"Shane, you gotta try this. They taste so clean." Dillon waved him over, and Holly watched Shane transform from a hard teenager to a sweet little boy again. Then he flopped down on his back and waved his arms and legs, laughing as Dillon flopped next to him to make snow angels. They popped up then jumped to a fresh patch of snow that was untouched by humans but with the occasional rabbit or elk print and made more angels. It was sweet, innocent fun that Holly couldn't tear her eyes away from. She could see Shane warming up to them, especially Dillon. He was coming out of his shell, and instead of always being the silent bystander, Shane was actually participating. He was finding out first-hand it was hard to tell Dillon no. Holly poured steaming cups of hot chocolate for everyone from the thermos that Ruth provided.

"Your mom thinks of everything," Holly said to Deacon as she handed him a cup. Deacon's cheeks were pink and he was fidgety. Holly watched him warily, wondering if he was having second thoughts.

"What's going on with you?" she asked. "You're acting weird."

Ignoring her question, he called out. "Hey, boys, could you come over here for a second?" Holly watched as they made their way across the snow, and when they gathered close, Deacon announced, "I have something important to ask your mom."

Confused, she watched him drop down onto one knee in his Carhartt coveralls. Pulling off his gloves, he reached inside his jacket pocket and extracted a black velvet box. A nervous smile tugged at the corners of his mouth as he gently pried it open with his fingers. In shock, Holly's mittened hands flew to her mouth. Nestled inside, one perfect, bright, shining snowflake lay cushioned there, sparkling when it caught the sunlight. Holly gasped and looked over at the boys. Dillon's mouth was wide open, and Chance had a small knowing smile spreading across his.

"Did you guys know?" Chance nodded his strong chin up and down and slung an arm around Dillon and Shane, pulling them together. The sight of her three boys made the moment even more magical.

It's happening. Something amazing is happening. Right now. To me.

Holly's cheeks hurt from smiling, and she caught

Deacon's hands trembling, his nerves obvious to only her. She looked down into the warm eyes of the man she loved and waited for him to speak. Time slowed to a crawl as she took in all the details. The flakes that drifted down from heaven and gathered in the collar of his tan Carhartt jacket. The pink flush of his cheeks from the cold. The way his eyes smiled and the corners of his full lips turned up when he said her name.

"Holly, I've known enough loss in my life to understand you have to grab love with both hands when you're given the chance. I love you. I love your boys. I want today to be the beginning of a beautiful life that we build together. I want to wake up with you and make you coffee every morning. I want to be by your side to help keep these knuckleheads in line. I want to take care of you, and travel with you, and fight with you, and cry with you. I want to do everything with you. All of it. Will you marry me?"

Speechless, she nodded and hot tears made icy tracks down her cheeks that couldn't stop smiling. The boys whooped and hollered in the background as he stood to kiss her. Deacon pulled off her mitten and slipped the ring on her finger, dipping his head to kiss it. "I have wanted to see it there for a long time."

"What do you mean?" she whispered. "I don't understand."

"This isn't about Shane, sweetheart. I've had that thing in the glove box for weeks now, waiting for the perfect time to give it to you."

"Really?" she asked, searching his eyes and finding the truth there. Everything good and pure rested in their toffee-colored depths.

"I knew a long time ago," he answered. She pounded her fists on his chest, laughing into the warm circle of his arms.

She was certain they were the only things keeping her from floating away in pure happiness.

"Come here, you timid little creature." He pulled her face up to his, meeting her lips with his, and then dramatically dipped her back into the snow before righting her onto her feet. He pulled her in tight for a hug, and she melted into him, both of them laughing buoyant and light. Behind them, the boys made gagging noises watching their over-the-top display of affection.

"You guys are gross!" Dillon shouted out.

"Yeah, get a room!" Chance teased them.

Holly laughed into Deacon's chest. She pulled back and looked up at him. He leaned down and pressed his forehead to hers.

"You've made me a happy man," he whispered into her kiss. "Now…" He paused, and a mischievous grin made his rugged face even sexier. "Let's get 'em!" He dropped to the ground, scooping up huge handfuls of wet snow and making quick work of packing it into balls. Holly joined in quickly, dropping down next to him on her knees, making ammo as fast as she could.

Chance was the first to register what was happening. He quickly bent down and made a huge snowball with two massive fistfuls of snow, then beamed it between Deacon's shoulder blades as an all-out war began.

"Are you sure you want in on this deal? They're savages," Holly apologized as she flung one at Chance, hitting his torso.

"Yeah, they are." Deacon ducked and then swatted a snowball down before it could hit Holly's back. "But they're *our* savages." Then he quickly bent down and formed three snowballs, pulled up the collar of his coat, and from behind a tree launched them at the boys. Twenty exhausting minutes later, Holly declared a ceasefire and passed sandwiches around. Deacon dusted off a picnic table and they sat down on the table, the thick snowdrift creating benches on the ground. Holly passed around the rest of the thermos of hot chocolate and folding camping cups to the boys.

She noticed Shane clutching his cup tightly and how he turned away from the group, protecting his food. His elbows were out like she had seen inmates behave in a prison documentary, and it was a dart to the heart.

The lake was quiet and still. Holly tasted a falling flake on her tongue. "It's like living in a snow globe," she said with a grin. "I didn't think this park could get more beautiful, but it did. See how everything is glittering and transformed into a sea of white?"

"She is beautiful," he admitted, squeezing her mittened hand, then turned to the boys, "I've been looking for some second-hand cross-country skis," Deacon admitted. "Do you guys want to learn?"

"Yeah! Can I get a snowboard?" Chance asked.

"Let me see if I can wrestle up a couple of those," Deacon offered. "I'm sure we'll be able to find something."

Holly listened to them talk, their voices jostling and jumbling together eager for Deacon's attention. Deacon was patient and quiet and engaging Shane. Asking his opinion and pulling him into the conversation. Deacon was a natural dad. He instinctively knew how to handle young men, and they looked up to him and respected him. He mercilessly teased them while they did their best to smack talk, savoring the attention he lavished on them. Deacon made it look easy.

This is how it is supposed to be. This is what a father does. I am so lucky.

She had to turn her head to hide her tears or risk being swept into the teasing herself. Warm inside her mitten, the ring circled around her finger. She rubbed her knuckles together, focused on the foreign object that would soon become as much a part of her as an extra appendage. This time felt different. It felt like it belonged there, and Holly couldn't remember being happier than this.

THIRTY-THREE

The next morning, Holly skyped Stacey.

"Hey, woman! I haven't heard from you in a minute. Thought maybe a bear got you." Stacey laughed.

"No bear attacks, but man, it has been *crazy* around here."

"Ooh!" Stacey enthused, thrilled by the notion of fresh gossip. "Tell me everything." She held up a sunny yellow mug. "I've got a fresh cup of Joe and nothing but time."

Holly smirked as she reached for her mug with her left hand and hoisted it in front of the camera, holding it there, then waited. The sun coming through the window refracted off the diamond and sent a prism to the ceiling.

"Wait… Whoa!" Stacey caught on right away. "Is that what I think it is?"

"Well, that depends. What do you think it is?" Holly teased her with an enormous smile plastered on her face.

"Oh my God! Congratulations!" Stacey shouted, shrieking into the phone. "Hold it closer. Let me see!"

Holly felt silly but couldn't help herself as she waved it in front of the screen like she was a twenty-two-year-old, hamming it up for the camera and making surprised faces until Stacey begged her to stop.

"You're going to make me pee," Stacey confessed. "You know you can't trust the bladder muscles of a woman over forty."

Holly laughed. This is what she loved about Stacey. She sighed a contented sigh. "Ahhh. He's incredible, Stace."

"I had a feeling."

"You did?" Holly was dumbfounded. "Why does everyone know what's going on in my life better than I do?"

"Because you don't see what an incredible woman you are. He'd be an idiot to let someone as amazing as you slip through his fingers. That Deacon must be a smart man."

Holly laughed. "He is." She shrugged her shoulders to her ears and smiled as giddiness fizzed up her spine, making her whole body tingle. Joy was the Alka-Seltzer of life.

"I don't think I have ever seen you so happy," Stacey admitted.

"I don't think I've *ever been* this happy."

"Aww, woman. This is the kind of love you deserve."

"It feels so good and easy."

"That's how you know it's right."

"So, what kind of event are we planning? Church wedding with the big fancy dress?" Stacey asked. Holly loved the immediate 'we' Stacey used when asking.

"Well, to be honest, we haven't even gotten that far. A couple other things have taken precedence." Holly recounted the story of the first night she met Shane, watching the shock appear in Stacey's bulging eyes.

"A gun?" she asked. "A teenager pointed a gun at you, and your first response was to make him pancakes?" She shook her head in disbelief, laughing at her friend.

"Well, when you put it that way, it does sound kind of

crazy," Holly had to admit. "But you know what I'm talking about, Stacey. We've had the same training. You've seen kids in rough home situations, coming to school hungry and neglected."

Stacey nodded thoughtfully and took a solemn sip of her coffee. "Unfortunately, I have."

"He just needs to be given a chance. That's all," Holly reasoned. "So, Deacon and I decided to start taking the steps to become foster parents."

"Really?" Stacey asked. "That's incredible. There is a massive need for loving homes for these kids."

"It's heartbreaking," Holly agreed. "If we can help out, we'd like to try. Deacon has a huge house on an acreage. We have plenty of room, and the boys can help out at the rescue."

"What a great idea! Being around dogs is so calming, almost like therapy, and it will give the boys a chance to step up and be responsible for something outside themselves." Stacey's voice got more animated as she spoke. "It's not exactly the same situation, but I just heard something on NPR about a program they introduced in the prisons that had such a profound impact. They tasked each inmate with training a service dog, and the dog bonded with them. It was incredible. To have contact with a living thing that didn't judge them for who they were or what they had done healed these broken people. It was so inspiring."

"That's awesome. I've seen what impact it has on my own boys. Chance is committed to the rescue. You should see how far he's come."

"That makes my heart so happy," Stacey gushed.

"You know, Deacon was on board with becoming a foster parent from the beginning. I'm kind of embarrassed to admit he had to convince me." She paused then continued. "There is no way I could even begin to consider being a foster parent without him. It felt like my hands were already so full. I didn't want Chance and Dillon to suffer."

"That's the difference when you have a real teammate," Stacey answered. "God, I am so thrilled for you both. You deserve this man."

"You think so?"

"Yes! Silly, I *know* so!" Stacey gushed. "You're the best woman I know. If anyone deserves a happily ever after, it's you."

"It's so funny, because right when I thought I didn't believe in them anymore, my fairytale found me."

"God, I wish I could reach through that screen and hug the shit out of you!' Stacey exclaimed as Holly laughed.

"I need to ask you something," Holly asked. "We haven't even given a thought to the wedding planning, but I want you here, beside me."

"There is no other place I'd rather be."

THIRTY-FOUR

Moving this time was easier. Holly left most of her furniture in place, intending to rent out the main house now, and only brought the pieces she was sentimental about to Deacon's. She sold the sofa in the barn, and they bought a new mattress and warm flannel sheets. Her massive dining room table that seated ten and had lived in the barn since she moved to Montana now had a real home at Deacon's, and Holly couldn't wait for the family dinners they would have gathered around it.

Deacon's house offered four bedrooms. One for Chance and Dillon to share, one for Shane, and one for guests. His kitchen was warm and cozy. He helped her paint the walls a calming blue, and all the oak trim was transformed to white. Deacon didn't fully understand her need to paint, clean, and refresh the space, making the rooms as open and airy as possible, but he could always be counted on to help.

There was a twinge of insecurity that remained when she thought about Deacon carrying Ashley over the threshold. No visible signs of her remained, and knowing Deacon's heart, she was afraid he put all the photos and mementos away for her benefit. One day, when she was cleaning out an old shelf in the attic, she found a small opal frame. Nestled inside was a much younger, grinning Deacon. His hair was an unfortunate mullet, and his strong tanned arm was draped around the shoulders of a beautiful brunette. She dusted it off and placed it on the shelf where all the family photos now lived. About a week later, Deacon noticed and asked her about it.

"She was part of your story, just like Mick was part of mine," Holly admitted. "I can't erase her or the impact she had on the man you turned out to be. She belongs there with the rest of our family."

Deacon's eyes glistened, and he pulled her in for a hug. She felt his warm breath in her hair. "I love the way you think. Thank you."

The sweetness and longing in his voice just reinforced his commitment to her, and as a result, she was able to unpack her feelings of insecurity and worthiness. Any comparison that she felt toward Ashley melted away.

She rearranged the kitchen, moving dishes around and configuring the cabinets to fit the way she liked to use them. At first, Deacon was frustrated. He was a creature of habit, and moving his forks and knives to the drawer to the right of the stove threw him out of whack.

"It's better!" she declared. "Trust me." She demonstrated, pulling open the drawer for the fork. "See? You don't have to go across your body. It makes more sense for this drawer to be their home."

He rolled his eyes. "Their home has been in the same place for twenty-seven years."

"Can we just try it for a little bit, and if you absolutely hate it, we can go back to the old way? Just give it one month."

"It's a good thing you're so cute," he said with a grin and agreed to the trial run. In the end, she won.

Two weeks later, Holly ran through the house, puffing up pillows on the sofa and sweeping the hardwood floors for the hundredth time.

"Relax, darlin', it's not a visit from the president. It's just a visit from the Department of Human Services."

"I know, but we're unmarried. I'm sure it's a shaky situation at best." She karate-chopped a pillow in the center, then turned toward Deacon who pulled her into his arms.

"You're a licensed teacher. There's no way they would deny you." He kissed her forehead, and Holly felt her pulse slow down and closed her eyes.

"The stakes are pretty high. Shane's been living with us. He could be removed anytime, and I just can't stand the idea of him going back to them or hiding in the shadows like some kind of wild animal. He deserves better than that."

"He does," Deacon agreed. "And he'll get it with us." He squeezed her hand and pulled her down on the sofa. "Just try to relax."

The gravel rumbled as a navy government sedan rumbled up the lane. Holly popped up and waited by the door, anxiously biting her lip. She smoothed the front of her green maxi dress while she watched the older woman dressed in a drab olive suit navigate the stairs to the front porch.

"Chance! Dillon! Shane!" she shouted upstairs. "Come down here please."

The staircase thundered as their feet ran down it. "Remember, I'll introduce you guys and our 'friend' Shane." She was torn in two from the stress of lying to a public official. She tried to adopt Deacon's stance. "It's better to ask for forgiveness than permission." But it tied her stomach up in knots. She was a rule follower, and going against the rules filled her with anxiety.

The social worker was a harried former redhead with streaks of gray who carried a battered briefcase and a clipboard. "I'm Alice Greenfield with the Department of Human Services, here to conduct your interview and home inspection."

"It's nice to meet you. I'm Holly, this is my fiancé, Deacon, my sons, Chance and Dillon, and their friend, Shane." The words rocketed out of her mouth fast, as they always did when she was nervous. "Can I offer you something to drink?"

"No, thanks, Ma'am." She set down her briefcase and pulled the clipboard out. "I've looked over your inquiry packet and have a few questions."

The inquiry packet had taken nearly a week to finish. A thick stack of documents Holly and Deacon worked to complete, verifying and documenting their ability to financially and emotionally provide for a foster child in their care. She also submitted the paperwork to begin their background checks.

"How long have you lived at this residence?"

"Twenty-seven years," Deacon piped up proudly.

"Have you lived together a minimum of twenty-four months?"

Holly hesitated, her mouth dry, and was shocked to hear Deacon answer for her. "Yes." Behind her, she heard a confused Dillon softly interject, "Wait… what?"

Ignoring his response, and clearly on a schedule, the overworked woman moved on to the next question.

"It says here you are a teacher?"

"I was. My life took a different path, but I have kept my

teaching license up to date and have completed all my continuing education credits."

The woman was all business and jotted down a quick note, then turned to Deacon. He smiled and said, "I'm a veterinarian and run a rescue where we train dogs to become service animals."

Holly noted he dodged the bullet of providing the breed and added, "My sons are actually part of the process, and we'd hope to offer the boys we foster opportunities to learn as well."

Alice nodded with a tight smile and jotted notes intermittently as she flipped through their paper application with purpose, licking her index finger before swiping the page up. The heavy silence weighed the room down. Out of the corner of her eye, Holly noticed the boys getting antsy.

"Is it okay if the boys get back to their video games?" Holly asked.

"Sure," Alice agreed. "We can begin the home inspection."

"Of course." Holly walked her into the kitchen, where the woman proceeded to open drawers and made notes.

"Is there a fire extinguisher?"

Holly crossed to the refrigerator and pulled it off the top. "Check," she said with her most winning smile.

Holly walked her to the bathrooms, where Alice quickly opened doors and drawers, and then into the boys' bedroom with the bunk bed.

"My boys share this room, and next door we have a bedroom set up for Sh…" Holly stopped herself, and then continued, "…a foster child, as well as a guest room." The day before, the room had been stripped of evidence that anyone was currently living in it. Holly stored all of Shane's belongings in Dillon's closet, desperate to keep up the façade of readiness. Knowing if it looked lived in, it would be a red flag.

Holly remembered the day she and Deacon showed Shane his room. Not understanding his days as a couch surfer were over, he followed them into the room they spent the day painting and setting up for him. When he realized it was his, his very own room, he shot them a real smile. He sat down gingerly on the edge of the bed, careful not to wrinkle the new quilt that rested there.

"Go on! Try it out!" Holly encouraged him.

With a grin, he laid down, stretched out, and laced his long fingers behind his head, his elbows jutting up like sharp triangles. "I've never had an actual bedroom before, with a *real* pillow." He wiggled his head on it, getting comfortable like Murph was apt to do.

After a few minutes, Shane walked over to the dresser and slid open the drawer, seeing clean stacks of new underwear and socks and gently used clothing that Holly picked up at the thrift store in Bozeman. He rifled through them and lifted a t-shirt to his nose, inhaling. "Smells so good," he said with a sweet smile. "They're so clean."

His enjoyment of the most basic things—clean clothes, new underwear, a pillow—made Holly's heart pang. She had taken those items for granted her whole life. To see them now with Shane's fresh, thankful eyes was a lesson in gratitude she was grateful to receive.

Then she walked him over to where a night light was plugged in. "This will come on automatically when it gets dark. So, if you wake up in the middle of the night, you'll be able to see."

His eyes met hers with a puzzled look.

"We want you to feel safe here," Holly answered. "I know sometimes when you wake up in a new place, it's hard to get your bearings. This way you won't crack a toe on a base-board," Holly continued. "You are welcome to eat whatever you want, *whenever* you want. The only time we will ask you to wait is the hour before dinner time. We try to eat together as a family as much as possible."

He nodded and looked away, breaking her gaze. The word family hurt to hear.

Deacon filled the long pause. "There are a couple house rules. If you make a mess, clean it up. You have to go to school and do your best. No skipping school, lying, and abso-lutely no drugs or alcohol."

Shane nodded quickly in agreement, and Holly softened her voice. "We are happy to have you here, Shane, and want you to feel comfortable. It takes a lot of work to run this acreage and the rescue, so we are going to need you to pull your weight around here. Everyone has responsibilities and chores. We are a team."

"And if I do all those things, I get a warm place to sleep, food to eat, and clean clothes to wear?" he asked.

"Exactly," Deacon said. "Do we have a deal?" He thrust his enormous hand out for Shane to shake.

"Deal."

Holly's focus came back to the social worker, who took a photo of Shane's bedroom and the newly installed bedroom furniture. The woman filled them in on how the system worked. Foster kids were often emergency placements, and they could get a call any time of the day or night. The state would provide a monthly stipend to pay for the basic needs of the child, and even though her Airbnb income was shaky at best, Deacon was able to prove a long-term history of good credit and a stable income. Together, they could and would financially provide for their family's basic needs.

Holly and Deacon gave Alice a tour of the outbuildings

and the rescue. The dogs were on their best behavior, somehow instinctively understanding the importance of this visitor. Tink and Daisy sat down, calmly ignoring Alice. After an hour of walking around the property, Alice relaxed and wrapped up the visit, saying, "I think that is all we need. I will submit this report and the photos, and you should get an answer from the state within a few weeks."

"That's it?" Holly asked.

"That's it," she confirmed. "Well, when you get approved, you will also need to complete our Foster Parent training program. It will give you some insight into how the process works, how to handle parenting boys who have likely been abused. There is a real need in the State of Montana for qualified foster parents for teens. They are the most difficult age group to place."

She gathered up her briefcase and the clipboard and offered a hand to Holly, who shook it, relieved that their time under the microscope was over. Now they had nothing to do but wait.

———

Later that night, Holly was reading a book when Shane sat down on the sofa next to her. The fire was roaring, thanks to Deacon stoking it before taking Chance and Dillon to Ruth's for supplies.

"You decided to hang back?" Holly asked, putting a bookmark into her book.

"I'm kind of tired," Shane answered.

"I bet," she commiserated. "Is there something on your mind?"

He shook his head no, but she knew otherwise.

"I'm glad you're here. I've been wanting to talk to you about school."

Shane's worry lines appeared and his forehead was pinched. He shrugged it off. "I hate school."

"You have to go back to school. We've been letting you lie low here, but once we start this ball rolling, you will have to go back."

"Can't I just get my GED?"

"Shane, one of the expectations of you in this family is to work to the best of your ability. I know how smart you are, even though you try to hide it."

The compliment threw him off guard, and he fidgeted on the sofa.

"You have to apply yourself now, even when you think it's lame or even if you don't think you'll be going to college. What if you change your mind in the future? I want you to have options. I want *all my sons* to have options."

The sentiment jerked him out of the apathetic mud he was wallowing in.

"I can't," he mumbled.

"Can't what?" she asked.

He pointed at the book still in her hands. "That."

Not understanding, Holly still struggled to put the pieces together. "What?" She looked down at the book. "Read?" she asked, shocked.

How could this be true? How could a boy get to be thir-teen years old and not be able to read?

"I missed a lot of school when I was little, and I'm not sure when it happened. But eventually, they assumed I could. I faked it because I didn't want anyone to make fun of me for being so stupid."

"Honey, you're not stupid. You just don't have a skill. In

fact, I would wager that you are smarter than most of those kids you thought would call you dumb. It takes a lot of intelligence to read the room and the context of conversations enough to be able to skate by undetected."

Shane smiled.

"It's true." Holly encouraged him. "Would you like to learn? I can teach you, a little bit every night."

He was unsure, but the idea of having Holly's undivided attention was appealing.

"When you can read, the whole world opens up for you," Holly continued. "You might even find it fun."

"I don't know about that." He was wary.

"You leave it up to me, buddy," Holly said. "I know I can find something that you will love to read. We'll start slow and build. It will be fun, I promise."

"Dillon warned me to run when you said that phrase," Shane said with a smirk.

"It will be!" Holly insisted. "We will start on Monday."

THIRTY-FIVE

In late April, a thick, white, official-looking envelope tucked in with junk mail and newspapers gave Holly and Deacon the answer they were seeking.

Ruth brought over two bottles of chilled sparkling grape juice and a pound of candy to celebrate. Holly baked lasagna and two loaves of cheesy garlic bread and set the table like it was a holiday. When the boys came home from school suspicious, they asked, "Why's the table so fancy?"

"We're celebrating!" Holly grinned.

"Celebrating what?"

"We got approved to be a foster family."

"Does that mean Shane will get to stay with us forever?" Dillon asked. He had grown close to Shane in the three months they lived together. Shane was endlessly more patient than Chance was, letting Dillon tag along on every task and answering his never-ending litany of questions.

Interested in the answer to Dillon's question, Shane was silent, afraid to show too much interest. When Holly caught his darting eyes that never really rested anywhere, always scanning for the nearest exit, she saw a glimmer of hope reflected there.

"We are one giant step closer to that," she answered. Holly was careful not to over-promise. Shane had been let down so much in his short rough life, and she didn't want to be another person added to the list of people who had failed him.

Bringing the hot lasagna to the table with oven mitts, the short spring nights still pitched the house in early darkness. Holly lit two tapered candles and called everyone to the table. She passed the salad and the creamy parmesan ranch dressing as everyone chattered away, except for Shane. As always, he was quiet and focused on eating. She noticed his cheeks looked fuller and had lost the grayed hollow look of malnutrition. He had gained weight in the time they had been together. Whenever it was time for a meal, he was always the first one who came running as if he'd miss out if he didn't rush to the table.

After dinner was eaten and the dishes were washed and put away, she sat on the porch with Ruth. It was a calm and cool night where the glimmer of spring promised better temperatures. Deacon brought them thick blankets and settled them on the porch swing before he headed back in. Rocking in a companionable quiet, the women reflected on the magnitude of the state's decision. Holly felt at ease alone with Ruth now, their relationship closer than ever. It was becoming a relationship that Holly treasured.

"You're doing good stuff here," Ruth remarked as Deacon came back out on the porch in his Carhartts, carrying a platter filled with mugs of steaming coffee for them.

"Here you go, Mama."

Holly smiled. "I love that you call your mother, Mama," she remarked. "It's adorable."

He flashed a grin at her. "Well, that's what she is." He pulled up a chair next to Holly and sipped at the coffee.

"This is progress for sure, but I keep looking over my shoulder, wondering what will happen when they find out we're harboring a runaway."

"He's much better off with you than in the system. Who knows where the kid would end up if he didn't land here?" Ruth took a sip then continued. "I don't want to be the bearer of bad news, but what if someone comes looking for him?" Ruth asked.

"We haven't thought that far," Holly confessed.

"I have," Deacon interrupted quietly. "His people are not good people."

Ruth nodded in agreement. "They've always been that way. A mess from the beginning. In and out of trouble with the law. Meth is a cancer on that family."

Deacon continued. "We need to go through the proper channels. Now that we've been approved as foster parents, we need to take Shane to the police and file a complaint of abuse."

"Do we have to do that?" Holly asked. "We just got him settled. I don't know how he's going to react if we force him to file a report. Even if it's in their best interests, it's difficult for a child to stand up against an abusive parent."

Deacon sipped the coffee slowly. "He can't hide out here forever. If we have a chance of saving this kid, we have to do it by the book." He sighed. "As much as I want to just erase them from existence, we can't. Like a bad penny, they will keep showing up."

"They will," Ruth confirmed. "Especially if they find out you have something they want. Promise me you'll be careful, sweetheart?" she asked, and Deacon nodded.

"I think we need to bring Duane in the loop, just so he can keep an eye on things. It's a small town and people talk."

"That's not a bad idea," Ruth agreed, "but Deacon's right. You have to file a report, get the legal ball rolling. It's going to get a lot worse before it gets better."

The curtain flicked to the side and caught Holly's eye. She got a glimpse of black hair and he was gone. "Oh no! I think Shane overheard us."

Deacon stood. "He's a smart kid. He's been in survival mode so long he doesn't know anything else. I'm going to go talk to him." Deacon went inside.

"Your son is a natural dad," Holly said to Ruth. "I've never met someone so good at meeting teenagers on their level. It's a gift."

"He was always good with children," Ruth answered. "And as the years went by, I started to think that he wasn't going to ever get to experience being a father. Seeing him step up like this is such a beautiful thing."

"You must be so proud of the man he is."

"Always," Ruth answered with a smile that morphed to a concerned frown. "But he's right; Shane is a currency. When his people figure out where he's been hiding, they will come, not because they want to be part of his life, but because they will use him as leverage to take anything that has value. I've never met a more entitled bunch of cruel people in my entire life."

Ruth grew quiet, and Holly tried to read her eyes but struggled.

"Promise me you'll all be careful."

"I promise."

"I've got to be going." Ruth stood, and Holly hugged her. She walked to her car as the words remained, still thick in the air.

Holly felt a jolt of fear surge up her throat. Torn between protecting her biological children and being an advocate for Shane. She stayed frozen on the porch, gliding on the swing in silence, lost in her own thoughts, none of them good.

THIRTY-SIX

The next morning, Holly pulled on her work clothes, threw her hair into a messy bun, and drove over to her acreage with Shane to prepare for the rentals for the weekend. Holly left Chance and Dillon at home with Deacon to shovel the kennels and dog runs after getting nearly eight inches of fresh white powder. April in Yellowstone still meant snow, but instead of the crowds of summer, you often had attractions at the park to yourself. Holly's Airbnb business began to pick up from the winter because April's lesser crowds meant a better chance for rare wildlife sightings as bears were coming out of hibernation. The town and the park weren't busting at the seams with people alighting from tour buses; instead, it was retired folks and naturalists who came to enjoy the park in a simpler way.

Shane sat next to her quietly in the van, giving her one-word answers to every question she asked. Unlocking the door to the cabin, she pulled out the cleaning supplies to get started.

"Will you go take some dry firewood to Elk Ridge?"

Holly suggested to Shane. When he got back, Holly pulled out a chair in her old dinette and asked, "Can we talk?"

He sat down and waited, staring down at his hands, unable to meet her eyes.

"I thought you might have overheard us talking about your future last night." His jaw tightened, but he said nothing. She reached out and steadied his knee that was jerking up and down anxiously. "Hey. You're okay. You're safe here."

"Am I?" he asked. His wild eyes were huge in his face as he finally swung them up to meet her gaze. Unable to contain his energy, he popped up and began to pace like a caged animal.

Holly started to explain, "We haven't exactly approached this living arrangement the right way… the legal way… and there can be ramifications for all of us. So, in order to keep you with us, we need to go through the appropriate channels. That will require us to file a police report and get child protective services involved. Courts usually rule to keep families together unless there is a legitimate reason they need to intervene."

He gulped and she saw the flame of fear light up in his eyes. "You mean a judge could send me back there? To them?" His voice trembled.

"I'm always going to give it to you straight, Shane." Holly started in with a calm voice, trying to diffuse his terror. "There is a small chance the judge could order you back to live with your biological family. Judges like to keep families together, or reunite them after the issues that caused the authorities to intervene are corrected with counseling or treatment."

He started to shake and bite his thumbnail.

"Listen," Holly said. "Tomorrow, we are going to go to the police station with you and file an official report. They will call child protective services. Deacon has already talked to his friends in the department, and he has arranged for you to be temporarily placed with us."

"Temporarily?' His voice hardened, fear raising the end of the word an octave.

"Trust me, it's a hoop we have to jump through. Then we can petition the court to terminate your dad's parental rights. You are going to have to submit to a full medical examination and tell the social workers what you've been through. I wish there was another way, but we have to get your abuse on record." She reached out to squeeze his hand. "It's important that you are truthful with everyone, especially the judge. He is appointed to look out for your best interests and make a ruling that protects your safety. In order for him to do that, you are going to have to tell him what has been happening in your home."

"Home?" Shane's sarcasm was so thick you could cut it with a knife. "That hell-hole could never be called a home." She couldn't argue.

"Do you have any questions about the process?"

Shane began to pace again and wring his hands. "I don't want to be a rat. Dad said there is nothing worse than being a rat."

Holly was stunned at the level of Shane's dedication. In the face of saving himself, he still had some sort of perverse sense of loyalty to a man that hurt him.

"Do you know what a dad is supposed to do?"

"What do you mean?"

"A father is supposed to provide for a child. That means financially, mentally, physically, and emotionally. Does your dad do any of those things for you?"

He was silent for a long moment, considering her words. "No," he whispered finally.

"Then he is not a father," she replied, "and you deserve better."

His shoulders caved and he began to cry. Holly moved closer and pulled him into a hug, feeling his thin frame trembling. "I know this is going to be scary for you, but you have to trust us."

Trust. The word made him pull away. He wrapped his arms defensively around his middle.

"Will I have to see him?"

"I'm not sure," Holly said. "But I promise you we'll be there every step of the way."

Wariness hunched his shoulders, and the conversation made him shrink. The progress he had been making during the last several weeks with them disintegrated in the wake of his fear. He was silent and sullen. The reality of what was ahead of him sunk in fully, in a way that even Holly didn't understand.

"Sometimes you have to be brave and stand up for yourself. This is one of those times. Deacon said sometimes you have to feel the fear, let it in, but push past it and do the things that scare you anyway," she recalled.

Shane crossed his ankle on his knee and began to pick at the loose rubber on his sole. "You know, that's really easy for people to say. They don't know what he's like."

He was a study of inconsistencies. A boy one moment, clinging to her in fear of facing his father, and the next, a man-child and survival expert. The contrast was so stark. Sinewy and taut, his body was all hard edges and sharp corners. Holly yearned for him to revert to the typical thirteen-year-old, where the biggest decision made was how to avoid doing the dishes and where food was plentiful at the pull of a refrigerator door.

"You are strong and resourceful. You should be so proud

of your ability to overcome," Holly commended him. "I'm not sure many boys your age would be able to survive camping by themselves out in the woods in the wintertime."

"Anything was better than going home." He frowned. "You do what you have to do," Shane muttered.

"Deacon and I want to give you tools to thrive, not just survive. The only legal way we can do that is to file these reports. Since you're a minor, the only way you can be removed from your father's custody is to charge him with abuse and neglect. I wish it were simpler than that, but this is the road we have to take to become your legal guardians." She reached out to squeeze his shoulder, and he shrugged her fingers off. Not taking it personally, Holly asked, "Do you have any questions?"

"No." He stood, and she watched him walk away with the weight of the world on his thin shoulders, lost in thoughts she wished he would share.

THIRTY-SEVEN

The following morning, she snuggled into the warm knee pits of Deacon. His bulky body heated the sheets and the mattress, leaving delicious patches of warmth she sought out and savored while the last vestiges of sleep trickled away. Morning light streamed in her room as Holly opened her eyes and pulled on a robe. At the window, she watched snowflakes drifting down from the sky. It sure was pretty, but she also groaned at the work it was going to take to clear the driveway yet again. Pushing snow and digging out during Yellowstone's temperamental spring storms was becoming a full-time job. Holly yearned for the warmth of summer to return and to breathe life back into the grounds.

She tiptoed out of the bedroom, her toes chilly on the wood floor, and out to the coffee maker. A few minutes later, she sipped on her coffee. enjoying the calm before the storm. Later that morning, they were going to put the plan in motion to become Shane's official foster parents, and she was hoping it would loosen the knot lodged in her gut from lying to officials.

Shane was a light sleeper, and she knew in a few minutes

his sleepy head would come down to the kitchen looking for her, a habit he began when they first moved to Deacon's house. She eyed the book they were reading together. Shane picked up sight words fast and graduated to *Percy Jackson and the Lightning Thief* in the short time she had been tutoring him. It was sitting on the kitchen table with a bookmark only a third of the way through, waiting for their morning ritual to begin.

But by the time she got to the bottom of her cup, he hadn't made an appearance.

That's weird. He must not be feeling well.

Deciding to check in on him, she padded up the stairs to his bedroom. At the door, she turned the knob slowly and pushed the door open with a creak, looking into the darkened room. Holly was surprised to see his bed was neatly made, but he was not in it. She felt for the light switch and flipped it on, the first spike of panic causing her heart to race. Yanking open the closet, she noticed his backpack was missing, too, as well as the new winter boots she had gotten him last week. Alarmed, she raced back down the stairs and burst through the door in their bedroom.

"Deak!" she called out. "Honey, you have to wake up." She shook his shoulder, and he growled before opening his eyes. "Deak!"

"What?" he mumbled, his voice still thick from sleep.

"He's gone," she blurted.

"What? Who?" His eyes were open, but his brain was having a hard time keeping up with the peppering of words this early and the terror on Holly's face.

"Shane. He ran away," Holly blurted the words, forcing Deacon from his drowsy state and sending him reeling to find his clothing.

"Why?"

"He was scared yesterday when we talked," Holly recounted. "I must have spooked him. If anything happens…" Her voice cracked. "I don't think I'll ever be able to forgive myself."

Deacon pulled her to him. "Hey. We'll find him. Make me a cup of coffee, and we'll get in the truck and go look for him."

"Should I wake up the boys?"

"Probably a good idea. They might know where he'd go."

She nodded, feeling more competent with a plan in place. She scurried to the kitchen to brew another cup of coffee and then went into Chance and Dillon's room to wake them up.

"Guys, wake up. We need you." Chance and Dillon stirred, and their eyes opened.

"What's going on?" Chance asked, clearly annoyed that he was being woken before ten a.m. on a Sunday.

"Shane ran away," Holly admitted. "Get dressed. We need to go find him. Dress warm. It's snowing again."

They started to stir and follow her orders. For the next several hours, they drove aimlessly, searching for him in town and on the roads that led back to his uncle's house. Holly's eyes scanned and scanned the endless drifts of fluffy white snow. Spring snow showers had the uncanny ability to cover the grounds in a full foot of snow in a matter of hours, making everything unidentifiable lumps. You could easily follow footprints and animal tracks when they were freshly made, but in hours, the tracks would disappear, too.

I should have bought him a new hat and gloves.

She thought about his long slender fingers and if frostbite would come to claim them.

Holly eyed the temperature gauge on the dashboard as the morning turned into night. Each tick lower of the temperature ratcheted up her anxiety. He was going to be cold and wet if he hid outdoors. If he took the chance and went back home, then he would be dry, but other terrors would plague him there.

————

Finally admitting defeat when the search became impossible in complete darkness, they had no choice but to file a police report and go home without Shane. Duane promised to keep them in the loop and would be doing a child welfare check at his uncle's home immediately. Holly was shocked at how much her heart hurt. Tears gathered at her lashes and blurred the acres of forest that whipped by.

Where are you, Shane? It's cold outside and wet. You don't have any food or shelter. Please come home.

Holly wondered if he even got the chance to consider their house his home. If he ever felt like he was part of the family. No wonder he sat on the outside watching warily. Endlessly waiting for the other shoe to drop, knowing that eventually this situation would turn out to be temporary, too, and he would be forced back into the woods or worse.

They rode home together in silence. Holly traced her finger on the steamed glass, willing her brain to conjure up some little detail, some little clue about his whereabouts. She looked down at her phone and then up, catching Deak's concerned eyes. He had been silent most of the trip, driving up and down every road within twenty-five miles. Shane was a needle in a haystack, able to disappear into the hilly and mountainous terrain.

"Nothing yet?" he asked, already knowing the answer.

She shook her head and swiped at a tear building up strength at her lash line. "Nope," she said softly. "Nothing."

Twelve degrees.

"Didn't he want to live with us anymore?" Dillon asked tearfully from the backseat. "I thought he was going to be my new brother."

Holly turned toward Dillon to reassure him. "We'll find him. He's just scared right now, and when you're scared, you sometimes do crazy things," Holly answered. She kept glancing down at the phone in her hand, willing it to ring. Checking and rechecking the volume on the ringer to make sure she would hear it. He probably darted into the woods. It was early spring, and he had all the skills necessary to survive. But the idea of him eeking out a wild existence was impossible for Holly to accept. In the short time he had lived with her, Holly had grown to care about him deeply. He needed a family, and Holly wanted to give him one. He was smart and resourceful, able to take care of himself, that much was clear, but Holly knew there was a small part of him that yearned for a mother, a connection, a real family.

Ten degrees.

"Are you guys sure you don't have any idea where he might have gone?" Holly asked the boys. She had drilled them for hours already while they drove, asking questions and getting nowhere. Shane had kept most of his cards close to his chest.

"He didn't say much about where he came from," Chance answered from the back. "I think he was embarrassed."

"His family is dangerous." Holly didn't want to scare Dillon, so she didn't go into more detail. "They hurt him, and he's afraid that if he stands up for himself, there will be repercussions."

"What's repercussions?" Dillon asked.

"Consequences," Chance answered for him, turning back to Holly quickly and shifting forward in his seat to whisper to

Holly. "We have to find him before they do. He showed me some of his scars."

"We can try again in the morning. It's no use in the dark." Deacon turned the truck toward home, and for a moment, Holly thought they might return and find Shane sitting on the front porch waiting for them. The idea of it gave her heart a jubilant burst of hope. A bubble that popped the moment they got to the end of the lane and he was nowhere to be found. She glanced at the temperature gauge one last time.

Seven degrees.

THIRTY-EIGHT

E ight sleepless hours later, she received a call from an unknown number. Holly quickly answered it, desperate for some word.

"Yes?"

"This is Athena Quick from the Department of Human Services. I'm calling you in reference to a child that needs emergency placement. We've been working in conjunction with the Garden Brook PD. Officer Wilson explained the situation and said that you've requested to be called in the event that we located the minor, Shane Winkler."

Relief flooded in.

"Yes!" Holly practically shouted into the phone, afraid to tell the woman they had been out looking for him all night. Worried that a wrong step here would draw attention to the fact they had bent the rules by keeping him at their home for months.

"The nurse is finishing up his physical and mental health exam at the hospital, and then he will be discharged. Can you take him later this morning?"

"Absolutely!" Holly cheered.

"I'll bring him to you after discharge. There was an altercation with his father, where he sustained some significant injuries. Assault charges were filed." The statement crushed Holly's joy.

"I understand," she choked out and ended the call, staring down at the phone in her hand. Holly was grateful he had been found, but the relief was tempered by the sadness of the pain he'd had to endure.

"He's coming home!" she shouted out when she found her voice again. "Guys!" she shouted upstairs. "Shane is coming home."

Deacon and the boys assembled in the kitchen.

"Why aren't you happier about this?" Dillon asked, picking up on Holly's pain.

"He has some injuries," Holly answered. "I don't know more than that, but we have to take good care of him. Spoil him a little and let him know how much we missed him."

The boys wandered away, and Deacon lumbered closer and pulled Holly in for a hug.

"What aren't you saying, sweetheart?" he asked.

"He went back home. Something happened, and they are charging his dad with assault."

"Maybe this will be a good thing," Deacon tried to reason.

"A good thing?" Holly scoffed. "That poor kid didn't need another traumatic event."

"I agree, but now there is documentation in the system. Now we have a much better chance at keeping him with us. He can settle in and begin to heal."

It was a bitter consolation.

"I guess," she muttered as she pulled out ingredients for his favorite cookies, giving Murph, Daisy, and Tink separate spoons to lick. She washed Shane's bedding and added an extra down-filled quilt to his bed. Two hours later, a police cruiser pulled up. Holly threw on her snow boots and ran outside with a whoop, forgetting her coat in the excitement of having Shane home. She couldn't wait to pull him into her arms for a hug.

Shane was standing at the cruiser with his back to her. When he shuffled to turn around, Holly's eyes widened in shock as she got her first glimpse of the black eye and broken blood vessels, the splint on his nose, and the sling that pinned his arm to his body. Holly bit the side of her cheek to stop the assault of emotion she knew would spread across her face. She gently wrapped her arms around him, afraid to squeeze him too tight, and murmured just out of earshot of the social worker, "I'm so happy you're home."

"Careful. He's got a broken collarbone," the social worker warned when he winced in pain from the hug.

"I'm sorry, buddy. Let's get you inside so we can get you settled." Holly walked him up the steps to the front door, her arm gently laced through his. Once inside, the dogs clamored around him. Shane winced as Daisy jumped up with her feet on his chest. Deacon immediately whistled, and Daisy and Tink sat, eyes cast downward.

The social worker handed Holly plastic bags filled with Shane's muddy and bloody clothing. Inside, pills rattled, trapped in their orange medication bottles. "Here's a copy of the report, and I will let you know when we are scheduled for court. The state will assign him an attorney who will be in touch. You will get a monthly stipend to pay for his expenses from the state. All the pertinent information is included here. He's been medicated, so he'll probably sleep for a while." She handed off the papers then disappeared. The sheer transactional quality of the exchange was hard to understand. This was a child. A young life in jeopardy, who was reduced to a stack of official paperwork and court battles.

"Are you hungry?" Holly asked, turning back to Shane sitting on the sofa, desperate to complete a task to make him feel more comfortable. An act of service to burn away the white-hot anger surging through her that welled the second she saw injuries to Shane's face.

"Just mostly tired," he mumbled. "Are those?"

"Peanut butter cookies? Yep, I made your favorite."

His expression flickered as the corners of his mouth turned up.

"Let's get you settled in your bed, and I'll make you a plate."

Holly guided him upstairs, and he sat on the chair, struggling to get his boots off. She knelt down and untied the boots and then pulled them off him. She wanted to ask him what happened, to tell him how glad she was to have him back, but it wasn't the right time. He was exhausted. She pulled back the comforter and the flat sheet, and he groaned in pain as he wriggled around, finally finding a comfortable position on his back. In less than a minute, he closed his eyes and fell fast asleep. All the dogs sensed the need to gather around him. Daisy gingerly climbed up next to his right side, avoiding the sling. She laid down her head, resting on his stomach. Murph took the foot of the bed and curled into Tink.

Even the boys looked shell-shocked as they gathered in the kitchen, and Deacon shared the details of the case Duane had given him. "His dad's been arrested for assault, with other counts of possession of meth and intent to deliver. He was cooking it in a barn on his uncle's property. Shane needs solid placement until a judge decides what's in his best interests."

"A judge could send him back there?" Chance asked with

innocent shock at the system and its obvious failing of children like Shane.

"He could, though it's unlikely. There is evidence of long-term and systemic abuse and neglect. Once a judge sees the report, he'll probably rule for long-term foster care and then, eventually, adoption."

Holly looked over the hospital discharge papers. Horrific key phrases jumped out. "Numerous healed fractures. Burn marks and cuts in various stages of healing." Her eyes welled up as she read each page and then handed them over to Deacon, who was as astounded as she was.

She gathered a plate of warm cookies and a glass of milk on a tray. When she opened the door to his bedroom, his eyes were closed. She put the tray on the table next to his bed and smoothed the hair away from his face. His right eye was an angry black turning into purple and almost swollen shut. A muffled whimper escaped his lips when she touched him. Behind his eyelids, his eyes darted back and forth. He shifted and rocked on the mattress, having a bad dream.

She bent down and whispered into his ear, "Shh, you are safe here. No one can hurt you now." Then she pulled up a chair and sat down next to the bed, keeping both her eyes on him, afraid if she turned away for even a moment he would disappear.

THIRTY-NINE

The bruises morphed from black to purple to green and then disappeared completely. The orthopedic surgeon in Bozeman decided that surgery wasn't needed to correct the break in his collarbone and sent him home to continue to wear the sling.

"You're lucky you have that sling," Dillion teased, clueless as Holly gasped. "What? Now he doesn't have to help haul firewood to the cabins anymore."

Shane laughed it off. "Dilly's right." He waved his hand in the air. "This thing will get me out of everything. All it takes is suffering through the most excruciating pain of your life to earn that privilege. Lucky me."

Dillon's eyes widened, two brown pools of worry. "I didn't mean it."

"I know, Dilly. It's okay," Shane said, trying to smooth the hurt that crisscrossed Dillon's face.

"Yeah, Dilly, you couldn't handle it," Chance weighed in, pushing Dillon to the side playfully. Then he tried to offer a silver lining to Shane, "Chicks dig scars, you know."

"Then this guy will be popular with the ladies." Shane

tried to laugh it off, but there was a twinge of pain that was lodged deep in his eyes.

A week later, Holly and Deacon reported to court with Shane for their hearing. After reading the lengthy reports that were part of his file and seeing his father was facing potentially years of jail time, the judge ruled that Shane would remain with Holly and Deacon in long-term foster care. There was a noticeable shift in his demeanor after the gavel banged. A lighter Shane walked out of the courtroom that day.

Holly pulled him in for a side hug. "You know what that means, don't you? You get to stay with us and have someone who cares about your grades, a couple brothers to boss around, but you'll also be promoted to the dreaded middle child position."

He grinned a real grin, and it lit up the darkened corners of his face. "Then my wish came true."

"What wish?" Holly asked.

"It's my birthday today, and my only wish was that the judge would let me live with you."

"It's your birthday?" Holly croaked out. "Why didn't you tell us? How could you keep that a secret from me?"

"Bad move," Dillon chimed in. "Mom lives for making us birthday cakes."

"Really?" Shane asked. "I've never had one of those."

"Never had a birthday cake?' Dillon couldn't imagine it.

"Never," he confirmed.

"Well, we're correcting that right now, mister. Get in the car." She barked orders at the boys. "We need to go to the general store, pronto." She turned to Shane, who was riding in the middle as Deacon started the truck. "At our house on your birthday, you get to pick your favorite meal for dinner."

Shane pondered his choices with a grin for the longest

time before settling on one. "Spaghetti and meatballs?" he asked shyly.

"You got it." Holly reached over and squeezed his knee as he jerked away reflexively. He was always so skittish, startled by noises and touch.

Someday, I hope I get to see Shane settle in. To let go of his apprehension and fear. To be able to touch him and not have him recoil.

Deacon pulled the truck into an empty space in front of the general store. Seeing his truck parked there, Ruth hurried out the front door with a big smile. Dressed in a simple dress, faded apron, and broken-in boots, her white hair was gathered on top of her hair in a bun. She pulled Holly in for a quick hug and beamed up at Deacon, who picked her up off the ground to hug her as she protested.

"Ruth, you have to come to dinner tonight. We have something huge to celebrate."

"You do?" she asked, her eyes crinkled at the corners and a soft smile painted her face.

"Yes, Mama," Deacon chimed in. "Looks like we get to keep this knucklehead around." He pulled Shane to his chest and ruffled his hair.

"*And* it's Shane's birthday!" Holly piped up as Shane glanced awkwardly down, the attention making him shyer and desperate to avoid eye contact.

"Well now, it's a tradition that the birthday boy gets to pick out anything he wants from the candy case."

At the prospect of a sugar high, Shane's head popped up. He smiled ear to ear and pointed at the cherry balls.

"Great choice," Holly said, nodding in approval.

Ruth opened a kraft paper bag and then pulled the silver scoop from where it rested by the scale. She scooped three huge scoops of the red candy into the bag and sealed it up.

"Happy Birthday." Ruth smiled at Shane as she handed him the bag. Shane had a secret smile of his own as he walked them over to Holly and handed the unopened package to her. Confused for a moment, Holly was caught off guard. She opened it and tried to hand the bag back to Shane, thinking he was struggling to open it one-handed, but he refused to take it.

"I want you to have them. I know you love these things, and I got the only thing I ever wanted for my birthday. I get to stay with you."

Holly's heart melted. Shane's sweetness hadn't been killed by the brutal conditions he grew up in. He was a dandelion blooming in concrete. Surviving against all odds.

"I couldn't," Holly said. "Pick something else out. It's *your* birthday."

Ruth walked forward, gingerly cradling a massive peanut butter cup, weighing in at 2 pounds. Shane's eyes widened at the sheer sight of it.

"Wow. Is that for real?" he exclaimed. "I've never seen one so big!"

She handed it to Shane. "It's almost as big as your heart for giving those cherry balls away. Just promise me you won't eat it all in one sitting."

Glee spread across Shane's features as he looked down at the gift with awe.

Holly laughed and put flour, butter, sugar, and cocoa into her basket. A glass jar of buttermilk and some powdered sugar were added next. When it got too heavy, Deacon took it out of her hands as they wandered down the rest of the aisles, adding pasta and sauce, a loaf of bread, and some garlic. At the meat counter, she added bison sausage and hamburger. A huge yellow onion, a container of cherry tomatoes, and two heads of garlic rounded out the shopping.

———

Two hours later, she rolled meatballs while Shane watched in the kitchen. Forever a teacher, she instructed him how to pinch the ground meat gently to incorporate the ingredients, careful not to over mix the meat. Unable to roll them himself, he sat and listened to the cooking lesson while Holly rolled the mixture into balls on a plate. Happy to have a way to help, he turned the knob and watched as the beef stock came to a boil on the stove, then used a spoon left-handed to drop them in a simmering pool of oregano-infused beef broth.

"You don't have to help me, you know. Dilly is right. You have a work pass right there on your arm. There isn't a teenager alive who wouldn't milk that situation."

"I *want* to help." He turned the meatballs with the spoon so all sides cooked evenly.

After a few minutes, she asked him to fish them out and showed him how to caramelize them in a cast iron pan, searing hot with a drizzle of olive oil.

"Do you like to cook?" she asked him as she turned the balls with the slotted spoon.

"This is the first time I've ever tried it," he admitted.

"I'm sorry." Holly tried to backtrack. "I didn't mean…"

"It's okay. How would you know that?" He stood at her side, his sling confining his arm to his stomach. "It was cereal and PB &J's if we were lucky. Maybe some ramen."

"Have you thought about what you want to be when you're done with high school?"

"Hmm? I don't know. Not really. When you grow up like I did, there isn't a lot of talk about the future or your hopes and dreams."

"Well, that makes me sad," Holly continued. "When you

take away a person's hopes and dreams, you take away their will to live."

He considered it as Holly added a can of tomatoes, garlic, and basil to the pan. "You can do anything, be anything, you just have to want to work for it. What do you like to do?" she asked.

"I like doing this," he answered as he stirred the sauce to keep it from scorching. "Food. I mean, I like being around food."

"You could be a chef, maybe go to culinary school?" Holly offered.

"Maybe," he mumbled, afraid to commit to something bigger than the moment they were sharing in the kitchen.

"You have plenty of time to decide. The key is to find something you enjoy doing so it doesn't feel like work at all. I loved being a teacher."

"So, why did you stop?"

"I adored the teaching, but I hated the other stuff. Fighting with the board and the phone calls from parents. Last year, I got the chance to try something new." She thought about it for a second. "Did you know that the average person changes jobs twelve times in their lifetime?"

"No."

"You have plenty of time to figure it out. The best thing you can do is be open to new experiences. To approach life as wide open as possible."

He listened, but she felt his walls rising. He stirred in silence.

"It's one of the bravest things you can do," she continued. "I know it's hard to see a future right now, where you are relaxed and happy and doing something you love, but you'll get there."

"I hope you're right." Shane's voice was hushed, and with

wisdom greater than his now fourteen years, he continued, ."But today, I'm happy. This is good enough for now."

Holly gently squeezed his good shoulder. He was an old soul, his truths hard-earned, but he was right. This *was* enough for now, and to look too far ahead would only waste her energy and tie her stomach up in knots. She had to admire the lessons of the universe. She thought she was the one teaching Shane, but she was starting to see that Shane had just as much to teach her.

FORTY

It takes a long time for a person who is used to living in chaos and drama to slow their brain down. Over the next few weeks, Shane had more good days than bad. He was relaxed and smiling more. The nightmares had slowed, and by the end of May, he was able to take the sling off, his arm skinny and atrophied from the lack of use. Holly infused their menu with his favorite foods and loaded seconds on his plate, happy to watch Shane gobble her food down. It was one of the easiest ways Holly could show Shane she loved him.

Still following the advice of Tim, she religiously ransacked all the boy's rooms monthly when they were at school. One morning, finding nothing but a bowl of rotten milk that was quickly becoming a biohazard, she was relieved to verify Chance's sobriety.

She found a more troubling discovery in Shane's closet. Under a pile of dirty clothes, she found cans of soup and bags of chips that had gone missing and unnoticed from the pantry. Crouched on her knees, she swept aside the quilt on his bed to find concealed boxes of macaroni and cheese and cereal. After doing some research and speaking to his therapist, she discovered this was a normal reaction to his fear of going hungry. That having a backup stash of food that he could see and touch would calm the fear in his heart. Rather than confronting and embarrassing him, she put together a basket of his favorite snacks and placed it on his dresser with a big bow. Holly added additional money to his lunch account so he could have seconds. She made dessert for every meal and cooked up a storm, leaving ample leftovers that he warmed up in the microwave every day after school.

The physical change in him was gradual but significant. His cheeks filled out, and he started to grow like a weed, requiring new pants and jeans every three months. He was already eye to eye with Chance, and she had a feeling he would tower over her within the next year.

She was amazed at how fast he learned. How quickly he picked up new vocabulary words and would then use them in sentences to show off. She introduced him to the world of Harry Potter. When she first put the massive tome in his hands, all eight hundred dogeared pages of *Harry Potter and the Order of the Phoenix*, his eyes were huge.

"This thing weighs a ton! It's going to take me forever."

"When you read all the books, then we can have a watch party. Dillon should have all of them around here some-where," Holly offered. "Don't cheat and watch the movies first. The book is always better!"

"Of course, you would say that." Shane was exasperated as he flipped through the book in his hands. "You're a teacher. You *have* to say the book is better."

"Just think how good you'll feel when you've read the whole thing," Holly cheered. "It will be a huge accomplish-ment." She handed him a shiny metal bookmark. "Use this to mark your place."

"I usually just fold the corner of the page I am on."

Holly inhaled sharply, her mouth agape in horror. "What? No son of mine is going to degrade books. It's sacrilege and goes against everything I stand for."

He shook his head at her, pleased as punch her use of the word son included him. It was a two steps forward three steps back process. Used to feeling like an outsider, he struggled to find his place in their family. Life was a roller-coaster. He would have stretches of good weeks, but then be plunged into fear and depression the closer they got to the custody hearings. There were times when he'd lash out and act out, getting mouthy with a teacher or being belligerent in class. On those days, Deak pulled him closer and helped him navigate his emotions and the guilt he felt at not living up to Holly's standards. He'd be too ashamed of the way he acted to face Holly. Eventually, he would come back to her, and her liberal forgiveness righted the missteps he took.

Every week like clockwork, Holly drove him to a therapist she found in Bozeman that specialized in family therapy and attachment disorder. She would faithfully sit in the waiting room for the fifty minutes of his appointments and then drive him home. Often, he was silent on the drive back, and since she knew firsthand how therapy was such internal work and exhausting, she tried to give him space.

She'd always ask, "Did you learn anything in therapy that you want to share with me today?"

Most times, he would say no and they would ride home in silence, but the closer they got to the final custody hearing, the more open he became.

"Did you know I'm at the age where the judge will take my feelings into consideration?" he mused, only six days from the next hearing. They were required to get a separate attorney for him, a guardian ad litem, to evaluate Shane and to decide what was the best for him moving forward. She would represent Shane in the custody hearing.

"Yep, that's right. A judge can do that," Holly confirmed. "It won't be the only opinion that counts, but your viewpoint will definitely carry some weight in his final decision."

"Who else matters?"

"Well, it's really up to the findings of your attorney. She will help inform the court. I know you have another meeting set up this week. The most important thing is to be open and honest with her. She doesn't have any ulterior motives. She doesn't have anything to gain. She is only there to be an advocate for you."

He sighed a heavy sigh.

"I know this process is difficult and you are exhausted, but it will be over soon," Holly empathized then asked, "What do you want to tell the judge when you get the opportunity?"

"I want to stay with you," he revealed, the words so wistful and filled with longing it broke Holly's heart.

"I want that, too, buddy."

"But what I really want is for you and Deacon to adopt me."

"You do?" Holly was surprised. He was only four years from adulthood, so it never crossed her mind that he would want to be adopted.

"I don't feel like I belong anywhere," he admitted. "I feel like I'm always a visitor floating through life. Almost like one of your Airbnb guests that someday will be asked to leave."

"I had no idea you felt like that." Holly turned toward him as she pulled the car into the parking lot at Ruth's general store and shut off the ignition.

She reached out a hand and squeezed his. Accepting physical touch was always a challenge for Shane, it was a process, but he was warming up to it. "You know what we want?" she asked him. "We want you to stay. We want to help you grow into the kind of man you can be proud of, and above all else, we want you to feel safe and protected and loved."

Tears welled at Shane's lashes, and he sniffed and turned away, embarrassed by the show of emotion.

"We want to be your home."

"I never had one of those." He revealed a sweet flicker of a sad smile. "That sounds pretty perfect."

Almost a week later was the final hearing. In the days leading up to court, he distanced himself and disappeared while still in plain sight. No amount of love or understanding could coax him back. It was almost like he was mentally preparing to be returned to his father. For the first fourteen years of his life, the system had let him down, and he didn't dare believe now, all of a sudden, all the wrongs in his life would suddenly be righted. He didn't let himself hope, because hoping would set him up for even greater pain if the judge ruled against him.

It was painful to watch him struggle and isolate himself. He would disappear into the bathroom with stomach aches and headaches. The tension and the stress manifested as physical pain. She didn't need to tell Shane how important the process was; he inherently knew. Holly stood outside his door at night, listening to his muffled cries, her knocks going unanswered. There was a deep crevasse of pain in Shane that he would not allow anyone to see. Deacon tried to keep him busy, and the dogs rushed to his side, sensing his despair. In their own way, they made him feel safe and loved and part of their pack. Even Dillon and Chance rallied around him, playing video games and joking with him to take his mind off the impending court date.

The morning of the final hearing, Holly's stomach was in knots. Deacon held her hand while they waited for their case to be called on the docket. On a hard wooden bench across from them sat Shane. Dressed in khaki pants and a button-down blue shirt, he looked like he was waiting for a job interview. His legs bounced up and down, expelling nervous energy for a few minutes, then he would bolt upright and pace down the hallways. Holly wanted to chase after him, but also knew he needed space.

"I'm going to go see how our guy is doing. Are you okay here?" Deacon asked, dressed for court in khakis and a button-down as he tugged uncomfortably at the green tie that constricted his strong neck. "I can't wait to get rid of this thing."

On the bench, dressed in a simple black maxi dress and conservative heels, Holly felt the same way. There was so much riding on this one hearing. Today, their lives would irrevocably change, and she had no control over the outcome at all. The decision was entirely in the hands of the judge and the recommendation by the guardian ad litem.

Holly gave the go-ahead and watched as Deacon jogged into step beside Shane, pulling his shoulder in for a side hug. Thankfully, she heard Shane's laugh ring out and her heart relaxed.

A few minutes later, they were called into the courtroom. The Montana state flag and American flag hung behind the elderly judge, perched high.

"The state of Montana versus David Winkler," the bailiff announced, and Holly and Deacon got to their feet along with Shane and his court-appointed attorney and shuffled forward. Holly wrapped her arm protectively around Shane's shoulders when she realized the boy had begun to tremble upon seeing his father.

"It's okay," she whispered to him. "One more hard hour and it's over."

The judge read through the thick manilla folder on his desk. He glanced over at a disheveled Dave Winkler, dressed for the occasion in an orange prison jumpsuit. The result of his arrest for drug trafficking.

"Well, Mr. Winkler, due to your previous incarceration for more than one year, and in light of your current incarceration, reunification is not in the best interest of the child. There's a history of violent behavior and reasonable efforts to rehabilitate you have failed. Therefore, it is this court's ruling that your parental rights have been terminated."

He turned to Holly and Deacon. "I understand the minor is in the temporary custody of foster parents Holly Simon and Deacon Cartwright?"

"Yes, Your Honor," Holly answered.

"Are you able to provide permanent placement for the child?"

"Actually, your honor, we would like to adopt Shane," Deacon said. "He is our son, and he belongs with us."

The judge cracked a smile. "I think that would be a magnificent idea." He banged the gavel. "The child will need to remain in your custody while the home study is conducted and you attend adoption classes. It's quite a lengthy process from what I've gathered, but pays incredible dividends." With a small smile and final bang of the gavel, he declared, "This case is remanded to family court."

Shane watched the officer place his father in handcuffs and take him away. The older man didn't even stop to acknowledge him, didn't even spare a glance in his direction.

When he was gone, Shane dropped to the bench. Holly and Deacon flanked him.

"What are you feeling?" Deacon asked, eager to comfort Shane.

"That was really tough," Holly empathized. "It's okay if you don't have the words to talk about it yet." She reached out to squeeze his hand, and he squeezed it back.

"I've been thinking and dreaming and having nightmares about this moment forever. I can't believe it's finally over." Shane sighed in relief as he sagged back onto the bench. "I never have to see that man again."

"That's right," Deacon confirmed.

"Did you mean it?" Shane asked Deacon, his tone hopeful. "Do you want to be my dad?"

"Damn straight," Deacon said softly with a smirk. "I'd be proud to call you my son any day of the week. We want you to be part of our family. What do you say to that?"

He burst into tears, and Holly was struck again by how mature he seemed one second and how young he seemed the next. They embraced him, holding him while he cried for a few moments.

"Is that a yes?" Deacon asked and then playfully pushed his shoulder.

"Hell yeah," Shane said with a grin.

FORTY-ONE

There was only one small legal hurdle Holly and Deacon wanted to clear in order to adopt Shane. They wanted him to feel secure in his position as their son, and to solidify it, they planned a fall wedding that would have them married before the final adoption hearing. Between the classes they needed to complete and the hearings in family court, they decided to tie the knot on Deacon's acreage under an old oak tree that would out-survive them all.

The days passed in a blur of activity, another summer under their belts. More forced family hikes in Yellowstone that Holly adored—being out in the fresh air, the sunshine on her shoulders, and a picnic basket full of food with the people she loved most in the world. Her Airbnb business flourished, repeat bookings were up, and she was building a real financial future for her family. The rescue was thriving, and between the two businesses and Deak's veterinary practice, the days sped by.

Stacey flew out in July, and in a weekend filled with cake tastings and bridesmaid dress fittings, helped Holly plan her backyard wedding for late September. Holly was so proud to show her friend the new life she'd created. They stayed in one of her cabins, and it was like an old-fashioned sleepover with her best friend. They stayed up late soaking in the hot tub under a sky filled with stars while sipping champagne. A vast contrast from the nights she spent decompressing on Stacey's back deck in New Hope.

Time rushed forward again, and on the morning of her wedding, the sunrise painted the sky a dusky peach and lavender. Each second that ticked by brightened the sky even more, giving way to a beautiful clear day where the views to the mountains from Holly's home were spectacular. Stacey had gotten in a few days earlier, and they spent the time checking off last-minute wedding details and having long talks while sharing bottles of wine. Holly's stomach ached from laughing with her best friend again, the best reason for pain in the whole world.

Trying to adhere to Deacon's traditional desire not to see the bride before the wedding, Holly and Stacey spent one last night at her cabin.

"It's your wedding day," Stacey sang out with a shoulder shimmy as she pushed open the door with her forearm, bringing in two steaming mugs of coffee. "Time to wake up, sleeping beauty."

Holly opened her eyes and stretched with a drowsy smile, sitting up to eagerly accept the cup. "Mmm. Deacon has my heart, but this coffee has my soul." After a few long sips, the caffeine hit her bloodstream and bubbled her to life.

"I'm so happy for you both," Stacey gushed, sitting on the edge of her bed.

Holly was giddy, excited, and anxious to see Deacon, knowing one of the best days of her life was about to unfold.

Stacey crossed the room to where her suitcase lay sprawled open, extracting something from it. "As your matron of honor, I would be remiss in my duties if I let you walk down the aisle without something borrowed. I wore this on my wedding day, so it's got a good track record." She held up a box to Holly and opened it, revealing a string of pearls nestled inside a bed of red velvet.

"It's so pretty." Holly reached out to touch it as Stacey popped the box shut, chuckling when it playfully snapped shut on her fingers.

"Julia Roberts has nothing on you." Stacey freed her fingers, then pulled her friend in for a side hug. "Soak it up, honey. This is the happily ever after you have always deserved."

Tears welled up at Holly's lashes. "You know what? You're right. I didn't think I believed in those anymore, and then Deak showed up and made me want to." She smiled as a tear dropped onto her hand. "And he's so good with the boys. Chance and Dillon adore him, but he's made the biggest impact on Shane."

"You know when you first told me you wanted to be a foster parent, I thought it was a terrible idea."

"What?" Holly was shocked. "You never told me that."

"I was afraid you were falling back into old habits again, giving away everything to everyone else. I really thought you needed to focus on yourself for a change and make yourself happy."

"I can see why you'd say that," Holly agreed. "I definitely had a history of giving everything away."

"But now that I can see you have a partner to shoulder the burden with, I'm not afraid for you anymore. Deacon will make sure you don't overdo it. And the boys, what a gift you are giving them! They get to see their mother happy and finally being loved well. I know you think Mick did some damage, and of course he did, but now they get to see the real deal. Up close and personal. It is going to change who they become and the type of relationships they go on to have. In a sense, you are all getting a second chance."

Holly studied her beautiful friend as the morning light washed across her features. This woman was always in her corner, always advocating for her best interests. She reached out to squeeze Stacey's forearm. "Thank you for always being my gauge for normality."

Coffee spit out of Stacey's nose as she shook with laughter. "Girl, you have to warn me when you're about to say something that absurd."

"It's true," Holly said. "You've always been steady. I finally learned I can add healthy grounded people to my life, and it increases my energy, makes me feel happier and more in control. And limiting the ones who suck me dry is an act of self-love. It took me a long time to learn this lesson, but I got it now."

"Yes, you do, and I am so proud of you." She glanced at her watch and popped up onto her feet. "Now you have *got* to get up and put on a button-down shirt, because we need to get over to the salon for hair and makeup. I booked you a session with a glam squad."

"A glam squad? Isn't that a little over the top?" Holly asked.

"Hey, if you can't go all out on your wedding day, then when can you?"

Holly laughed and stood with a stretch. Hanging from a hanger on the back of her closet door was her dress. It featured a fitted empire bodice with an A-line skirt that was wrapped in yards of ivory lace. In an effort to fit into it, she had eaten small, birdlike meals and skipped the wine for the month leading up to the wedding.

"I can't wait for Deacon to see you walk down the aisle," Stacey raved. "I hope he knows what a lucky man he is."

"He does. I try to remind him every day," Holly joked as she walked to the window and opened the curtains, revealing the view that she adored. It was what sold her on the property to begin with. Just four hundred and eighty-eight days had passed since making the single best decision in her entire life. Moving to Montana had shot her life off onto a trajectory she never saw coming. A little over a year ago, she was a scared mother starting over, and she was terrified. Today, she was starting over again, this time giving her children the one thing that had been elusive. Stability. A strong foundation with a man who would become the father figure they deserved. A man who would willingly step into the sloppy void that Mick left and help heal them all.

Her fingers caressed the lace on the most beautiful dress she had ever worn. It was an incredible find at a consignment shop in Bozeman, but even second-hand, it was more than she'd ever spent on a single garment of clothing in her life-time. The sweet sales girl wouldn't take no for an answer when Holly gasped as she pulled it out and then hung the hanger on the rack so she could check it for holes and stains.

"Trust me, you need to see it on. The hanger doesn't do it justice. Are you looking for a special occasion?"

"Yes," she answered. "A wedding." She felt foolish that she still felt such a thrill, getting married in her forties, but got over it quickly when egged on by the blonde clerk.

"Well, now you gotta try it on, honey." Before Holly could protest again, she strode over, pulled it off the rack, and dragged Holly by the hand back to the changing room. She swept the cream-colored curtain to the side. "Do you need some help getting into it?" she offered.

"I think I can manage."

"Now, I have one request."

"What is that?" Holly asked the excited girl.

"I must see it on you." She waved a finger at Holly. "Don't you dare put it back on the rack and sneak out of here without letting me see you in it." Holly laughed, busted for being so transparent by the perceptive clothier. After she caught a glimpse of the price on the tag and estimated it would take a week's worth of guests at the Airbnb to pay for it, she preemptively crossed it off her possibilities list, but decided to try it on for fun.

Not exactly wearing the right bra for this, she thought as she caught a glimpse of the old sports bra she was currently rocking.

It's like dress-up, she convinced herself as she pulled the lace-up and over her head and arranged it to settle off her shoulders. The lace dropped like a curtain to the floor. She reached behind and contorted her body in an effort to pull the zipper up. Feeling accomplished as it slid up her backbone, fitting like a glove, she finally spun around to see herself in the mirror.

Her eyes widened and her breath hitched in her chest. Her reflection was a total transformation. The delicate boning under the ribs pushed up her breasts and created the illusion of creamy cleavage. She turned from side to side, enamored with her mirror image. Surely, this room was outfitted with those funhouse mirrors, giving her the optical illusion of a svelte and elongated frame. She couldn't pull her eyes away.

"Are you doing okay in there?" The salesgirl's voice jolted into her reverie through the curtain.

"Yes."

"Come on out and let me have a look at you."

She took a deep breath and yanked open the curtain.

"Oh my, you're a revelation," she gushed. Her wide-open

smile sincere as could be, the clerk's hands wistfully clasped at her chest. "This is it. You have to get it. This is *your* dress." She quickly knelt down and tugged on the hem. "I can tailor this for you. Will you wear heels or flats?"

"I'm not... I..." Holly stammered. "I need to think about it."

"What is there to think about? Life is short. Wear the dress!"

"It's just that it's a little more than I planned on spending. Actually, a lot more," Holly confided.

"Well, if *that* is your only objection, I can work with that." She looked up into the air while she mentally crunched numbers and calculated. "How about I rent it to you? The fee will be one-fifth of the purchase price."

"You would do that?"

She looked around the store and then leaned in, her voice dropping to a low whisper. "You look like the kind of girl I can trust. I fancy myself a kind of couture matchmaker, and that dress is your fashionista soulmate."

Holly grabbed her arms excitedly and began to jump up and down. A pile of organza and lace instantly reduced her to a silly sorority girl. But it was *the* dress. "Yes!" she shouted out, giddy and excited. "Yes, yes, yes!"

She wanted *that moment*. The moment where the music swells, and the air is scented with peonies and roses and at the end of a long aisle, where the man she loved waited, ready to promise to love her for the rest of her life. She wanted to take his breath away. Holly didn't get it the first time around and had tried to talk herself out of wanting it. That it wasn't necessary and a frivolous desire, but that was a lie. She treasured that moment more than anything, and now she was finally going to get it.

"Hey, Mama," Chance said as he walked in, pulling her

focus back to the schedule at hand. "Deacon wanted me to come by and see if you need anything?"

"Come here." She opened her arms and he walked into them. She squeezed her eyes shut, drinking him in, the scent of Irish Spring and fresh grass. "I love you, you know." Her voice broke.

"Stacey! She's crying already! You were supposed to make sure she didn't do that!" He pulled back and grinned at her.

"That's not fair! You gave me an impossible task. You know what a sentimental goo ball your mother is."

Chance laughed in agreement. "At least we tried."

"Wait a minute," Holly exclaimed. "Are you taller than me?" She was seeing it for the first time. Chance was filling out and getting stronger, and now he towered over her by a solid inch. "You are! God, when did that happen?"

"You see me every day." He laughed exasperated as she brushed her thumb softly across his chin dimple. Now there was a roughness surrounding it. He had grown sandpapery stubble. The realization whisked fresh tears to her eyes. "Come here, you sentimental sap." Chance grinned as he pulled her tighter to him. "You deserve a man like Deacon. You won't have to do everything yourself or fight your way through life anymore. I know Dad wasn't the best husband." His voice trailed off as it hurt him to make this admission out loud.

"You don't have to say this," Holly whispered.

"Yes, I do." Chance pulled back to look into her eyes and continued. "I can see that Deacon makes you happy, and you deserve to be happy."

"He does."

"I just can't bring myself to call him Dad," Chance said. "It doesn't feel right."

"Oh, honey, Deak doesn't expect you to."

"But he has done more for me than anyone ever has. I want you to know that I see that."

Holly fanned her tear-stained face with her hands. "Dude, you are killing me with these revelations. My mama heart can't take all these feelings!"

"Wipe your tears, woman!" Chance exclaimed. "I've been given strict orders to be your personal chauffeur today and to get you to wherever you need to go, but most importantly, at four o'clock, you have to be back here walking down that aisle or Deak will have my ass."

With one more sweet smile, she caressed his rough cheek and gathered her things and Stacey for the drive to the salon.

FORTY-TWO

"And, here we are!" The sweet stylist swiveled the chair to face the mirror, and Holly gasped. Her hair cascaded down her shoulders in soft, shiny waves. The stylist continued to twist her curls into perfect position as Holly stared at her reflection.

"It's beautiful," she said. "Thank you." She glanced over at Stacey, who gave her a wink in the mirror and was seated in the chair next to her while another stylist twisted her blonde locks into an elaborate French twist.

Holly was whisked to another small room lit by a million soft warm white lights.

"Tell me what you're looking for."

"I don't usually wear very much makeup," Holly admitted. "Maybe something natural with just a little extra oomph since it's my wedding day?"

The makeup artist nodded and then swirled her away, advising Holly to shut her eyes. Holly felt short bursts of air and then a fine, cool mist coat her cheeks and forehead.

"I'm airbrushing your foundation. This is a buildable

coverage for one of the most important days of your life. You know the photographs are around forever."

Holly smiled and felt a little tug of regret. She wanted to hire a professional, but it seemed silly for a second-time bride who was over forty to splurge on such an extravagance, so she nixed the idea.

An hour later, the artist swiveled the chair to the mirror, and Holly gasped at her reflection again. The woman in the mirror was still her, but her eyes appeared larger, her skin smoother. It was like seeing herself filtered but in real life.

"Wow," she whispered.

"Wow is right," Stacey said, edging closer. "You look incredible."

"I'm going to have to make sure Deak takes a good long look, because it's all downhill from here." Holly laughed with self-deprecation and drained the last of the mimosa in her flute.

"All she did was make sure the outside matched the beauty of the inside," Stacey stated sweetly.

Holly fanned her face and tipped her chin up to keep the tears at her lash line from falling. "No more sappy. I can't take it. You guys are killing me today."

Stacey laughed. "Alright, freak, let's get some food in you and head back to the ranch."

————

Five hours later, as the sun sank lower on the horizon and cast longer shadows on the enormous trees flanking Deacon's property, she was dressed in her gown and ready. She pulled the curtain back from the window, and a flash of movement caught her eye. A photographer with real equipment was snapping photos of her looking out onto the site they had chosen for their ceremony.

She stepped back when he opened the door and walked inside. "I'm Sam, your photographer. Congratulations! Deacon hired me to make sure you don't miss a moment. This day will be such a blur, and he wanted to make sure you had beautiful photography to remember every little detail."

A wide smile spread across her face.

"Does Deak know you or what?' Chance said from the doorway. She whirled around, her skirt swaying and swishing as the photographer snapped away. Dillon popped up behind him as they walked into the room with Shane following behind.

"Look at all my guys." Her eyes drank them in, wearing identical charcoal tuxedos with a small spray of stephanotis pinned to their lapels. Their hair was clean-cut and shaved close around the head with longer waves on the top. Still, Dillon clamored to copy his older brother. "Come here." She opened her arms wide, and Dillon and Chance came closer for a hug while Shane hesitated.

"You look beautiful, Mama." Chance embraced her gently. "I'm afraid to hug you too tight. I don't want to muss you up."

"Shane, you get over here right now," she playfully insisted, and he finally took steps toward her.

"You look so dashing." She pulled him in for a hug then pulled back to caress his cheek. "So handsome."

"Can you help me put these on?" he asked, handing her the cuff links. When Holly fastened them to his cuffs, he seemed to relax.

She reached out a hand toward Dillon's, bent down face to face with him, and kissed him on the nose. Then she pulled back as the photographer snapped and snapped, recording the most precious of memories. "Come closer to me, guys. Squeeze in." When her arms were full of wool and testosterone, she bit her lip to stop the tears from ruining her makeup. "I am such a lucky woman. I love you all so much."

"We love you, too," they chorused together. She offered her hands to them, and they formed a tight little circle. "It's been the three of us for a while, and then we got to add Shane, and today we are going to open up and add one more set of hands."

"You're such a mush ball," Chance said with a grin.

"Guilty as charged." Holly chuckled. "I can't help it. Today, I have so much love for all of you, my heart is bursting. I never thought I would get to feel like this."

"We're happy for you and Deacon," Chance said, speaking for them all as Dillon and Shane nodded.

"He's a good man, and he is going to be good for all of us," Holly added. "Group hug," she sang out and gathered them to her, squeezing them close.

"Are you ready to walk me down the aisle?" she asked them and they nodded. With a nervous smile, Shane opened the door and began the procession.

"Don't forget this," Stacey said, her lavender dress swishing as she walked to where a bouquet of wildflowers rested in a glass. She pulled out a towel and dried the ends before placing it in Holly's hands.

"Soak it up. You deserve this." Stacey gave her a quick hug and then opened the door before disappearing down the aisle where, just faintly, Holly could hear music playing.

Standing at the door, waiting for her turn to begin the procession down the aisle, she was lost in a rush of emotion. She wished her dad could have been at her arm, but when she glanced over at Chance, standing so tall and so strong, she felt peace fill her heart. Everything was exactly how it should be. Even though her dad wasn't physically there, she knew he would be proud of the new life she'd fought to create. He would be impressed by the mother she had become. He would have been her strongest supporter. She felt him close, and her heart squeezed, wondering if he was on a cloud somewhere with her mother looking down at them.

I am happy, Dad. I finally have a man like you in my life. I hope you are proud of me.

Dillon opened the door and then rushed back to her side.

"You guys are so handsome," she gushed. "Let's remember this moment forever. This one, right here, right now."

She turned and looked back over her shoulder and saw the lace draped behind her, glad that she decided against a veil. She wasn't twenty anymore, and all it would do was get in the way of the hugs she wanted to give. Instead, the stylist had pinned a gardenia near the comb over her ear. She felt beautiful, like she was floating on air. The music swelled, and she exhaled.

"Okay. Let's do this." She smiled at her two boys who had become young men as they stepped through the door and out into the soft golden light. On either side of the makeshift aisle, her new friends and Deacon's sat in simple white folding chairs. It was a small, intimate gathering of fewer than thirty people. As they walked down a path strewn with pastel rose petals that scattered in the light breeze, heads turned, necks craning to get a glimpse of her. Her heart swelled as her gaze focused on each face. Cal and his family, Stacey's family, Deacon's friends, and in the very front, Ruth leaned in with her phone, recording every precious second of her son's face. Deacon stood tall with his hands clasped together in front of him, looking so handsome in his dark grey suit. His eyes were glued to hers. She tipped her head to the side with a sweet smile turning up the corners of her mouth. She'd never seen him dressed in formal wear, and he was so handsome he took her breath away. She saw him wipe away a tear quickly, and Holly felt happiness bloom in her center like a rush of butterfly wings. Deacon exhaled, laughing at himself as he wiped more tears away the closer she got to him.

Halfway down the aisle, Chance stopped and passed her hand to Shane. Chance and Dillon solemnly walked down the remainder of the aisle, high-fiving Deacon as they passed him and found their places in line behind him.

She could feel Shane trembling with all the eyes on him. "Walk me the rest of the way, handsome."

He smiled and took steps toward Deacon. She shuddered, remembering how thin and frightened Shane was when they met. It had taken a long time to break down his walls, but they had done it. Deacon, Holly, Chance, and Dillon had shown him what it was like to have a family. To be part of something bigger than yourself, where everyone contributed and was accepted and loved. It healed him. Holly knew the scars remained, and as much as she wished she could take them away, it was part of his story. It was where he had come from, and to eliminate that would also eliminate all the work he had done. It would discount his resilience and his tenacity. The Shane walking beside her now was almost a man. A man with a future and hopes and dreams. Nervous, his smile was tight and his cheeks were reddening. He never liked the spot-light. She gave him her biggest grin, and they walked closer, landing in front of a very nervous Deacon.

Shane turned to hug her and whispered, "You look beauti-ful, *Mom*." The words were rough as his voice caught in his throat. She choked up and squeezed him tighter.

"That's the first time you've ever called me that," she

whispered back and then brought her hand to his cheek, leaning in so only he could hear her.

"I love you, *son*," she whispered, and her eyes crinkled as she took his trembling hand. Tears broke free, cascading down both of their faces. Looking down, he completed his task and walked her slowly and carefully, with such respect and reverence, to where Deacon stood. He placed her hand in Deacon's larger one and then he fell in line behind Dillon as the music softly ended.

The sun set deeper, casting the sky into a showy display of pastel waves—pinks and purples, soft baby blues, and the puffiest, most beautiful clouds. The setting sun transformed every surface it touched with its amber light. Tracing the lines and planes of Deacon's hair and body. Outlining this massive man with glowing light. Filtering through the lace of her floor-length skirt. It was a magical fairytale moment. Gathered under a cove of trees, tea lights dangled from thick branches. Flower garlands draped down, and Holly stood in front of Deacon ensconced under this lush canopy.

She looked up at this man she adored. A tear trickled down his cheek, and she reached up to brush it off with her thumb.

He laughed at himself and grabbed her hand, kissing the back of it. She leaned into him as he wrapped his arms around her, touching her forehead to his, and heard him whisper, "You're so beautiful. I'm the luckiest man alive." Then he tipped his head and kissed her as their friends laughed.

"Whoa there, Nelly!" the minister said. "We haven't gotten to that part yet."

Holly and Deacon laughed as the rest of the world fell away. She heard every word the pastor said, but it was surreal. A blissful event was unfolding around her, and all she could focus on was the love that shined from Deacon's eyes.

They enveloped her in warmth and safety she had craved her whole life. Her gaze drifted behind him, seeing Chance, Dillon, and Shane standing in line so strong and proud in their tuxedos, and her heart burst.

Shane took a tentative step forward, holding a book in his shaking hands. Taking his place next to the minister, in front of the congregation, he looked into Holly's confused eyes with a quick nervous smile before opening the bible.

What's happening? This wasn't part of the plan we walked through last night at the rehearsal.

Deacon gave him a nod of encouragement, and in a strong, unwavering voice, Shane began to read. Holly's heart caught in her throat, and fresh tears coursed down her face as she concentrated on the words that were all the more poignant coming from Shane. It was a perfect full-circle moment and joy coursed through her as goosebumps broke out down her arms.

"Love is patient, love is kind. It does not envy, it does not boast, it is not proud. It does not dishonor others, it is not self-seeking, it is not easily angered, it keeps no record of wrongs. Love does not delight in evil but rejoices with the truth. It always protects, always trusts, always hopes, always perseveres. Love never fails."

He closed the book and claimed his place behind Dillon with a proud smile.

When the sun lowered, it was time to say their vows. Stacey reached over to hand Holly her notecards and a tissue.

"Deacon. Loving you has changed my life. I never knew this kind of love existed. When we arrived here in Montana, I was scared but determined not to show it. Starting completely over sounded like a great idea, but the nuts and bolts of it were so overwhelming. So, I have to thank Ruth for looking out for me and my boys, and for offering up her only child as a guardian angel for us. From nearly the very first day we moved here, you have strived to make my life better. Showing up with sleeping bags, saving our dog, fixing leaks, you always look for ways to make me and the boys happy. I am so grateful that you have so much love in your heart for not only me, but for all of my sons, Chance, Dillon, *and* Shane." She choked up and had to take a few deep breaths to continue. "I promise to love you all the days of your life and to like you during most of them," she said, and the audience chuckled.

Deacon's head tipped back as he laughed deep and booming under the treed canopy.

"I promise to force you to buy yourself new boots when you need them. To help you on your mission to put more of your dogs into the hands of veterans where they belong. I promise to encourage your dreams and to help you shoulder your burdens. I promise to give you the last bite of cheesecake and first spoonful of peanut butter. I promise to accept every challenge we face together as your teammate and to always put our family first. I will love you all the days of my life." Tears traced down the rugged lines of his face, and he unabashedly allowed them to, unafraid to show the depth of his emotions publicly.

"Holly," he started boldly, no need for notecards as he dove into the depths of her warm eyes. "You are my best friend. Sorry, Cal." He looked out into the audience with a chuckle. "I knew I was in trouble the day I saw you sitting on your living room furniture in the front yard with one of our summer thunderstorms coming. I tried my best to fight it, but my truck always swerved toward your lane. I had to force myself to stay away. I thought Montana would swallow you up whole."

The crowd laughed, and Holly smiled as a tear slid down

her cheek. His voice was so sincere it was wavering. He had never strung together so many feeling words in one sentence, and she was riveted.

"It didn't. I was drawn to you, but my heart was shut down. I didn't know if I could feel anything ever again. I know I might have used Mama as an excuse to visit initially, but then you kept finding me. It is almost like there was a thread that connected us from the beginning. Maybe we are all born with strings connecting us to the important people in our lives. Because when I met you, I felt a tug toward you that I hadn't felt in years. It was familiar and inescapable. I couldn't fight it if I tried. I love you. I love our children.

I promise to tuck you in every night and bring you coffee with two shots of cream and four sugars."

Her eyes crinkled in a goofy, lovesick grin.

"I promise to teach Chance, Dillon, and Shane how to be men, how to stand up for what they believe in, and how to protect and take care of the people they love. I promise to scrape the ice off your windshield in the winter, even when it's below zero. I promise to make the bed when I am the last one out of it. I promise to keep you safe and give you a strong foundation that you can believe in. I promise to become the kind of father to your sons that I wish I had growing up. And when we're old and gray, or maybe I should say older and grayer, I will still hold your hand, and grab your butt, and kiss you in public because you are the most beautiful woman I have ever laid eyes on. When you look at me the way you do, I believe I can do anything."

The minister asked, "Do you have the rings?"

Dillon stepped forward and quickly dumped them in the minster's outstretched hand. Deacon's broke free and rolled down onto the ground. Dillon flashed red, and Ruth stooped to pick it up and handed it back to the minister, giving Holly a wink.

"Holly, I give you this token of my never-ending love and faithfulness, joining my life to yours forever."

"Deacon, I give you this ring as a symbol of my love for you and my desire to be your partner forever."

"By the powers vested in me from the great state of Montana, I now pronounce you husband and…" He didn't even get out the whole sentence before Deacon pulled her to him, gathering her waist in his impressive hands and pulling his new wife into a deep kiss as everyone cheered.

Chance, Dillon, and Shane quickly passed cones of rose petals to all the guests, and as the photographer snapped away, Holly and Deacon walked back down the aisle under a flurry of satiny soft petals tossed into the air like fragrant confetti. Holly laughed as Deacon leaned down and swept her up into his arms in a fireman's carry as the crowd cheered. Kissing Holly, he walked into the beginning of their new life together. Both of them looking forward, never back. Holly laughed into the air.

Maybe there is such a thing as happily ever after, after all.

ONE YEAR LATER

On a crisp fall day, where the maples were fully dressed in their yellows and reds, they waited for the hearing that would make Shane an official part of their family. Shane towered over Holly's five-foot-four frame now, and she gazed up at this young man who, in just forty-five more minutes, would officially become her son.

"Can you believe this is really happening?" she asked him.

"We've been waiting a long time," Shane confirmed. Holly reached up to stroke his freshly shaven cheek, already becoming sandpapery with fresh growth.

The sun hit Deacon's belt buckle as he held up her phone to take a photo of Holly with her boys.

"Get closer to your mama," he demanded with a smile. They shuffled closer to Holly, dressed in a long burgundy dress, wrapping their arms around her, and she felt her heart swell with pride. Her gaze rested on each of their faces for a moment, acknowledging how far they had come. Dillon was standing eye to eye with her now. His arm wrapped around her waist; he was forever her snuggle bunny, affectionate and loving.

When they started the adoption proceedings with Shane, Dillon had a lot of questions. The biggest one he dared to ask one night as they were washing dishes after dinner.

"Can Deak adopt me, too?"

Stunned silent, Holly didn't even begin to know how to answer him. Relief flooded in when Deak answered for her.

"What made you ask that question?"

"I miss having a dad," he admitted and looked down at the suds, blowing them into the air.

Deacon's eyes met Holly's.

"I bet you do," Deacon empathized. "I'd be honored to fill in for your dad until you see him again, and for Chance, too."

Hearing his name, Chance wandered over to the conversation.

"What do you think, buddy?" Holly asked Chance.

"I think it would be okay."

It was more than okay, but Holly understood his allegiance to his father. Chance loved his dad and missed him terribly.

"You wouldn't have to call me Dad or anything," Deacon offered, quickly understanding Chance's hesitation, "but is it okay if I call you son?"

Chance thought about it for a long minute then nodded. It was beautiful to see the way Deacon cared for her children. He didn't need the title or to make a public show. He was a father behind the scenes and where it really mattered. He was the one helping guide and shape them into the men they would become. With Chance and Dillon's blessing, it became an adoption of three boys instead of one.

Over the last year, Holly and Deacon continued to take

emergency foster placements. One of the boys was six months from his eighteenth birthday. Chance asked him, "What happens to you then?"

"I'm on my own," he answered bitterly. "Aged out of the system. There's lots of resources when you're a minor, but they are fewer and farther between when you're my age."

"What are you going to do?"

"I don't know."

Chance chewed on it. It was a problem so huge, it seemed impossible to solve. A few months later, during Chance's junior year, his final sociology project accounted for twenty-five percent of his final grade. Chance had worked for weeks on it, putting together a PowerPoint presentation he was sure would knock their socks off. When Holly asked him about it, he was tight-lipped but promised he would share it with them when he was finished.

The day before his official presentation, he invited them to their darkened living room. Cagey and excited, he bounced on the balls of his feet as he handed them a perfectly bound, printed copy of the presentation.

"Wow." Holly was stunned as she turned the thick copy over in her hand, marveling at the sheer professionalism of it. "You've really put a lot of thought into this." She handed it off to Deak.

"I can't wait," Deacon encouraged as the sofa creaked under his weight.

"Me neither. Let's get started."

He clicked onto the first slide. "Little Hope" By Chance Simon. Holly recognized a photo taken of her house, and it surprised her. The next slide was an aerial photo of her land. Chance began his carefully researched presentation then segued into statistics, focusing on teenage boys and the rates of poverty and crime of children in the system as they aged out to eighteen. The biggest common denominator of young adults that landed in prison was homelessness and poverty.

Chance passionately described the reason. If they couldn't find a legal job with self-sustaining income, then they were one car repair away from becoming homeless. Most find themselves driven into drugs and petty crimes just to stay alive. It was an endless cycle of poverty that churned and kept these young men imprisoned and hopeless.

His solution was to build a colony of tiny homes, each under three hundred square feet, with a bed and hot plate and a huge shared bath house for showering. Young men would have to earn their right to stay there by working in the rescue or by learning construction techniques to build even more tiny houses. Each teen would be assigned a mentor that would help guide them and shape a valid career path to ensure their independence and free them from the system.

He planned on teaming up with the local technology school for paid internships, and once a student was able to save a nest egg for emergencies and had obtained a skill in a field that was self-sustaining, he would graduate the program and be ready for integration into regular life.

Holly was stunned as she watched Chance deliver his passionate solution to a problem that plagued Montana. As slide by slide clicked by, Deacon sat up taller and leaned closer to the screen. Studying Chance's presentation with extreme interest, his hands clasped underneath his chin. When the lights came up, they were both silent.

"Mom, you could tutor the ones that didn't graduate." The stirring in her belly confirmed that something huge was taking root. She could. She could do that.

"All these guys need is a little hope."

Holly saw the pieces of the puzzle pulling together. No longer scattered on the table and senseless, she saw the outlines of the bigger picture. *This* was her purpose. Her excitement began to match Chance's. She jumped up on her feet and started to pace, wearing down a track on the carpet as deep as the one Chance was making. Over the next two hours, they flushed the entire plan out, had three lists of action items to complete, and began to take baby steps to make Chance's sociology presentation a reality.

The big idea filled Chance with confidence. It gave his life direction and he would not be deterred. Even when the first zoning meeting at the town hall didn't go his way, he rallied, and at the next spoke with so much conviction and determination, the zoning committee didn't know what hit it.

His final declaration sealed the deal. With steadfast strength, he leaned in, resting his forearm on the podium. His deeper voice was thick with emotion. "Sometimes you find your purpose, and sometimes it finds you. Little Hope will find it's home, somewhere, someday. I believe that home should be in Garden Brook." The room burst into applause, and after a vote, the board unanimously agreed to allow Little Hope to begin construction.

Holly's heart burst with pride, and a peace filled her that had been missing. Chance was going to be okay. His life was shaped by the hell they had gone through, but he was stronger for it and it had transformed him into a man that was on fire for positive change. He was going to make a difference in the lives of so many people, and Holly had never been more proud of her son.

As they waited on the courthouse lawn, her sentimental gaze shifted to Chance, who was graduating in a few months and pursuing a career in addiction counseling. At first, she was shocked to hear his career aspirations. She remembered when he came home lit up with a fire in his belly, high on a deep sense of purpose created by finding his path and claiming it for the first time.

"I know what I want to do with my life," he'd declared proudly, thrusting a thick booklet from Montana State University into Holly's hand.

"What's this?"

"I want to major in psychology, become an addiction specialist."

"Really?" Holly was shocked.

"It makes perfect sense," Deacon weighed in like he always did. Holly was in awe of the ease that he entered into fatherhood. He was built for it. Patient with high standards. Willing to get down in the trenches with her when Shane acted out and was sent home for a three-day suspension for punching a boy during lunch. He peeled away Shane's violent act and distilled it down to the reason. The driving force of the wound that drove Shane to act out in the first place.

"You always said, you need to start with what you know," Chance explained. "I know firsthand how easy it is to lose control of your life. I know I hated going to Sierra, but I learned so much about myself there. Kent and I have been talking about it for a few months now, and I feel like this is my place in the world. This is where I can do the most good."

Deacon reached out to squeeze his shoulder in support.

"That's what it's all about, son. I am so proud of you."

Chance visibly puffed up in the wake of Deacon's praise. Holly stepped closer. "So proud, Chance. You will really bring a great perspective to addiction and be able to help so many people. I'm just worried about the toll it will take on you emotionally."

"You worry about everything," Chance teased.

Deacon nodded with a smirk. "That's true. I don't worry

about anything because I know this one has already worried enough for all of us."

Chance laughed. "He's got your number, Mama!"

"Hey!" Holly exclaimed, wounded. "I guess you're right. We worry because we love. It's part of being a mom." She paused then continued. "What can I do to help you?"

They settled into filling out college applications and searching for scholarships and financial aid. In the end, it was the essay he wrote about his time in treatment that earned him a grant that completely paid for his first year's tuition. Holly got to see Chance buckle down and work toward a goal he set for himself. She got to see Chance's determination to realize his dream, and it was one of the most rewarding and satisfying moments of all of her years of motherhood.

Her eyes finally landed on Shane's blue ones. Of the three boys, Shane had changed the most. Over the last year, he settled in and found his place in their family. At first, he struggled to accept the love they all wanted to shower over him, looking for ulterior motives and doubting every good thing they told him. Going to weekly therapy and focusing his energy on training the dogs with Deak, he was able to rewrite the fear that had been etched into his soul with every slap and harsh word that had ever been spoken. He began to flourish. The boy that had broken into her home was a terrified wild animal. No different than an angry bear, destructive and driven to survive. The man he was developing into was softer around the edges and slowly becoming more trusting. He was recalibrating from the inside out, better able to control his fears and insecurities. It was a rocky road over the last year. Fights at school and suspensions. A bad decision to sneak out with the car and come home tipsy the weekend he learned his father was up for parole.

Holly and Deacon saw these feeble attempts to self-sabotage for what they were. A child who needed them to prove they weren't going anywhere. That even if he did his worst to drive them away, Holly and Deacon would stay. They would stand and wait. They would correct and set strong boundaries. They would lavish their time and attention on him and show him deed by deed and day by day their total commitment to him.

"Smile!" Deacon said as he snapped a couple photos. "Come on, Shane, use your real one."

Ruth piped up, "Give me that camera and get in there with your sons!" Deacon handed it over and claimed his spot next to Holly.

"Say 'happy family'!" Ruth called out.

"Happy family!" they chorused together.

"Okay, one fun one!" Ruth snapped away as they all pulled faces and stuck their tongues out.

Holly looked at her watch. "We've got to get in there! Our case is on the docket at ten."

The boys ran ahead to open the door for Ruth, jostling each other in a competition to be the first one to hold the door open for the grandmother who doted on them.

"Well, look at them." Holly laughed. "I think we've finally turned out a few gentlemen." She turned to Deacon with a smile. "Good work, Daddio."

Holly walked into the courtroom with her boys and her husband, and twenty minutes later, they walked out legally declared a family. Her place in the world had changed immensely, and she didn't regret a second of it. She knew it was all interconnected. Every bad thing that happened put her on the path that redirected her to the place she landed today. Holly felt a rush of gratitude fill her soul as her gaze lingered on all the members of the family she and Deacon created. Feeling complete finally, as a woman and as a mother, she fought for and won the complete and total joy that zinged up from her belly.

She leaned in to kiss Deacon and said, "Thank you. Thank you for giving me this life that is so much better than before."

He smiled and squeezed her hand. "I'm just getting started, darlin'."

THE SWEETEST DAY: A DELUCA FAMILY BAKERY NOVEL

Real love doesn't exist... or does it?

Pastry cream runs through Gionna DeLuca's veins. Forty-something, curvy, and content with her life, she makes extravagant wedding cakes to celebrate other people's love stories. Believing she will never need one for herself.

Surrounded by a long legacy of loving relationships in her family's bakery, a brutal heartbreak forces Gionna to shut down and build unscalable walls. She resigns to live her life fiercely independent and tries to find happiness and success on her own terms.

Until a younger mohawked sous chef walks into DeLuca's and challenges everything she thought she wanted. He pushes Gionna's boundaries and forces her to confront her fears and failures. Demanding she open her heart to the risk of love or remain stuck and unfulfilled in a life she is beginning to outgrow.

The Sweetest Day explores one woman's misconceptions about the existence of forever love and the danger and reward of putting your heart into the hands of another.

Available on Amazon, BN Nook, Apple iBooks, Kobo, Google Play.

Order now at: https://tealbutterflypress.com/products/the-sweetest-day

READ MORE BY THIS AUTHOR

The best way to buy my books is direct at tealbutterflypress.com
There you can save 20-25% and find autographed paperbacks.
They are available at most booksellers too.

I write under two pen names, Ninya for Non-Fiction and Blair
Bryan for Contemporary Fiction.

Non-Fiction

Scotland with a Stranger: A Memoir

Treehouses with a Teenager: A Memoir

First You Then Him

Fiction By Blair Bryan

Back to Before

Better than Before

The Sweetest Day

The Funologist

When Wren Came Out

AnaStasia Lived Two Lives

Steamy Sexy Series Velvet Guild

Velvet Guild Collection 1

Velvet Guild Collection 2

Velvet Guild Collection 3

Velvet Guild Collection 4

Velvet Guild Collection 5

ABOUT THE AUTHOR

I've always been a risk-taker, so at 44 I decided to write and publish my own books. It has been a roller coaster ride with a punishing learning curve, but if it were easy, everyone would do it. I write under the pen names of Ninya and Blair Bryan.

I love to travel and a trip to Scotland with a complete stranger was the inspiration for my memoir. I also seem to attract crazy experiences and people into my life like a magnet that gives me a never-ending supply of interesting storylines.

If you love a good dirty joke, a cup of coffee so strong you can chew it, and have killed more cats with your curiosity than you can count, I might be your soulmate.

Visit me online www.tealbutterflypress.com

Join my facebook reader group: https://www.facebook.com/groups/ninyons

9 781956 109030